PRAISE FOR HOVERING ABOVE A HOMICIDE

"There's not a point guard in the nation who's got a better handle on combining hoops and mystery than Tom Kelly. Catch a clue and pick up a page-turner that's nothing but net!"

—Danny O'Neil, *ESPN*

"Tom Kelly's captivating *Cold Crossover* introduced us to Coach Ernie Creekmore and a town full of sharply-drawn characters. *Hovering Above a Homicide* is another terrific read. It's filled with vivid characterizations, spirited dialogue, and more than enough plot twists to keep you hooked well into the wee hours."

—Robert X. Morrell, MD, MBA, Raleigh, N.C.

"This book is for anyone who likes suspense, high-school hoops, and terrific storytelling. I thought I knew all-star basketball but I learned a lot from this book. Coach Ernie Creekmore is a compelling character."

—Craig Smith, *Seattle Times* sportswriter, 1976-2008

"Kelly sends Coach Creekmore running and gunning for the truth behind his all-star team, including who's gunning for him. Lots of dealing and dishing in high school hoops including kickbacks stashed like stinky sneakers in a fancy gym bag."

—Bob McCord, Tucson

THE ERNIE CREEKMORE SERIES

HOVERING ABOVE A HOMICIDE is the second book in the Ernie Creekmore series featuring a longtime high school basketball coach who calls upon his years of experience, resources and small-town logic to help his fishing buddy and the county's chief criminal investigator solve murder mysteries.

In the first book, *Cold Crossover*, Linnbert "Cheese" Oliver, a hard-luck hero in the Northwest town of North Fork, is reported missing from a late-night ferry. And for Ernie, his father figure, friend and former coach, the news hits hard. Ernie's suffered too much loss and pain in his life—his wife, a state basketball championship, a serious medical malady—and he just can't accept the idea that Cheese might have taken his own life.

"The Cheese" was the best basketball player Ernie Creekmore coached in his nineteen years at Washington High School and the best shooter Ernie had ever seen. The unassuming great-grandson of the town's founder, Linn Oliver could do no wrong. He was the talk of the town—until he missed the final shot in the 2000 state championship game.

Working with the county's Harvey Johnston, Ernie uses his new contacts in real estate and old hoops resources to trace Cheese's movements. Meanwhile, hints at possible foul play turn up in pieces of North Fork's rough-and-tumble history in fishing, logging and railroading and the past and present violently collide in a series of heart-stopping moments that peel back layers of secrets, gold and twisted family ties that refuse to stay buried.

All the best!.

[signature]

Hovering Above
a Homicide

Hovering Above a Homicide

AN ERNIE CREEKMORE MYSTERY

TOM KELLY

Crabman Publishing • Rolling Bay, WA

Published by
Crabman Publishing
Rolling Bay, WA

Copyright © 2014 by Tom Kelly

ISBN-10: 0977092062
ISBN-13: 978-0-9770920-6-2
Library of Congress Control Number: 2014919117

The characters and events in this book are fictitious. Any slight
of people, places or organizations is unintentional.

Book design by Bill Cameron.
Cover photo by Alberto Chagas.

Cataloging-in-publication data is available from the Library of Congress.

10 9 8 7 6 5 4 3 2 1

Printed and bound in the United States of America

For Jimmy Rags
The pride of Alhambra and Minneapolis
Ah, the laughs!

ONE

Elmo "EXCELLENT" SERVICE continued to dog it.

The last straggler on the court for Saturday morning basketball practice, the six-foot-six stringbean forward needed an eternity to lace up lustrous patent leather Jordans and cinch calf-length Carolina baggies so that the sponsor-stitched elastic band on his white compression undies was suitably exposed.

A chronic complainer, Elmo proceeded to strut through layup drills, skip out on his turn to lead a three-man weave, and then saunter over to the water fountain when his coach blew a whistle to remind his players about the need to get the most out of each and every practice.

"Are you with us today, Elmo?" barked Ivan Scuttle, the Port Edwards coach. "Because it sure as hell looks like you are thinking about last night. Now, move it or get the hell out of here!"

Hands on hips, the player raised his chin and massaged the front of his neck. "Seems like Elmo's moving pretty good," Elmo said. "'Sides, Elmo got in pretty early last night, given the demands on Elmo."

Scuttle strutted toward him and pointed at his chest. "Well, I demand a hell of a lot more than I'm seeing so I better see it soon."

I smiled and shook my head. After nineteen years of high school coaching, and five more of full-time scouting, I've learned that the best method of evaluating a player's physical skills, attitude, and energy is to measure him against another player of his caliber. Catching that matchup often is impossible, especially in small towns where one kid's abilities clearly transcend those of anyone else in the ZIP code. But by arriving unannounced at a practice session, often you can find what makes a player tick, verify he's a leader, and gauge his genuine impact on a team.

I studied Elmo's indolence from the creaky balcony of the Port Edwards High School gym. It was cold, dark, and a terrific place to hide, particularly for coaches charged with selecting an all-star team. Like me. The rarely used upper corner smelled and felt like a dusty choir loft in a downtown church.

But in my mind, the bandbox building built in 1953, "The Home of the Roughriders" inspired an even loftier reverence for me than the old stone church in the town square. Flawed and funky, uncomfortable and hostile to opponents, the landmark gym was the Fenway Park of state hoops and the last remaining gymnasium from a bygone era dominated by canvas shoes and satin shorts gathered at the waist with flat silver buckles.

It was old-school, and so was I.

"All great and precious things are lonely."

The familiar cynical delivery floated from behind me. I turned to see a rumpled Harvey Johnston draped across the top three rows, his brown overcoat streaked with rain.

"John Steinbeck," I said. "*East of Eden*. But you must be referring to this wonderful, remote venue."

"Perhaps it is merely you in your cherished element."

I coughed out a surprised laugh and continued to survey the floor.

"So is it your opinion that Mr. Service would provide excellent service to your select team?" Harvey said.

"Actually, I was trying to figure out how the kid ever got his nickname," I said. "His work ethic needs jumper cables. Clearly, he doesn't view practice as an important athletic experience. Seems 'Sluggish Service' would be more appropriate."

"Might the origin have come from a sportswriter looking to make a name for himself?" Harvey said. "Then again, maybe this young man's coach thought it might be compelling in a headline."

"I seriously doubt that. This is the kid's third school in three years."

"Really?"

"The two previous coaches probably had their fill of him. I've got a feeling we're looking at a self-named product here."

We observed Scuttle crouching crab-like, overemphasizing the need to remain low while defending the dribble-drive.

"Randall!" Scuttle yelled to a player at the far end of the gym. "You keep your butt between your man and the basket on defense or your butt will be on the bench!"

Harvey chuckled at the animated teaching moment.

"Frankly, Ernie, I thought you'd had enough of coaching this game," Harvey muttered. "What's it been? Four years since you've been on the sidelines with a real team?"

The realization brought a deeper exhale. "Actually, it's been five. The guy who was going to handle the all-star team took a job out of state. The organizers needed a warm body and I was probably the only one available. Besides, the team sponsor's from North Fork and was loyal to me and our teams at Washington High."

Sliding a clipboard further down the bench next to me, I turned and faced my old fishing partner, who just happened to double as Skagit County's chief criminal investigator.

"Now don't tell me you came all the way up here to tell me how to tie a new killer fly. Rivers are still too high and there's no fish anywhere. How the hell did you find me, anyway?"

"I telephoned the office. Cookie said you were going to check out a new listing on the Skagit and then maybe come up here and catch practice."

Sneakers screeched on the hardwood floor below. A fat forward tumbled to the deck and began rubbing a knee, the result of Elmo's flagrant moving screen. "Ouch," I murmured. "That's nasty, Elmo. Geez, at least help the kid up."

Harvey chuckled and walked my way.

"Ernie, there's this young man over at Loyola High," Harvey said, sliding onto a bench, elbows on thighs. "You ever scout Trent Whalen?"

"Kid's a hothead." I said. "A tornado of emotions, I'm told. I don't recall if he played last season or sat out."

"But don't you think he'd be a logical candidate for your regional select team?"

"I remember him as an accurate shooter around the basket and a solid defender with excellent size. Got a box-out butt." Twisting on the bench toward Harvey, I whispered, "But I'll tell ya, partner. I don't need kid who's spent a ton of time at the corner of Bad Temper and Lousy Judgment."

Harvey looked away and dropped his chin.

"Candidly, he could use your help, and so could I."

While Harvey was a big-time buckets fan, he'd never lobbied for a player. That included the years when I coached his nephews at Washington High.

"I'd like to see him become a better communicator," Harvey said. "On and off the basketball floor."

"Why?" I said, swerving toward him in my seat. "That's quite the in-depth observation from a casual observer. Do you mind telling me how you fit into this?"

Harvey stood and stretched, arms overhead, hands clinched. The stair-stepped rows allowed him to tower above me like an NBA center.

"His father was the realtor shot to death—"

"Are you kidding?" I gaped. "I know exactly who he was. Who could forget something like that? His murder was splashed all over the papers for days."

"Along with a photograph of me with egg on my face and the DA seething in the background."

I glanced toward the rafters, recalling the front-page photos of the white body bag being carted from the red brick colonial.

"Tim Whalen. Decent guy, well respected. Three or four years ago, one of my customers showed an interest in one of his listings. It didn't go anywhere, but he treated me well."

Harvey said nothing.

"The last I heard—"

Harvey grimaced and plopped down next to me. Expecting a sermon, I scooted my bottom a bit farther away.

"——is that my department hasn't made any meaningful progress? Yes, and I regret to report that is still the case."

"Serious?"

"This might be the least amount of evidence of any major crime I've been around. Early in the investigation, we thought we might have had a line on a drifter from down in California, but he had a solid alibi."

"So, what do you think Trent knows?" I said.

"That's just it. The youngster has pretty much clammed up on everything. He could prove to be the prime mover in the case or he might not know a thing. But he's had little to say on any topic from the beginning. He was off at some early-season hoop tournament when the dad was killed."

The timeframe was hazy yet the only tournaments I'd missed usually involved fishing. I shook my head.

"It might have been that Mazatlan trip," Harvey offered. "Remember that long weekend when I was swamped? Anyway, Master Trent has become the master of one-word replies. You should examine my officers' notes."

"I take it he didn't say much?"

"You could count the sentences with more than one syllable on your left foot. Now he seems to just mumble to his mother and it is getting under her skin. I witnessed her fly off the handle one time because of it. She is a tiny, attractive gal who can look quite formidable when she becomes upset, even next to her hulking son."

"The kid was probably stunned out of his mind," I said. "Try to remember the guy lost his father, Harvey."

Harvey managed a *You must be joking* laugh that sounded more like a cough. "He's just not given us anything to work with."

Smiling, I turned and faced him. "High school boys are hardwired to mumble. They practice on their parents. You should hear some of them talk after games, even after they've scored thirty."

"Well, he's an only child, she can't break through to him,

and it's driving her crazy. I guess Tim was way too involved in his son's basketball, but there are no other men we know of in Trent's life now. You're the kind of man who can get a youngster like that to open up. "

I smirked and shook my head. "You do remember my degree is in English Literature and not Grief Counseling."

A sharp whistle summoned the players to center court. They hovered around their coach in a semicircle, eagerly awaiting the next drill. Elmo Service stood with his back to his coach, swayed from side to side and stared up at the rafters.

Harvey brushed the side of my knee with the back of his hand, seeking my attention. "I've seen you work with students and players for years," he said. "I know you've solved a lot of classroom shenanigans because you've got a magic touch with kids."

"Right," I sneered.

"I just thought maybe if he made this select team, he would get close enough to somebody to give up something."

"Geez, Harvey! Do you want me to coach him or interrogate him? *If* he makes the team, and that's a big *if*, do you think he's going to bare his soul just because he's an all-star basketball player? I mean, all of a sudden he's an elite selection, so, therefore, he's bound to tell all? Besides, there's a ton of talent out there and I've caught hell already from a handful of coaches and parents for not even giving their kids a look."

Harvey rolled his eyes like a player ordered to pick up dirty towels for arriving late to practice.

"Look, Ernie, I'm not exactly sure what I'm asking you to do. But yes, please consider speaking with the youngster soon. We're nowhere with this case and the months are piling up."

I folded my arms and leaned closer. "Why all the renewed interest now?"

"A pair of my detectives recently went back through all the evidence, statements and alibis. At least one of them thinks Trent had the time and motive to go into that house and shoot his dad to death."

"Whoa. That's a big move, Harvey. For a teenager? During a tournament?"

"Other coaches watched him that day at the tournament, so the kid was there, at least for a while. His mother was at some stained-glass class at a girlfriend's house."

"That sounds a little flimsy. Did you ever like the mom for the murder?"

"Not really," Harvey said. "But the gal who taught the class has a bumpy past and was about as friendly as a blowtorch when we pushed her about exact timeframes. The woman acted as if we'd broken all the glass in her artsy-fartsy studio."

"You think she's hiding something?" I said.

"We don't know … Anyway, she said she'd known Samantha Whalen since high school and confirmed Mrs. Whalen was in the studio when Tim Whalen was murdered, but it was like pulling teeth. And hers aren't so good. Terrific figure, though. Imagine an aged Madonna after chomping on a case of Copenhagen."

Harvey peeled through his notebook. "Anyway, this lady was a real piece of work. Here it is, Paula Soijka. Does that seem Scandinavian, or Russian? Regardless, she told my detectives that anytime she had to communicate with the police, she came out on the short end of the stick. When we checked her out, we found two drug-related assaults more than a decade ago down in Centralia and Vancouver. We spoke with Soijka twice in person and probably will visit her again. She apparently was ill both times and my officers couldn't wait to get out of there."

"I'm sorry, Harvey. I'm confused. If coaches at the tourney said Trent was in the gym, why do you now feel he had something to do with his dad's death?"

"Teams take breaks between games, correct? You of all people should know that. This young man's team had a layover after the second session and he had plenty of time to get to the open house his dad was hosting. Please, just do me a favor and consider him for your team."

I glared at him, stunned. He flashed me a *Why not?* twitch.

"So, one day your guys decide to charge the kid with whacking his father. And maybe, if I'm lucky, the cops come in to my practice, cuff the guy and take him away in front of the rest of the players!"

"That's not what I anticipate."

"But think about what you are saying, Harvey!" My outburst drew inquiring glances from the court below. Embarrassed, I continued in a lower, slower voice. "First you ask me 'just' to talk to him and now you want me to put him on my team. Why don't you figure out what you're going to do with Trent Whalen and leave me, and basketball, out of it?"

Steamed, I descended the back stairwell, trying to stay a few steps ahead of Harvey as he followed me out.

"Look at it this way," Harvey said. "You know how to ask the right questions at the right times with these young people. In fact, I even had to slow you down on the Cheese Oliver case. I'm positive you remember your effort on that."

He quickened his pace to remain at my side.

"But that was different, way different. This could be a day-to-day involvement with a prime suspect in a murder case, for crissake. Think about the other team members involved here. If the kid is a nutcase, I'm knowingly putting them in harm's way!"

"If I thought that was true, I wouldn't be asking you to do this."

"You say Tim Whalen was too involved in his kid's game? Just wait until other parents get wind of this. Then, you'll really see involvement. No thanks, Harvey. I don't need the aggravation."

He tugged on my elbow, and turned to face me. "I'm afraid you don't fully understand. The police commissioner, the DA, the mayor all are turning the screws on my department, Ernie."

"And the press," I continued. "Can you imagine if this thing goes sideways? God in heaven, I can see the headline now: ALL-STARS INCLUDE PREP PERP. Writers I've known and respected for years would write me off."

I rested my hands on the side of my face and shook my head, visualizing what could be.

"Please, Ernie, just visit with the young man."

"No way. My plan was to reenter coaching gracefully. I'm sorry, sir, but this is at the other end of the scale."

"For all we know, Trent may turn out to be a wonderful kid," Harvey said. "And, he could be a terrific addition for you. We need to keep him focused during this time on something that he loves, and we know he loves his basketball."

"Read my lips. *No.* I'm not going to sacrifice team chemistry with that kind of distraction."

"Ernie, do I have to write up a desperation proclamation here? I'm up the proverbial creek." He glanced at the floor and stared down the hall. "OK, as my friend, as a man who has yet to return my favorite steelhead rod, please just have a conversation with the kid!"

My head began to hurt. I tried to ease the sting in my eyes by gently massaging the lids. I took a deep breath and let it fly.

"All right," I said. "Now listen closely. I will attend a game on the Loyola schedule. No one will know when or where or if I am there to see a specific individual. If I like the way Trent plays, I will consider a conversation with him at some point. No promises, got it?"

"Understood."

I turned and half-pointed at him. "Harvey, we do this my way. All of it. If there's the slightest rumbling that I'm going to a Loyola game, or if I went there only to see Trent Whalen, then I'm out the door."

"With all due respect, and without putting the cart before the horse, what must occur for that conversation to take place?"

I shook my head and stared at the floor. "I knew you'd do this to me."

"No, really. What would be your expectations if you were able to observe him?"

"Frankly? It will be more about body language, how he flows with his teammates, and treats his coach. If he's a fit and if he can play, we'll talk. But I'm telling you right now, even if we have that talk, I would never give him a spot on the team that somebody else has earned. I would never take him just to take him, and I mean that. You've got a lot of *ifs* in front of this one, Harvey."

"When you're looking down a dark hallway of locked doors, you hope like hell there's at least one you can jimmy open."

"Which is exactly what I did to your garage door last week when I returned your steelhead rod."

Harvey's jaw fell open with an almost audible clunk.

As we stepped down the hallway, Scuttle strode toward us with Elmo Service bobbing and weaving closely behind.

"Ernie!" the coach called out.

"Ivan the Terrible," I replied.

"I guess I thought you might call before you came." He whirled a handful of folded papers toward his star. "I'm sure you know Elmo Service."

"Not formally," I said. I introduced myself and Harvey as my friend and a prep hoops fan. The youngster reluctantly clasped our hands, like an elderly woman offering a greeting in church.

"Elmo?" Harvey said. "I'm just curious. How did you acquire that nickname?"

The young man stretched, arms extended far behind his back, fingers interlaced. Incredulous, he sniffed and looked away as if we were the only two uninformed people in the lower forty-eight.

"The ladies," Elmo said. "See what I'm sayin'?"

Scuttle frowned, blinked toward the floor and shook his head. "Well, we're just about ready to get Elmo re-taped. Seems he tweaked an ankle just now. I hope you get to see him at full speed because I think he can really help you for that spring break tournament when our playoffs are over. Lord knows enough scouts have asked about him."

"I guess I saw him at full speed earlier today," I said.

Elmo perked up and swayed back and forth. "Right, Elmo was movin' pretty good in some of them drills. Had it dialed back a notch, though. Not sure if the guys could keep up with Elmo." He cocked an eyebrow and gazed at me.

Grinning, I told Scuttle I would be in touch and began heading for the door. Harvey suddenly turned.

"Excuse me, Elmo," he called. "Do you recall ever playing against Trent Whalen over at Loyola?"

The player checked for scuffs on his slick sneakers then wiped the back of his hand across his mouth.

"Elmo got into it with that sucka in a summer league game down at Rainier Vista. As usual, Elmo was mindin' his own bidness when the dude goes all Ali. Throws this nasty-boy punch. Both benches empty. Coaches come break it up. Course, Elmo hel' hiz own."

"You two guys have a history?" I asked.

"Not really, man. Dude's a hothead of the first order. Scary strong, too. Gets that crazy look in his eyes like he's gonna rip your face off."

TWO

Elmo service's unimpressive performance had me second-guessing, albeit briefly, my decision to return to coaching. While I'd hoped for more from the kid in his new environment, I wasn't exactly surprised. The lackluster showing screamed *I'm too good to be here* and created more research and decisions for me regarding frontcourt candidates.

Much to my chagrin, Trent Whalen loomed as one of the few logical choices. There just weren't a lot of bangers his size who could rebound and run the floor.

"That bubbly weather woman on television would say our rain has turned to showers," Harvey said, opening the door to his county-issued Dodge as we stood in the gym parking lot.

"Never could understand it," I said. "Change the name, it's still rain. Maybe not as consistent, but it falls from the sky and gets you wet."

Harvey turned, stood in the V between the door and the driver's seat, rested his arms over the window, and swirled a key ring like a six-shooter. Raindrops beaded on the sleeves of his brown London Fog.

"How are these players different, Ernie? Correct me if I am wrong, but a few years ago a young man like Excellent Service would never have transferred to another school just to play basketball."

"That's a topic that we need to take out of the rain," I said.

"I've got a feeling I'm in for more of a surprise than I thought, even after five years away. My gut says kids haven't changed that much, but parents have changed dramatically. A buddy of mine coaching in Idaho went 25-0 last year and said it was his hardest year as coach. Because of the parents. They're more concerned with attracting college scouts, which alters the behavior of the kid, his coach … the entire family.

"A good example was Ivan Scuttle just now. He didn't say one word about his team, the playoffs or the kind of season he's had. His primary concern was that he wanted his kid on the select squad. The focus has shifted from school teams to all-star teams, especially for the parents."

"From what I've heard," Harvey said. "Trent's father was no picnic on the sideline. Apparently, he was one of those helicopter parents, way too much involved and constantly hovering above his child."

I nodded in recognition. "Tim Whalen relocated Trent, you know. The explanation that was given for the move was for better basketball exposure."

I extended my hand as an intro to my exit. "See ya."

Harvey slumped behind the wheel and fired up the engine.

"I'm going to get together with my officers again on Monday morning. After that meeting, I'll figure out if there is any new or additional information and if the department is still leaning toward the young man as the possible perp. I'll be in touch."

He shut the door and pulled away, splashing through chuckholes toward the chain-link gate.

*　　*　　*

While I'd seen Tim Whalen at state realtor meetings and seminars, the only person I knew who had worked with him was Elinor "Cookie" Cutter, my all-business boss and the broker at Big River Realty.

I'd planned on heading her way and quizzing her about what made Whalen tick, if I could get my ancient VW bus to cooperate. The motor often needed every ounce of ignition juice to start, and this time slumped into a silent stutter before turning over. The heater took an eternity to kick in, and the thought of a son having any role in his father's death didn't make things any warmer.

Heading for Interstate 5 and the fifteen-minute drive back to the office, I recalled the last time I'd seen Tim Whalen alive. Two years ago in the first round of the district playoffs, Everton played Bellarmine Prep down in Tacoma. While scouting Bellarmine's two sophomore guards for a Division 1 coach in Texas, I was blown away by the continual commentary of a loud, irrepressible parent. Hands cupped around his mouth, he sat in the third row behind the Everton bench and yelled, mantra-like, for the entire first quarter:

"Be hard to guard, Trent! Hard to guard!"

Tim Whalen became so annoying that the kids in the Bellarmine student section jeered back with a repetitive group cheer (*"Trent, NOT hard to guard."*) before one of their parents drove Whalen from the bleachers by roaring a nasty verb followed by a quick personal pronoun. Moments later, Whalen resumed his relentless remarks from behind the bleachers in the corner of the gym. At halftime, he huddled with his son going to and coming back from the locker room.

By the time I hit the Division Street exit in North Fork, the sun streaked through the scattered clouds and spun a brilliant rainbow above the Skagit Flats to the west. Only a few spots remained in our agency parking lot, so I angled the bus into a spot on the street, saving the primo space for a potential big-bucks tourist flying up the freeway from Sea-Tac Airport. I'd heard a rumor about a tiny agency losing a California buyer when a chauffeur couldn't park an aircraft carrier-sized black limo. Since then, I've always surrendered my spot in the lot in case the limo showed.

Edith Utley, our senior salesperson, whose ubiquitous frosted beehive hairdo complemented her full-length broom-stick skirts, greeted me with her usual sartorial evaluation before I could reach the friendly confines of my cubicle.

"Oh, Ernie," she mused. "The pleated trousers are a wonderful addition to the new you. And so crisply creased as well." She continued to eyeball my entire person. "Come to think of it, I don't think I've ever seen you in a button-down shirt. A recently laundered one, anyway. Well, let me say from one old teacher to another, keep up the good work."

Shaking my head, I continued toward my desk. "And— what, Edith?" I asked. "You'll give me a passing grade at the end of the semester?"

She glared down the hallway, her dark beady eyes narrowing as I moved farther away. "If you weren't so huffy, I'd tell you that Cookie—"

"Cookie what, Edith?" barked the boss, approaching from behind. "Did you tell Coach I wanted to see him?"

"I was trying to do just that, but he—"

Cookie dismissed Edith with a quick wave. "That's fine," Cookie said. "I got him now." She glared at me and snapped her head back with a *What's up?* sign. "Now, please tell me you wrote up an offer on that cabin on the Skagit?"

"No, but it won't be hard to sell. It's got a warm feel to it and far enough out of the flood plain. Plus, I hooked a fat Dolly Varden on a fly right out front of the place last year and told just about everybody I know. Let me circle back with those guys, plus get the info in front of couple of retirees. Buddies of my dad."

"What? I thought you had an old fisherman in tow today, somebody in your pocket. That's why I suggested you head up to the river. Hell's fire, Coach. I could have lined up my own customer to go out there but didn't want to get in your way."

I smirked and stuck out a stop-sign hand.

"Look, I absolutely checked it out and went straight from there to scout a kid up at Port Edwards. He was supposed to be a likely candidate for the select team I'll be coaching at spring break." I glanced away, avoiding eye contact. "Doesn't look like he's going to work out."

She snickered, shook her head and pointed toward her office. "You told me you might go to Port Edwards, but I thought you turned that job down." She twisted briefly in my direction. "Didn't some parent raise a stink about your MS? Thought you might infect his kid or something?"

I laughed and eased into the leather armchair opposite her huge walnut desk. "I can't believe some of the ignorance out there. I'm always having to conduct some basic MS education."

"How've you been feeling lately, anyway? You actually look quite normal. Goofy, but normal."

"I expected as much, coming from you." I snorted and looked away. As much as the woman hammered me, she had my back. "Actually, I've been fine. There have been no major incidents other than the constant tingling in my hands and feet. No real pain. I take the weekly injections and hope for the best."

My hunger pangs were so loud, I was afraid she would make them a separate agenda item. "Before we brainstorm more names and numbers for the Skagit cabin," I said, "can we talk about Tim Whalen?"

Cookie sat up straight in her seat and dropped her pink Space Needle pen onto a yellow legal pad.

"Why?" Her eyebrows curled slightly. "Coach, the poor man's been in the ground for months."

"I'll get there in a minute, but humor me for a second. What words would you use to describe the guy?"

"Well, OK." She looked at me askance. "He was definitely a conscientious, efficient agent. Mr. Organization. And, I'll tell you what: His death probably changed the way real estate is sold around here. If you want to know why real estate agents now operate in teams, just thank the Tim Whalen case. That accelerated the practice. I think sales agents are nuts to go into some of those big, dark homes alone."

She shook her head and swiped unseen dust from her notepad before continuing. "Everybody has the perception that we need help with all the paperwork of a transaction. Sure, that's a part of it. But a huge piece, especially for older women, has become more about safety. We no longer go to meet unknown clients in homes we've never seen. There's a reason we say 'Meet me at the office' before we go out on a showing. "

"Hey, it even made me think twice," I said, "and I'm bigger than the average bear."

After a lengthy pause, Cookie said, "Why on earth are you asking about Tim now?"

"His son's a bruiser and has turned himself into quite an imposing basketball player. Some people believe he would be a useful addition to my select team."

"Little Trent?" Cookie said. "The last time I saw him, he was about up to here." She held her palm at the height of the desktop.

"Well, Little Trent apparently was a late bloomer and is now Big, Bad Trent. He's pushing six-foot-seven and two-thirty. A person like you could hide behind him all day. Did you go to their house often in those days?"

"Oh, no. When I was working at Imperial National with Tim, Samantha—never call her Sam, by the way—was teaching school and taking classes at the UW to get her master's. So, Tim sometimes brought Trent to the office when an offer was coming in, or to get work done he couldn't do at home. Realtors do it all the time. Trident even had a kids' room with toys, games and a TV."

"Did you get a chance to see Trent with Tim much, or was it basic daycare maintenance stuff?"

"On the contrary," Cookie said. "Most of the agents would just throw their kids in there, hope they'd behave, and then go deal with a customer in the conference room. Not Tim. He'd spend a lot of time making sure Trent was squared away, had a board game or puzzle he enjoyed, plus a backup. It was like the kid was ADD or something, but I don't think that was the case."

"Really? Why do you say that?"

"Tim had this way of going beyond showing with Trent. It

was as if he never took a break from over-the-top nurturing with that kid. Then there was that incident around the Fourth of July."

I sat up straighter in the chair. "I'm sorry. I have no clue what you're talking about."

Cookie took a deep breath and paused before exhaling. "I guess it wasn't really common knowledge. Trent and a buddy were horsing around with some firecrackers. Evidently, the pair tied up a mouse—maybe it was a lizard, I can't remember—and blew the thing up in a neighbor girl's playhouse. Her parents were so upset that they moved away before school started in the fall. I got the listing when they put their home on the market. They didn't even mention the firecrackers until the house sold."

"Good God," I laughed quietly. "Don't tell me the people moved just because of that? Lots of young guys do dumb stuff with firecrackers. Growing up in Yakima, we began saving our weekly allowance in early June for a big trip to buy firecrackers on the rez. We'd have contests to see how far we could flick ladyfingers. You know, like old cigarette butts? Hell, we'd blow up rotten apricots in our orchard, stick cherry bombs under coffee cans. Other guys got more creative."

Cookie looked out the window at an elderly couple shuffling down the sidewalk. "This might have been more than a young-guy thing."

"Why do you say that?"

She pulled a new pencil from a slim pack in her top drawer and rotated slowly.

"About a week later, the little girl's kitty-cat was found tied to the bike rack at the elementary school. Part of its face had been blown off. Cops thought it probably was some sort of combo package or those little silver M-80s. Trent denied knowing anything about it."

"Hmmm. Maybe Tim had a reason for staying on top of that kid."

"He was always on him, all right," Cookie said. "He was too attentive. We never saw other parents act that way. I mean, Charley and I had three kids who weren't angels, but we gave them lots of chances to figure things out for themselves. And, you know, they turned out OK."

I slumped in my chair and gazed out the window. I knew problem parents came with the coaching territory, but *I* never got to find out how closely I would hover. While we always dreamed of having kids, including one who wasn't afraid to post up his dad in the driveway, Cathy died before it could happen.

A few players came close to filling the gap as near-surrogates but we never got the opportunity to raise one of our own. I probably would have been overbearing anyway, demanding a relentless man-to-man defense rather than a lazy two-three zone.

Cookie halted my reflection with an elevated back-to-business tone.

"And speaking of figuring things out, let's get your old fly-casters on the phone," Cookie said. "Get their drift on that Skagit River cabin. And I don't mean drift boats."

"Right, I'll do it today. You know, though, that my guys are old and conservative with their cash. They certainly won't buy anything sight unseen. They'll have to get out there, poke around, and then go over the structure with a fine-tooth comb."

She nodded repetitively. "I know, I know. Old farts take

forever to roll the dice. Just get them out there." She reached in the top drawer, lifted another notepad with *Skagit* underlined at the top and perused half a sheet of pencil comments. "I know you usually have a pocketful of buyers for riverfront listings, but a young guy asked me last week about a headquarters for a guide service. Apparently, he wants to rent out the bedrooms and have his clients float the river for steelhead and chinook."

She flipped the pad in front of her, crossed her arms and gave me her best *What do you say to that?* look.

"Those two upstairs bedrooms would be perfect for visiting anglers," I said. "There's a view of the river bend. A guy could live downstairs, cook breakfast, rent out the upstairs to paying customers."

"Knowing your experience on these rivers, I'd almost suggest that you open up shop there. I said *almost.* You've already got too much basketball in your life, and not enough real estate."

Perhaps she was right. I'd brought my basketball notes into the office and left my work material in the bus. But while trudging back out to the street to collect two forgotten listing files, I felt my life probably contained just the right proportions of property and hoops.

As I swung the driver's door open to reach the folders, I discovered a white paper sack scrunched under the brake and clutch pedals. It smelled like French fries, and its bottom was smudged with grease. Unrolling the bag on the brown vinyl seat, I found ten hundred-dollar bills wrapped in a stained napkin. A message scribbled in blue ballpoint read:

To Insure Excellent Service

THREE

THINKING CLEARLY WAS not something that came naturally on an empty stomach, but the queasy feeling resulting from the sleazy, cash-in-the-bag discovery produced an unappealing outlook on everything.

Heading back downtown, I edged the bus into a vacant spot on the street in front of Tony's. The landmark waterfront restaurant hosted not only monthly Big River Realty meetings but also Rotary, the Washington High School Fighting Crabs Booster Board, Eagles, Masons, the St. Brendan Holy Name Society, and summer wedding receptions needing a last-minute solution for a backyard downpour.

By the time I entered the dining room, my appetite was back. Big-time. Savory smells seeped from huge ovens beneath the mammoth metal hood. Every day, they kicked out fresh-baked focaccia, legendary cannelloni, and hand-thrown pizza.

George Berrettoni, wrapped in a starchy chef's coat and hat, unloaded racks of garlic bread into the dining room steam table for the early buffet crowd. The towering Italian taught with me at Washington High for two decades before taking over the books of the family business and assisting his father in the kitchen.

"Well, this must be Celebrity Saturday," George roared as I approached a table for two shoehorned into a corner near the far wall. "First the distinguished criminal investigator and now the coach."

"Is Harvey here?" I said.

"The man just left. He was slamming down a meatball grinder when his cell rang, and he was off faster than a prom dress. He mumbled something about being late for some county fundraiser."

"Well, I bet that really perked him up. It sounds like another wonderful chance to write an obligatory check and wear a shirt and tie until midnight."

George pushed me away with a good-natured open hand to the chest. It was part of his M.O.; if he didn't touch me three times in a visit, I'd probably question his heritage. I sat down. He loomed above, looked both ways, and then slunk closer as if ready to divulge the combination to the restaurant's safe.

"Talking about midnight, I heard you've been seen out late with Harvey's secretary," he said. "What a body on that thing and man, does she know it. Old fisherman like you, she probably beats up your bait box. I'm tellin' you, Ernie, if my Evelyn weren't around, that woman would be smack dab in my crosshairs. And I'll tell you what, man. I'd be locked and loaded."

"It's true I've had dinner a couple of times with Margie McGovern."

"And?" He waited wide-eyed and long-necked for my reply, like a turtle rousted from its shell. Given his gusto, I felt he might drool on his table.

I stared across the room, beyond him, knowing the questions were bound to come sometime, yet stunned by George's boundless energy in asking them.

"And I took her to see the Huskies beat Arizona down at Hec Ed."

"And?"

My tiny wooden chair seemed to shrink. It needed a padded seat. "And, I will probably see her again but I wouldn't rule out the possibility of dating another woman who is not as—"

"Hot to get you in the sack? Tear your clothes off? Aggressive, eh? Seriously, tell me!"

I closed my eyes and dragged my hands down my forehead and face. "She's so darn deep about everything. Everything is the third degree. She'll take my hand, look me right in the eyes, and ask me what I bought at the store. I mean, who cares? Actually, I'm beginning to wonder if she finds anything important the least bit interesting. Many times, she can barely hold up her end of the conversation when it comes to the things that bring out her passion."

"Hey, give me a holler if you ever need some help bringing out her passion, baby." George raised his head and snickered. "Talk about a guy who's always cookin'. In more ways than one. No, seriously. It's good to hear you're back on the horse after all this time, you just happened to pick a stallion coming out of the gate. Hey, really, Cathy would have wanted you to be happy, enjoying yourself."

George finally pulled up a chair, rested his meathook forearms on most of the table. A small Chianti bottle held a stubby red candle; a jagged wax cascade crusted its wicker sides.

"So, you come over from the office?" he said. "I saw listings have been picking up over there. Sales better than normal, too."

I was relieved to be off the subject of my rust-coated love life. "For this time of year, activity has been surprising. That is, at least for me. Maybe there are simply more retired teachers and coaches this year looking for waterfront homes and cabins."

George swayed in his chair, prompting a creak from its spindly legs. His eyes scanned the room. "Cookie was here last night for our month-end meeting. The numbers are way up over last year. You know, the best decision Pop and I ever made was to front her the money to start that place seven years ago. That doggone office has made a profit from Day One. Our piece of that agency darn near nets what we get out of this place every month."

I twisted in my chair, fidgeting to get more space between my knees and the bottom of the table. "She's shrewd, organized, and one tough chick," I said. "When you think about it, she's got all the buyer niches covered. Edith and Martina dominate the blue-haired-widow network. Ted handles the military moves. Graham schmoozes the high-tech first-timers, and I've got the old teachers, coaches, and fishermen."

"She seems to have a knack with the out-of-staters," George said. "Big-time bucks from southern Cal seem to come her way."

"She may be tiny, but she negotiates like a mobster. I've seen her reach through the phone line, grab another agent by the neck, and get exactly what she wants, especially when it comes to price."

"My kind of girl," George smiled briefly, then creased his forehead. His thick black eyebrows sloped up like enormous backslashes. "Say, Harvey did pass along the fact that you had decided to return to coaching. Some sort of county select squad?"

"Yeah. I was kind of late being asked to the party. I guess they saw me as a last-resort guy ... Did Harvey say anything to you about specific kids?"

"Not at all. But I was kinda pissed to find out just now you're getting back into the grind."

"You know that I've actually been thinking about finding a way to ease back in for about the past year."

George snorted and looked around the dining room, then lifted a *How's it goin'?* nod to a waitress shuffling in to begin her evening shift. "Yeah, you brought it up a couple of times but you never said you'd officially pulled the trigger."

"I know. I know. I probably owed it to you to tell you sooner."

"Damn straight you did," he sulked. "So, what's the sharp hook that brought you back now?"

I took a deep breath and grabbed the edge of the table with both hands. "In the end, it was the chance to ease back into it with a short-term setup."

"Kinda like easing back into it with Margie McGovern," George grinned. "You animal. Babe's got legs longer than I-5."

I shook my head and glanced at the floor. While Harvey Johnston's secretary was the first woman I'd dated more than once since my wife died, she was not my idea of a first-round draft choice, and I didn't know how long my interest would hold.

"As I was saying, there's a three-day tournament coming up at Seattle Center," I said. "The Seattle Center Spring Hoopfest. The idea is to get all the good kids in the state together in one place, players from big schools and small schools, and eventually pick an all-state touring team for the summer. I guess they think the counties north of Seattle have enough top-flight kids to have their own team. Some of the remote counties will team up."

"King County will be loaded. The Seattle inner-city kids will kick everybody's ass."

"You'd think so, but who knows? Some guys just won't play. Others might not get chosen."

The bouncy redheaded waitress changed into her uniform in record time, perhaps to impress her boss. She pulled a pad and pen from the white pouch sewn into her apron.

"What can I get you to drink, Coach?"

"If Arnold Palmer is back there, I'll take him on the rocks."

She nodded and scribbled. "George, how about you?"

The proprietor shook his head, and she strolled toward the bar.

I leaned back in my chair and folded my arms. "George, do you remember the night we went down to Snohomish to scout the point guard? They were playing Everton in a holiday tournament."

"Sure. About a year and a half ago. The little guy lit 'em up for about twenty-five points. Didn't he keep about four D-1 schools in the dark before signing with Texas?"

"Right, he did and he's been seeing some minutes as a freshman. But do you recall there was a fight that night? There was a rugged kid from Everton ready to take on the world?"

George ran a hand down his five o'clock shadow. "Yeah, I remember, but it takes two to tango, and tangle. He was a bulky white kid, sophomore with an attitude. Just kinda snapped. Didn't he transfer after that season?"

"Yup. He's now over at Loyola, and he's a prospect for my select team. He's also the son of the agent found shot in that home for sale. Harvey's detectives haven't found the guy who did it. Not even close. Maybe it's stuck in his craw, or it's a slow time in the crime game, but the man is back on that case. Big-time."

George sat up, removed his arms from the table, and stared off over my shoulder. When the waitress arrived with my drink, he said: "On second thought, Shirley, maybe I will have a club soda. With a lime."

We fell silent for a moment. "Coach, there was something about that night that stuck with me," George finally said. "At the half, I hopped down from the stands to hit the head. When I came out of the can, here's this guy in a coat and tie, pinning a player against the wall in the corridor. Guy's got his forearm in the kid's throat; kid's on his tiptoes. I get closer and the guy eases off, and the kid runs toward the gym floor."

"And the young man was Trent Whalen."

"Bingo."

"And the guy doing the pin job was his father?"

"I can only assume so. I guess I didn't know for certain, because I'd never seen his dad before. You would think no other man would be in that situation."

Pulling a pen from my shirt pocket, I noted the incident on a napkin and pondered a possible timeframe.

"I know it was more than a year ago, but do you remember if Trent looked injured or scared when the guy turned him loose?" I said.

"No, the kid was just pissed. Not scared at all. Got the feeling he was stunned by what the guy did and where he did it. Then he got this wild look in his eyes, and I thought for a second the kid was going to throw a punch. What a sight that woulda been. Player in uniform going to blows with his dad? At halftime? Lordy lord."

Stuffing the napkin in my shirt pocket, I popped the top back on the ballpoint and rotated the pen with my fingers. "I'm supposed to see the regional basketball contact for this select club tomorrow at an open-gym session in Arlington. I need to ask him about the number of kids I can carry on the team and his expectations. There's also a six-foot-five player who's supposed to show up from a little school in Rolling Bay. While I've never seen him in person, I hear he's got wonderful wheels and can really score."

"You mean just like Margie McGovern?" George grinned.

FOUR

THE CLUSTER OF retired coaches seated in the stands at Arlington High was a Who's Who of western Washington basketball, and Augustine "Coats" Coatsworth seized the moment to hold court. Directly behind him, a dazzling logo of a streaking eagle, wings aloft and talons flashing, covered the mid-court circle.

"Now, I'm not going to ask you to go down there tonight and coach these kids," Coatsworth said. "But these all-comers clinics are near and dear to our state coaches' association and give us all a chance to see next year's best juniors and seniors all in one place. Lord knows all of us are far too old to run these things.

"That is, other than Coach Creekmore here, who I persuaded into taking on the North Counties squad in the Seattle all-star tournament." Light laughter was sprinkled with a few surprised looks. "Just take a few notes on these guys, supply any background you might know and get your remarks to me. I'll make sure the info gets to the all-star coach from that player's particular area. I thank you all for taking the time to be here."

Since leaving the classroom and full-time coaching, this was the way I spent most of my Tuesday and Friday nights. Scouting. Individuals and teams. Now with the new select-team job, I'd spend weekends in different high school gyms throughout the Puget Sound region. The drill was about the same: Climb the portable wood bleachers to a row high above center court opposite the teams' benches and zip open my notebook. While getting settled, I'd wave politely to familiar faces, even rise to greet an old crony who would ask about the whereabouts of a former player.

"You know why we have these tryouts at Arlington High?" shouted Coatsworth, whose baritone snapped me back into the present. "Because they got the best damn popcorn in the county, Ernie. These nice folks didn't bring it in a plastic bag. No, sir."

His starchy blue-and-white-striped button-down shirt appeared uncomfortable and ready to crack. Basketball-orange wingtips looked like tiny aircraft carriers and barely fit on the cramped floor beneath the benches. A fresh fifties flattop, led by greased-up bangs, revealed the scalp down the middle of his head.

"A lot of people would say it was because the school decided to resurface the gym floor," I smiled. Despite the makeover, the building reeked of quaintness even without the popcorn. Old athletic shoes, wrestling mats, aging cedar wall planks.

"Well, that too," Coatsworth continued. "Plus they let us use it for free. The coaches' association doesn't even have to pay for the lights. Those penny pinchers at places like Edmonds Prep seem to want a hundred bucks if a kid takes a shower."

Below us, energetic players in blue/white reversible tops sprinted single-file to the four corners of the court, pivoted, and casually backpedaled to the foul line. The court's bright, glossy finish magnified the high-pitched squeal of new sneakers.

"See that clown up there in the black and orange?" Coatsworth said, pointing to the far corner of the gym. "The jerk gave the girls at the door the hardest time."

I glanced toward the top rows and identified the target.

"He just said he was from Arizona Southern, then scribbled his name so you couldn't read it on the sign-in sheet. Don't know how you tell if he's affiliated with one school, several schools, or even a professional agency."

"Why not wear a shirt, look presentable?" I said.

"Trying to be cool, I guess, to impress kids. I mean, look at him. He's still got his sunglasses on. I plan to have a talk with him." Coatsworth turned briefly toward me. "You know the type?"

"I do, yet I've been away from coaching a while and things have probably changed."

"You have no idea, Ernie. It's gotten absolutely out of hand."

"When I was coaching at Washington High, any scouting was usually done by a college assistant. Some were cagey. They don't want anybody to know they're after a kid they might see as a diamond in the rough. Other times they are afraid they'll get a bad rep for tracking a mediocre prospect."

Coatsworth backhanded me on the arm to get my attention.

"Ernie, it's a new game. Some of these scumbags fake like they're assistant coaches but they're just professional brokers. They're out for the cash. Period." He shook his head. "Some get paid for steering kids to a particular college. If they think a kid can play for money someday down the road, they'll suggest an agent. Brokers, agents, consultants, counselors, coaches. There's a supermarket of hoop services out there. Some guys are a one-stop shop; others just basketball pimps. There are some, of course, still clean as a whistle, offering legitimate athletic scholarships."

"Right, but how many of today's elite young studs can realistically make it in the NBA?"

"It's gone way beyond that, Coach," Coatsworth said. "Europe, Australia, Asia. You dangle a couple hundred grand under a kid's nose and a lot of them snap it up in a second. Hell, steer a kid to a European team and the agent gets ten percent. Do that a few times a year, you're talkin' some serious coin."

A smooth shooting guard, about six-foot-four, buried consecutive jumpers from the right corner, high-fived his rebounder, then swapped places with him under the hoop. Directly behind the new shooter, a woman with short blonde hair, designer jeans and a puffy Patagonia parka took her time planting her impressive figure in the second row. When she leaned forward to scan the teams, most eyes in the bleachers scanned her. She appeared to relish the attention.

Coatsworth beamed at the group diversion, then resumed. "A bunch of us attended a tournament in Texas last summer. Coaches and agents lined up shoulder to shoulder to talk to kids. It was crazy. One college coach was getting popcorn at halftime. At the concession stand, he bumps into a guy who has sent him kids in the past. The coach finds out the same guy was in town only to take a player's dad to dinner just to meet an agent."

"That would put the coach in a tough spot," I said. "You don't want to offend a guy who's been helping you, but you don't really know who's zoomin' who."

"I'll tell you what, Ernie," Coatsworth said, "all-star team coaches like you are getting hit, too. You become very influential in a young man's life. Especially with all the scouting that you do. You're bound to get guys saying they are only looking out for a kid's future when they're really in it for themselves."

I lowered my head like an old man heading into a confessional. "I'm afraid I've already been found."

He acknowledged with quick nods. "Doesn't surprise me. It's one of the reasons we offered you the job. We were fairly certain you would do the right thing. They'll come after you again. There's really no place to hide, especially at an important game or tournament. You'll be found."

After the teams exchanged buckets on the floor, Coatsworth continued. "The fact of the matter is money. High school coaches' salaries are so crappy that a lot of them, even guys with so-so records, get approached to steer one good kid somewhere. They've got kids, mortgages, car payments like everybody else. The pressure to cooperate can be intense."

While I've scouted from every section of a gym, I'd learned that some scouts often arrive guarded and secretive and sit in the least populated section of the bleachers. I preferred to steer clear of them. Some sport full nylon warmups with their school's colors and logo. If surprised by a peer, they'd respond with a friendly nod and the revered title *Coach*, like doctors acknowledging each other in a hospital corridor or religious sisters in a convent dining room. A contemporary's last name is always preceded by the title (*Coach Crichton, Coach Heathcote*) and few first names are voiced unless the man is a neighbor or relative. Extremely popular nicknames (*Fitz, Lefty*) are the exception.

Even more identifying were the signature shoes and the pretentious posture. College coaches are never seen in sneakers other than their school-contracted editions (usually provided by the same company that produced their warmups). And they answer "just scoutin'" when little kids wander up to see what the men are scribbling about.

Given Coatsworth's comments, I wondered how many of my fellow scouts were actually college assistants and how many were merely go-betweens looking to make deals.

"Ernie, are you going to have enough talented bodies to compete in this deal?" Coatsworth said without looking at me. Part of any coach's in-gym MO is conversing without ever making eye contact; their gaze rarely leaves the action on the floor. "The last thing I wanted to do was set you up for failure on your return to coaching."

I glanced into my open folder and shuffled a few pages. "Looking down the lists you gave me, I'm encouraged by the possibilities. I've had a chance to see most of the kids during the season. Besides, it's only a weekend tourney so if we stink, we won't stink for long."

The big guy laughed. "Man, I know what you mean. I've been there and some of those lopsided games can take an eternity. The good news is that I know there are some kids up this way who can score. I just hope they can defend—Any muscle available who can block out and go get it? Play like you used to play?"

I snorted and looked away.

"Maybe I've got a soft spot for rebounders," I said. "But there are only two or three big bodies that seem to stand out. Now I just have to make time to see them on the court; find out how much they want to be part of this. "

"Well, if one of them is Bowers over at Burlington, forget about it. He went down with a knee last night. His father indicated on the phone that the boy tripped while hauling bales in the barn. The family physician called a while later and said it was an ACL, so the youngster is done for the year. Too bad. He's a big fella who can really get up and down the floor."

Coatsworth turned and mouthed a "thank you" to a portly, gray-uniformed custodian hugging the handle of a push mop at the base of the bleachers. "Then there's a Bible slammer over in Stanwood, but I don't think his mama will let him play on Sundays. She says it's reserved for the Lord."

I slumped back against the row behind me. My thinnest position, power forward, was getting thinner fast.

"I need to see the Whalen kid over at Loyola," I said.

"Right. He probably should be in the mix. To tell you the truth, I half expected to see him in the stands today." He craned his neck and perused the stands. "Loyola's got a non-league game tonight. The young man churned up a few waves when he jumped from Everton, though. The move brought back the old public-private school argument, especially when the school's out of the district. However, the bigger fuss recently has been recruiting. The publics say the privates recruit any eighth-grader they please."

"There were some coaches who were really upset by that move," I said. "Know it was for basketball only."

"Proving it, though, is darn near impossible," Coatsworth said. "You can't keep a parent from pulling a kid from a public school and sticking him in a private."

I lifted a shoulder in a *Who knows?* move.

"I guess the father was a big-time helicopter parent," Coatsworth said. "He just wouldn't stop interfering with the kid-coach relationship and the program. Didn't they find the dad dead shortly after all that mess? Realtor, right? Did you know the guy?"

"I met him a few times and we talked on the phone, but he worked with a different clientele. I doubt if there were a lot of retired teachers in his Rolodex looking for rustic cabins."

"What a tough deal. A kid losing a dad at such a critical age. Let's hope someday they find the guy who did it. I'm sure the family could use the closure."

He slid a handful of extra evaluation forms into his lap and turned toward me.

"I never told you this, Ernie. But as you can imagine, we had other candidates for your North Counties position. Some pushed hard. One who approached us, actually, he didn't come forward—his representative approached us. Can you believe it? A coach having an agent for a position that doesn't pay? He was quite surprised by our final decision, saying your MS zapped your energy, and that you could never put the time and effort into it that's needed. He obviously wanted this deal."

"Look, Coats, I've been upfront with you from the get-go. Nothing's changed. I probably don't catch the ball as well on the fast break as well as I used to, but I can still coach and have got plenty of juice. I'm told nobody can even tell."

"Right, but hear me out. The members on the interviewing committee felt the guy probably wanted the job for the wrong reasons. They said he was after the personal exposure to players and the individuals the kids now lure. What he didn't know is that I've got a brother-in-law with multiple sclerosis who's a ski instructor at Crystal Mountain. He was diagnosed ten years ago. He takes his drugs and says he's never skied better or played harder."

I stood and stretched. As my hands lowered toward the

floor, I angled my fingers away from a spattering of spilled popcorn. *Using a disease to leapfrog over somebody else?* It'd never even occurred to me.

"Maybe I shouldn't even have told you," Coatsworth said. "But I got the feeling some of the coaches who are here today were also surprised that you looked so good. We need to get people thinking that everybody with MS is not an immediate candidate for a wheelchair."

I also wasn't a nominee to sit next to them and buddy-up in a gym. A few had deemed me contagious. Two greeted me as if I had just been fired from a longtime job. I could feel the wincing glances from a handful of other coaches, especially the older guys from communities out in the sticks.

After a long pause, I said, "Tell you the truth, Coats, I first thought MS was a fast, ugly track to a death sentence. I was as ignorant as the next guy. So, I'm not surprised by anybody's reactions. And if somebody really wanted this job bad enough, maybe they would play the disease card against me. Who knows?"

Coatsworth rose. "I better go see if our next group of players need anything in the locker room. I suggest you spend a little time with the coach at Everton. He's a young guy; I believe this is his third year. It might be beneficial to get his take on the Whalen transfer."

"Will do," I said. "He's on my list, but I've got my hands full at the moment just in the organization of all this. I've got to find some guys who can play so the district team can compete in Seattle. I've got a feeling you didn't choose me to do this so that I could fall on my face."

"No, I didn't," Coatsworth laughed. "As I said, you don't

need a faceplant just coming out of retirement. Besides, it could prove to be a big ding to my reputation."

I nodded warily and looked across the court where two Evergreen State assistants appeared to be comparing notes. "Thanks for the concern about my future."

Glancing down at the scratched Timex I'd purchased at Ace Hardware, I wondered how and when the hint of condensation had gathered atop what had to be the number 4. It was time to stop guessing what was behind the fog on a number of issues, including Margie McGovern, my desire to coach, and smokescreen reps masquerading as college assistants. I vowed to find the engraved watch given to me by the school district and upgrade the Timex.

"I'll go see the Everton coach, but I've got to push a few other items off my plate before I do. If Whalen's a coaching challenge, I've got to muster more bandwidth than I've got at the moment before I meet with him."

The blonde woman in the second row stood, hands on hips.

"Nice body," chirped a voice from above and behind us. "She sure likes showing it off, too. How old do you think she is?"

"Hmmm, tough to tell from here," another chimed in. "But I'll tell ya, I wouldn't mind takin' that to the rack. And I don't mean to the hoop."

Swooping up a huge yellow patent leather purse, the woman relaxed a grimace long enough to shoot a practice smile to a pair of portly seniors and disappeared behind the bleachers.

"It certainly doesn't appear that she found who she was looking for," Coatsworth said as he headed toward the corridor between two sets of grandstands.

"Tell her I just cleared an empty seat for her right here,

Coats," said one of the coaches seated behind me. Coatsworth smiled and pointed a *You got it* finger toward the voice.

Spreading a handful of player profile sheets on the bench in front of me, I considered the time-consuming work ahead. I began to mentally bracket my region's schools and wondered who I would ask to assist in scouting and coaching the select squad. Linnbert Oliver immediately came to mind, along with Dr. Timoteo Mesa, a longtime friend and volunteer trainer at Washington High.

As I scribbled a question mark next to a player's listed height, the bleachers jiggled slightly and the smell in the gym suddenly turned to fresh peaches. The blonde woman who had drawn all the stares plopped down next to me, her black jacket nearly touching my sleeve. The move caught me off guard, like a car pulling into the slot next to mine in a near-empty parking lot.

"A man over there said you were Ernie Creekmore," she smiled, her words flavored with what appeared to be a last-minute Lifesaver mint that briefly made an appearance when she spoke.

"Well, that man was correct."

"I wanted to introduce myself." She snapped her shoulders back, forcing her considerable breasts forward. A couple of the men behind us cleared their throats and shuffled their feet.

"I'm Samantha Whalen, and I have a son who is a basketball player at Loyola High School." She offered her hand, fingers pointing curiously more toward the floor than at me. I shook it. She allowed one hard downward stroke before yanking her hand back atop her purse.

"Nice to meet you," I said.

More squirming above us rattled the bleachers. I didn't share the fascination, raw- physical or otherwise. This lady dripped high-maintenance, the type of person who would be allergic to my off-day pleasures like kayaks and crab pots.

"I was hoping to meet my son, Trent, here," she said while combing the stands, chin high. Her plum lip gloss was too perky for the setting, yet it was early and she looked like a woman who had other stops to make. She swirled toward me, her knee bumping mine. "I understand you will be coaching a team in some all-star tournament in Seattle."

"Correct again."

"Well, I believe my Trent is in your territory. There are some sort of boundaries for all these teams and he falls within your particular boundary? Something like that?"

"You are now three for three."

"Well, you probably know he is a very good player, and he is now getting a lot of interest from college coaches and other people."

I folded my hands in my lap. "What other people are you talking about?"

"Well, I guess people like yourself who want him to play in tournaments 'n stuff."

I suddenly felt the commitment involved in dealing with the peripherals of a big-time team. While I had to explain to some parents why their child did not make my old high-school teams, this would be a completely different game. Entitlement cards would be played, and this was only the first.

I straightened up and faced her. "Mrs. Whalen, I don't ..."

"It's Samantha. Please."

"I was going to say that I don't know if I want him to play

for our team in the tournament yet because I have not seen him play in a long time and know very little about him. I do plan on seeing him on the court soon."

She slung the purse handle loops over her wrist, slapped her hands on her knees, and lifted her rump off the bench into a half-squat. And leaned in closer. I thought she flashed me a tiny wink but I was too dumbfounded to judge. I did, however, feel a soft pat on my back.

"I'll be in touch," she said before sidestepping down the row toward the exit.

*　　*　　*

I stopped by Tony's for a cold one, and George sent me home with a carry-out foam carton stuffed with enough fettuccine alfredo to feed an Italian army. Coasting down the driveway, clutch pedal to the floor to save the neighbors the dreaded pop-pop arrival of the bus, I killed the engine and glided to a stop in the garage. I swung down from the driver's seat with a handful of property files, the beer now adding to the weight of a heavy day.

Sauntering toward the back door, I dropped my keys while trying to pin a manila folder under my arm. Bending down in the darkness near the threshold, I observed that the door was slightly ajar, its bottom weather strip angled slightly above the mudroom's checkered laminate floor.

I'd left the house earlier via the main entry, recalling how I parked my coffee mug on the porch's wicker table in order to lock the deadbolt. Since a boatload of out-of-town coaches plus half of my former players still in the county knew about the extra house key in the garage refrigerator, I was more in-trigued about the identity of a surprise visitor looking for a cold beer rather than concerned about an uninvited intruder seeking valuables. *Valuables? Like old issues of Sports Illustrated or state tournament programs?*

With both hands fumbling with food, keys and files, I backed into the door, using my rear to swing it open. I won-dered why I even bothered to lock the place. I mean, this was, after all, North Fork, Washington.

"Welcome," I shouted. "Now, who is the latest party crash-er? Forgive me if I somehow missed the memo."

No reply.

I plopped the files and keys on the washing machine, flicked on the mudroom light, and sidled into the kitchen with the still-warm carton of pasta that I slid abruptly across the counter toward the sink.

"Don't tell me you're already in the sack," I called, head-ing to the spare bedroom. En route, I slammed into the knife drawer beneath the kitchen counter, nearly taking a chunk out of my left thigh. Tilting forward, I attempted to rub away the pain while silently closing the drawer. I could feel my cool and calm sliding away to anxiety and alarm. There were no known secret female admirers in my life, but I was running out of catchy intro lines.

"Ah, the night is young, and so are we."

Curling my arm into the room, I waved my hand in small arcs on the bedroom wall, searching for the light switch.

"I've even got ..." My gut grew tighter as the single overhead fixture illuminated an empty room. No strange jackets draped on furniture; no indentations on the tight plaid bedspread. "...

fresh pasta."

I could feel the moisture on my forehead as I looked constantly over my shoulder down the narrow hallway. Unzipping my jacket, I wrapped it firmly around my right forearm, knowing that any blade would have to work its way through heavy canvas and goose down before it pierced my flesh. I continued with a now-guarded tour of my own home.

"The king has come home to his castle," I roared. "Has no one afforded him the courtesy of a proper greeting?" But the last sentence lacked the uppity flair I intended; a peculiar dryness had settled in the bottom of my throat.

The guest bathroom was next on the left. The chrome doorknob, cold to the touch, turned without sound, and I planted one of my size-thirteen boots in the middle of the emerald tile floor. Flicking on the bar lights above the mirror, I immediately backhanded the vinyl curtain the entire length of the shower. Norman Bates without a knife.

I managed a fake cough, deliberately left the lights on, and edged around the corner toward my bedroom.

"OK," I yelled. "Is anybody home?" I waited a few seconds. "I mean, it is *my* home."

An unwanted stranger in my bedroom would be the supreme violation. The door was wide open. I coaxed a shaking hand around the molding and leaned closer, pressing my body tight against the hallway wall. Inching my head into the opening, I could discern nothing more than the silhouetted rolltop desk and headboard and the far end of the bed. I swept my hand along the wall for the light, and was relieved to find my home court unoccupied and just as I'd left it.

Not exactly show condition, especially for a female guest,

but far from a stage-four disaster. The bed was not actually made, but the covers were pulled and straightened. Neither sheets nor pillows were exposed. Edith would be appalled but I was rather pleased. Shirts were hung in the closet, not draped on the leather recliner, and tennis shoes and dress shoes were properly aligned beneath a handful of Poinsettia Cleaners-wrapped sport coats and suits. *Yep, personal maintenance progress.*

The glow of the streetlight danced off the mirror above the living room mantel, tossing beams across the round oak table in the adjoining dining room. As I reached for the standing lamp in the corner, a dark green Chevy Nova cruised slowly down the street, inching to a stop directly opposite my front door. I hesitated, then twisted the tiny knob, lighting the room and revealing my presence.

As the car quickly pulled from the curb, I hustled to the picture window as it accelerated around the corner toward downtown North Fork. Nova or Buick Apollo? Old and ugly, definitely domestic. Four doors.

My breathing returned to near normal when the car sped away. I continued a strange, fake-cavalier exploration of my own digs. "I can see I arrived too late for this chalk talk," I mumbled, flinging open the coat closet adjacent to the front door. The raincoats hadn't been moved in months; my goofy assortment of faded ball caps were still neatly stacked on the shelf above, bills and team logos pointing out.

Completing the circuit through the book-crammed den and back toward the kitchen, I felt compelled to perform at least a cursory inspection of the cleaning closet, the last remaining unopened door in my usually cozy Craftsman. Years ago, I rigged the door for Cathy with a pop-out, hands-free switch that triggered a light upon entry.

As the bulb flickered in its tiny tomb, I discovered no surprises but no longer expected any. My dad's old canister vacuum cleaner, an orange-ribbon mop I got suckered into buying at the Puyallup Fair, and a monster bag of Costco charcoal briquettes dominated the floor space while a stack of old sweatshirt rags, cans of WD-40, Mr. Clean, LiquidWrench, and an extra bucket of OxiClean lined the side wall.

Note to self: The WD-40 is not in the garage.

I stepped into the kitchen and turned on the overhead light. Atop the steak-stained, pot-scarred butcher block table sat an enormous, dark chocolate layer cake on a foil-wrapped square. Brightly colored jimmies swirled into its round top.

The lines of a basketball.

The note, scribbled in familiar blue ink on yellow paper, appeared unevenly ripped from a tablet.

Elmo will be the frosting on your cake

I didn't know whether I should smash it or eat it.

Turning away, I splashed water on my face at the sink and yanked the paper towel roll so hard that a dozen extra sheets whirled onto the counter. The leaders made it to the floor, completing a white paper roller coaster.

I threw the pasta in the fridge, locked then latched both doors, and slumped onto the sofa, praying Jimmy Fallon's impersonations would take my mind elsewhere.

The call to Harvey could wait. I didn't want to gamble he'd take me off the case simply because somebody might want to break a few of my limbs with some compact angel food.

FIVE

MARTINA KELLOGG DETESTED her role as the substitute office receptionist and cherished every chance to let others know just how she felt about it.

Five-foot-eight and exceptionally thin, her spindly bird legs made me wonder how they could ever support the rest of her body. The taut skin on her face was now lined with the creases of time, and no one would ever guess her to be younger than her sixty-eight years. Cookie had her sit up front during Peggy's lunch breaks and vacations because Martina not only was the agency's least productive salesperson, but she possessed a deep, proper, traditional tone like a dignified housekeeper in a *Masterpiece Mystery*. Martina could swap her sinister, vinegar-tongued office delivery for a smooth, caramel-laced telephone greeting in the time it took to push the call-waiting button.

When I discovered her scowling down the hallway, headset temporarily coiled about her long, narrow neck, I tried to shrink behind my wastebasket. She looked like a grandma en route to a mandatory telemarketing class.

"There's a woman asking for you at the front desk," Martina barked. "Evidently, it has nothing to do with real estate. And, quite frankly, this is not the place for you to conduct your personal business. She punctuated her statement by snapping an orange WHILE YOU WERE OUT note in front of me. The telephone box was checked. The caller was *Scott Hazelton*, and the message read *hoop promoter*.

"I don't even know this guy, Martina. And, as far as my personal life goes, I doubt if the visitor has got a lot of juicy gossip potential for you."

She huffed, and I mimicked the huff back at her. "Well, I need for you to come up and deal with her immediately. Hopefully, that can be done outside the building."

"I'd hate to have Big River Realty get the reputation of rejecting women in distress."

Martina folded burgundy paisley sleeves across her chest and bowed one heavily penciled eyebrow. "She certainly doesn't appear as if she's anywhere near distress. And"—she cringed—"you wore a Pendleton shirt to *work*?"

The woman paging through HOUSE BEAUTIFUL in the waiting area appeared to be the physical antithesis of Martina Kellogg. Her tan legs, crossed high in front of her on the faux-leather loveseat, were long and athletic beneath an expensive charcoal skirt. When she rose to greet me, she flashed a wry, almost satirical grin I sometimes found in women sitting confidently at a bar. A nicely cut white long-sleeve blouse topped with a creative silver necklace accentuated a fit, impressive figure.

"Coach Creekmore, we've never met. I'm Diane Chevalier."

Behind the front counter, Martina leered and faked a cough.

"Pleased to meet you," I said.

"I've seen your picture in the newspaper alongside some of the properties you have for sale."

"It's reassuring somebody other than myself checks those pages. We spend a lot of money for those ads but we're finding most people now first discover us online."

"Yes, well, I'm not here to talk about a house. At least not right now. I'm renting a home near Warm Beach. Your information in the paper reminded me that a mutual friend suggested I get in touch." Her cell phone blasted the opening bars of The Doors' "Love Her Madly." Dipping into her purse, she palmed the phone and checked the caller ID. "Excuse me. I need to take this." She fired off a couple of quick yeses, nodded as if in agreement, then said, "Call me in an hour."

She stashed the phone back in her bag, rearranged her shiny brown hair with a quick shake and spoke. "Sorry about that. The trials of transition. I'm managing my company on a cell and laptop for the time being until we get set up in my garage or find a small office."

Diane dropped her hands and extended her fingers, as if to halt and hold the moment. "Right, well, I have a son who is a high school junior. He really enjoys basketball, and I understand you have been coaching around here for a long time. Since he'll be new in school, I thought I might ask you for some recommendations."

She looked and spoke like a woman in charge, yet with a playfulness and innocence of someone much younger than a mom with a kid in his late teens. Her hooded eyes, once I got to explore them, appeared speckled with a deep green and carried an invitation to something more. Not unlike my wife's eyes once did.

"I see. I'd love to visit over lunch sometime, but my time is a little short right now, unfortunately. Can you tell me a little bit about him."

"Well, he's six-foot-nine and still growing. Timoteo Mesa over at the clinic mentioned to him during his physical exam that you might be a helpful resource."

Bending slightly, I attempted to hide my enthusiasm with an extended stretch. "I see. You just provided two notable pieces of information from a well-respected individual. Would you have a moment to follow me to a place where we could talk?"

"You should be advised that the conference room is reserved for most of the day," Martina announced. Then, toward me in a surlier tone that Diane could obviously hear, "Please do not inconvenience others with non-work-related conversation that could more appropriately be held elsewhere."

In front of me, Diane cowered in jest. As we whirled and walked back toward the entry, Martina displayed an extended sneer as she settled in behind the phones.

"I know if Mrs. Chevalier should choose to visit us again," I said, "I'm sure you would offer her some of those imported shortbread cookies you hoard in your desk. The ones you bring out for special occasions? They *might* make her feel more welcome."

SIX

THE JESUITS WHO run Loyola High School are more than proud to note that it is one of the oldest continuously running educational institutions in the state.

Started in a one-room house on Native American land just west of Marysville in the 1879, the good fathers waited nearly eight decades before they decided to build a gym/cafeteria. When a wealthy benefactor donated a former dairy farm just south of Warm Beach for a new all-boys school in 1946, the priests raked the back forty for a football field and a baseball diamond but relied on the school's cafeteria for basketball. A single ring of steel folding chairs surrounded the court. Wrestling pads protected players from flying onto the stage when fouled after a layup. When the Cubs made the playoffs, games were moved up the road to Stanwood High, much to the chagrin of the archrival Spartans.

When a well-heeled grad gifted a huge waterfront piece of Camano Island in 2000, the school finally built a suitable basketball facility, yet tried to cut corners and save costs by installing a bright, slick but extremely inexpensive "all-purpose" polyurethane floor. Two years and several broken ankles and torn ligaments later, Loyola tore up the floor and invested in top-quality maple, making the gym the best playing surface in the county.

The new floor, complete with a snarling lion cub logo at

midcourt, attracted players like Trent Whalen. The school's reputation for discipline, order, and the high percentage of students going on to four-year schools helped as well.

The bad news about a newer building is that there's no place to hide for a scout. Few have balconies, and all the pull-down bleachers are open and in full view. Bring a clipboard and you stick out like a sore thumb. It was the main reason many scouts have gone to tiny handheld devices to record observations and tendencies. If the place is packed, I can sometimes sneak up into a corner behind the teams' benches and eliminate the straight-across sight lines of coaches and assistants, but I still run the risk of being identified by a competitor or reporter. Guys like Greg Smithson from the *Seattle Tribune* know every coach in the state and are never shy about asking who I was scouting and why.

For some reason, perhaps fueled only by my own expectations of a terrific contest between the Rainier Vista Vikings from Seattle's Metro League, I expected a larger crowd. I thought more Skagit County fans would turn out to see the speed and quickness of the inner-city black kids against the strength and toughness of the mostly white farm boys from nearby dairies.

Not tonight.

Eager to observe player body language and how coaches interacted with their troops, I chose a row opposite the teams' benches just above the foul line and near the top of the bleachers. I waved to a couple of retired coaches and nodded to several semi-familiar faces who turned in their seats when I pulled out my pencil. Above me and to my left sat a couple of no-neck bullet-heads in red windbreakers who most likely had dreams of converting one of tonight's guards into a running back or a power forward into a tight end.

Like Trent Whalen.

As I settled in for the player intros, a chubby man in rimless glasses who looked like a sixty-year-old bank teller shot me a half-wave from his beltline. I had no idea who he was but he clearly knew me and was headed my way. A slightly larger version of Danny DeVito, complete with the flyaway collar and sweat beading on the balding forehead. He sat in the row below me and offered his hand. It was soft and damp.

"Manny Cossetti. Good to finally meet ya, Coach. Really heard a lot about ya."

"Really?" I looked around to determine if anyone was listening. Or watching.

Cossetti's baggy black blazer, adorned with an ornate golden lion crest, stank of stale tobacco. He looked like a Jacuzzi salesman at a home show.

"Wouldn't be surprised if several of these players ended up in that Seattle torn-na-munt. Say, let me give you my card. Before I forget."

He lifted a black leather satchel on to his lap. He opened it just a crack and tried to block it from my view with his lumpy shoulder, like a magician concerned that a child might look too closely at his bag of tricks. I slipped it into my coat pocket without reading it, and simply nodded to a litany of his unintelligible comments without making eye contact or saying a word.

I turned to the game. Trent Whalen stood strong despite the Rainier Vista flurry, imploring his teammates to take their time and run their offensive sets. I could not help but smile at his massive baseline screens, lumberjack legs spread shoulder-length apart, hands crossed at his navel as his teammates ripped by close to his body, rubbing their opponents into his sturdy frame.

Unlike most high-school kids, Whalen blocked out on every shot and not only on his assigned player. When a shot went up, he surveyed the scene and instinctively went after the Viking who stood the best chance of grabbing the rebound, often riding the opponent away from the play and nearly off the court. As I expected, there was no backing down, even when a Viking got in his face for spreading his elbows high and wide.

While he missed three of five short jumpers and did little to astound me offensively, it was clear Trent Whalen could play the game. And by the time the first half was over, I knew he could play for me.

I headed toward the snack stand, and was joined moments later by a smiling Manny Cossetti, waddling in the door from the parking lot.

"Smoke and a client call," Manny said. "Now I'm set for the second half."

"Excuse me, Manny. But what exactly do you do?"

"Variety of things, really. You pick and I roll. Ya falla?"

"I'm sorry. I don't."

"Mostly try to obtain the maximum amount of exposure for my clients."

"And a client can be …?"

"Just about anybody. Law firms, shoe companies, athletes. Ya falla?"

I blinked and shook my head. "Help me understand how you are compensated, for say, helping a high school athlete."

He peered at me as if I had just arrived from the moon. "Well, if the kid is good enough to go to the pros, maybe to Europe or Asia, I'd get a percentage of his professional contract. And maybe a little finder's fee on the side."

I crossed my arms and swayed side to side. "But so few of them go on to that level of play. Most talented kids can't even get a ride to a D-1 school."

"True, and some college coaches show their appreciation if I can encourage a young man to attend their school or summer camp."

"I see," I said, looking both ways down the hall. "Camps, too, eh ...? Excuse me. It's time for my popcorn."

"I'll walk with you."

As I pulled a bill from my wallet to hand to the vendor, I heard Manny's voice from behind me.

"Did you get my email? I sent it the other day about exploring possibilities."

"I did. And I'm not quite certain what 'fulfilling the best interests of my players' means."

Clutching the bag and a napkin, I returned to the free space near the wall. Manny followed me like an aggressive panhandler.

"Look, Coach, I know you are relatively new at this fringe stuff, but there are a lot of college coaches who are going to be extremely eager to speak with you once your select roster is set. Division 1, D-2, even the Ivies, who don't even give athletic scholarships. They are going to need kids and the best place for them to start is to get to the guys who have the most influence on where they end up. All-star team coaches like yourself. You are the center of their universe."

"So you get paid for getting me to have lunch with them? I don't like it."

He bent backward and glared at me, as if accused of a crime he did not commit.

"Compensated, sure," he said. He stepped closer and opened a hand like an usher directing me to a seat. "But, hey, look at it this way." His tone was confident and excited, like an inventor explaining a proven product. "Let's say you have a kid that you love that no school knows about. The guy can really play but for some reason he's not on anybody's radar. The young man wouldn't stand a chance of getting a free college education unless you told a college coach about him."

I hitched my shoulders. "I can always pick up a phone and call assistants, head coaches that I know."

"And what if you miss? They say he's not a good fit for whatever reason. Or, the school's scholarship allotment is gone. You gonna feel good about telling the kid you went to bat for him but failed? No!"

"I believe I could find the right coach who—"

"What I'm proposing is getting you in front of some college coaches you might have never thought about contacting. Ya falla? Guys you had no idea were interested."

I tossed some popcorn in my mouth and looked down at the stained-concrete floor, a soda-pop-sticky concourse the color of a muddy winter stream that missed the janitor's mop.

"Ever hear of a guy by the name of Scott Hazelton?" I said.

Manny flopped his too-short arms across his middle and widened his stance. "One of the newer kids on the block. Most of the guys who have been around awhile call him Mister BS. That's bait-and-switch, among other things. His pitch and promised prizes depend on the type of agent he's running for."

"What do you mean, 'running for'?"

"The kid's a runner, not an agent. Runners find ways of getting close to players then introduce, link, and otherwise hook 'em up with professional agents. Sometimes coaches. That's 'cuz agents need to funnel cash and other goodies to kids through an intermediary or third party. These 'runners' then get paid in a variety of ways—lump-sum cash, premium tickets, part of a signing bonus, maybe a piece of a coach's shoe contract."

I glanced down the hallway in both directions. Dance team members screamed past, concerned about fixing their hair before the second-half tip.

Manny raised his eyebrows and pulled gently on his primary chin. "Man, you have been gone a long time."

"Tell me something," I said. "How do these agents and runners know a player is even going to sign with them once a payment has been made?"

"Most of them don't, and the savvy kids really take advantage of it. They'll string an agent or school along, stashing cash for months, sometimes years. The agent just looks at it as a cost of doing business, knowing full well that a lot of the time the cash will be gone and the kid will go somewhere else. Schools, too. You hear stories all the time how some hotshot assistant babysat a kid for a year only to have lost him at the last minute to another school. It becomes pretty evident when the kid is seen around town in a new Escalade with custom chrome rims."

"OK, so I guess I'm really naïve. I always thought that a guy who was interested in a kid only represented one school. But now that players actually plan one-and-done college careers, they could be speaking for a variety of people?"

Manny leaned in closer, his short black facial stubble shined with perspiration. "Coach, every one of these guys could be a double or triple agent. Basketball espionage at its best. The days of the good ol' booster with the car dealership steering a kid to his alma mater are gone. Now, as soon a young man shows even a remote chance of one day playing for money, there's a good chance the runner will tell 'em he can help with not only a school but also a professional contract."

"So, how is what you do different from what they do?"

"I never take money from a school. Ask any coach. I'll gladly take four good ducats down low at the foul line for the biggest conference game of the year. Final Four? Even better. But as much as college basketball is big business, I do my part to keep cash out of the college game. But if a kid's going pro, anything goes. Play for pay? Hey, I'm in. The agent's gonna get a cut and I'm entitled to my share for doing the legwork."

"Know anything about a bag full of money on the floor of my bus?"

Manny's shoulders drooped and his head bobbed lower. He looked as if I had hit and run his car.

"Seriously? That kind of stuff is sleaze central. Not my style, Coach. Besides, none of the people I represent would allow it. If they ever found out I did something like that, my future would be toast."

His voice trailed off as the Loyola players sprang from a locker room door in front of us and jogged casually down the hallway en route to the band-jamming gym. The assistant coaches followed. Bringing up the rear was the head coach, flanked by a rangy man in pleated black trousers that folded perfectly atop gleaming cordovan loafers. His slicked-back, gel-coated hair would have made Pat Riley proud. It was duck-tailed above the cardboard-like collar of his baby-blue calypso shirt.

As the coach neared the double doors, the two men stopped, smiled and faced each other. They energetically clasped hands and slapped backs, two synchronized pats popular among longtime male friends. But at halftime of a star-studded regional game?

"You asked about Scott Hazelton?" Manny said, nodding toward the gym door. "Take a look for yourself."

*   *   *

Eugene Slaughter dragged four fingers through his curly red hair outside the Loyola locker room, just steps from the spot where I'd spent the halftime break with Manny Cossetti. The Cubs' coach dabbed a hankie at the perspiration on his forehead, coughed briefly into a fist, and asked a reporter to repeat a question.

"As I mentioned earlier, we just made too many mistakes down the stretch when the game was on the line," Slaughter said as if plucking a line from a rehearsed script. "You can't expect to beat a team as good as Rainier Vista when you turn the ball over as much as we did tonight."

I smiled. Been there, said that. *Way to be original, Gene.*

Greg Smithson also cringed at the stock answer. When I caught his eye, he nodded my way.

"Do you think Whalen's elbow was deliberate?" Smithson said.

Bam. Clearly, the most important post-game question to

the handful of reporters present, but only Smithson had the guts to ask. Slaughter shifted his feet, then propped the sole of his shoe against the wall as he leaned against the off-yellow cinder blocks.

"No, I don't, and I spoke with Trent about it," Slaughter said. "Rhodes was playing up on him tight. When Trent caught the ball and pivoted, his arms were already out." The coach demonstrated the move in the hallway, palms above his head, elbows hovering at ear level. "When Trent turned, he simply caught Rhodes in the nose. Yes, there was a lot of blood, but it looked worse than it really was. Nosebleeds always do."

Smithson pulled me aside and asked to be invited to our select team practice. I mentioned I'd just begun selecting the team but would stay in touch. As the last of the reporters closed his notebook and sauntered away, I shuffled toward Slaughter.

I knew a little about him, thanks to George Berrettoni, my unofficial scout with a constant ear to the ground. Slaughter spent five years with a downtown Seattle commercial real estate firm scrambling to find tenants for a developer's new skyscraper. Married with two young children, he traded competitive fourteen-hour workdays for a calmer life in the country.

Resituated in northwest Snohomish County, Slaughter and his wife both turned to teaching and coaching. George said Slaughter's career change produced a financial hardship, transitioning from lucrative real estate commissions to rather meager school salaries while the girls remained enrolled in an exclusive Seattle academy. Slaughter's wife earned more at a public middle school than Gene did as chair of Loyola's history department and head basketball coach. The Jesuits have never been known for excessive salaries.

I stepped up and introduced myself.

"Please, I know who you are," Slaughter smiled, extending his hand. "I mean, is there anybody around here who doesn't?" I grinned awkwardly, and winced through his knuckle-crunching grip. "I just wish you would have seen us on a night when we played hard for all four quarters."

"You were up against a talented team with a coach dedicated to details. That team seems to be on a roll. Counting tonight, that's three impressive wins in a row."

Slaughter shook his head and gently angled a shoulder against the hallway wall. His thin tortoiseshell frames nearly disappeared in the hair along the sides of his head.

"You played, Coach. I played. Did we just *battle* more than kids today, or am I just crazy? I mean, it was as if our kids didn't think they could really win. Or didn't deserve to win. Rainier Vista made that eight-point run and our guys acted like it was supposed to happen. The only guy with any real confidence was Whalen and he doesn't shy away from anybody. I don't know, maybe I have to find a better way to teach toughness."

"Speaking of toughness," I said. "I could use a guy who can mix it up on the Northwest select team we're putting together for a Seattle tournament. I came tonight to scout Trent Whalen and also wanted to get your opinion as to the type of teammate he would make."

Slaughter popped off the wall, slid the silk tie from his button-down shirt and carefully folded it into the breast pocket of his tweed coat.

"I think he'd be a terrific addition," Slaughter said. "But you know who you want and what might work best for you. He'll be out of the locker room soon, so you can see for yourself. I'm not backing the guy just because I'm his coach and I'd like to see him and our school in the newspaper. The kid's a born leader, a coach on the floor. All my guys like him, respect him. He knows where everybody should be at all times. And lord knows he doesn't take any crap from anybody."

I nodded. "I guess what I wanted to ask you is if he also creates any crap."

He shook his head. "I can honestly say that I have not seen Trent initiate any BS during a game. He's not a cheap-shot artist. After some of the problems on the court at Everton, some of our opponents have come after him, trying to get under his skin. I'm not saying that there haven't been any confrontations, I just haven't seen him start them."

"Right, but it takes two to tango."

"Yes, it absolutely does," Slaughter said. "And Trent could have done a better job in how he responded in some situations. But he's not out there roaming around, constantly looking for a fight. A lot of people think he is, but nothing could be further from the truth."

"What has he said about his time at Everton?"

"He hasn't really said that much to me, other than his parents felt Loyola would better prepare him for college."

Slaughter straightened up and crossed his arms, as if his initial interest in meeting me had descended into discomfort.

"Remember, all that went on before I got here," Slaughter said. "When the awful incident happened with his dad, I was still in real estate. Barney resigned after school started last September and he was in the middle of all the transfer stuff. I'd heard some secondhand buzz but I didn't know much about the real history of any of it. When Barney departed, the varsity team kind of fell in my lap, and I was the new guy in the building."

If Slaughter was aware of the police's renewed interest in Trent Whalen as a suspect in his father's death, he was doing an admirable job of concealing it.

A trio of wet-haired Loyola players emerged from the steamy doorway, their team-logoed Cubs gym bags slung over their shoulders. As they sauntered down the hall, Slaughter called out, "Next time, guys. Next time." Heads down, none of them altered their strides.

Slaughter shook his head and stared down the corridor. "We'll get better," he murmured. "Games like this help you get better." He wheeled toward me, as if emerging from a momentary daze. "So, the big guy takes forever to dress. Usually one of the last out of the shower," Slaughter said. "I understand he's going to have a lot of options, and maybe not just at the collegiate level. There could be some international clubs coming after him pretty hard."

"I see," I said. "Well, I'm afraid I'm not in the position to offer something that intriguing. There's been talk of a possible Northwest traveling squad after the Seattle Center Spring Hoopfest, but all that is still way down the road."

Trent Whalen swaggered from the locker room and lofted his bag in front him. The canvas cylinder skidded to a stop at the base of the hallway wall near his coach's feet. A stiff Levi's jacket covered at least two layered shirts. The combination made his shoulders look huge. His forehead still dripped with sweat.

"Didn't git 'er done, Coach," he said, head down. "We were in it for a while, but couldn't finish."

Slaughter slapped the player on the back. I moved in closer, awaiting an intro.

"Trent, I think you know Coach Creekmore. He's putting together an all-star team."

"Sure, Coach." He nodded in my direction. "I've heard a bit about it. How ya doin'?"

I stepped to the middle of the hallway and extended my hand. He looked at it briefly then quickly looked away, rejecting the handshake.

"Trent? Coach Creekmore is in a position to add you to a very special team."

"Look, no 'fense," Trent said. "But I'm playing well right now and can't afford to get sick. We've got important games coming up and I owe it to my team to be ready."

Slaughter slid back against the wall, feet flat on the floor, his mouth wide open.

"Excuse me?" He shot Trent an icy look.

"Let me help," I said. "Unless Trent is referring to some nasty transmittable bug I know nothing about. I've got multiple sclerosis. I was diagnosed about seven years ago. Apparently Trent believes it's contagious."

The player crossed one massive Wolverine work boot over the other, folded his arms, and peered down the hall.

"Well, it certainly is not and I can personally guarantee you that!" Slaughter shouted. "I'm just stunned that—"

"Don't be, Coach. Trent's not the Lone Ranger. A lot of people don't know how to be around a person with MS. I was with a couple of coaches down in Arlington the other day who reacted just like Trent. It happens more than you might think. No worries."

Slaughter shook his head as if still annoyed and approached his star. "Look, you've got nothing to be worried about here. Nothing. I see this as a great opportunity for you because select teams this far north aren't that common. I'd say we're lucky regional officials have put this together and Coach Creekmore is here tonight."

Trent stared at the floor. "You're right. We haven't had an all-star team since Cheese Oliver played at Washington High. What was that? Five years ago, anyway."

"It's been seven," I said, easily recalling the best player I ever coached. "There were a couple of efforts since then but somehow it never happened. It always came down to big school-small school allocation. The little guys felt they weren't getting a fair shake, that they were rarely given a chance to make the team."

"How about this time around?" Slaughter asked.

"We are definitely open to everybody," I said. "In fact, from what I've seen so far, I think some of our biggest contributors could come from some of the smallest towns."

"At least we'll know that they'll make free throws," Trent said.

Slaughter squinted and scratched his head. "Hmmm. Why do you say that?" he said.

"'Cuz kids from small towns got nothin' else to do."

Slaughter coughed out a laugh, caught by the big-city line of his own player in his own gym. I smiled in respect for a kid with the pluck to zing his coach.

After a moment Trent said, "Coach, what guys you scoutin' mix it up on defense? Lot of dudes I know got all-star attitudes. Only want to run and gun. Nobody wants to hit the boards."

I nodded. He'd scored a point in a game he didn't know about. "That's one of the reasons I came to see you."

Trent shifted his weight from one leg to the other. "Well, always willing to do dirty work. Be nice to get some help, though. Inner-city kids like to 'timidate, see what they can get away with. Say white guys can't play. 'Specially kids from the sticks. Played in enough open gyms to see what goes on."

I smiled guardedly, attempting to hide not only my delight in his off-season effort and experience, but also of his understanding of the challenge ahead.

"You lookin' at Elmo Service up in Port Edwards?" Trent asked.

I flicked my shoulders to indicate uncertainty. "*Looking* would be the optimal word there," I said. "How would you feel about being on the same team with him?"

"Man never saw a shot he didn't like. Seen him go an entire half without passing the ball. If he gets it in the low post, it ain't comin' out. Even if he's triple-teamed."

I grinned, knowing he was probably correct. "So, you wouldn't be expecting a lot of help from Elmo under the boards?"

"You kiddin'? He's way too skinny to push people around under there. You stick a big butt on the guy, he'll go flying. Only rebounds he might get hit him in the back of the head when he's running down the floor."

If this kid was a clandestine monster, at least he had a sense of humor. "Well, I'll be in touch. There's still a lot of scouting and evaluating to be done and time is getting short."

"Hey, thanks for comin'," Trent said, now shaking my hand. "Wished we'd played better ... Love to be considered, though.

And please be on the lookout for another guy who doesn't have to shoot it every time down the floor."

"Will do."

Slaughter stepped in front of me and lowered his voice. "And if you need another assistant coach, let me know. I might be able to bring some people to the table who could solve a lot of your funding issues."

"I'll keep that in mind," I said, wondering if I would have to take him as an assistant coach to get his sources. "Did I make it sound like we were hurting for cash?"

"No, but a traveling team always needs help with expenses. Air fares are going up, hotels. And everybody knows how much food these guys can put away."

Air fares? Was I the last guy to know this was the first stop on a sophisticated traveling show?

I raised my hands in a slow-down sign. "First things first. I need to solidify the Seattle team, play that tournament and then we'll see what happens. Besides, we may not even be good enough to consider traveling. Prestigious events don't just invite anybody."

Trent Whalen picked up his bag and stepped toward the door.

"So, Coach Creekmore, do you know who's gonna be helpin' you 'sides my old coach?" Trent said.

"That's a good question," Slaughter said, hands on his hips. "How much room on the bench will you have for assistants?"

"Wait a minute," I said, as my clipboard slipped out of my hand and bounced on the concrete floor. "Who said anything about an assistant? I've always asked Dr. Timoteo Mesa to help me with—"

"This guy was a lot younger than you," Trent said, pointing to his coach. Slaughter frowned and shook his head. "Sorry. Anyway, he comes up to me after a game in Marysville. Maybe two weeks ago. Said he was representin' a Northwest prep team, that my old coach from Everton would be one of the coaches. Wanted to know if I might be interested."

"You don't say," I said. "Do you remember what this man looked like?"

"Dressed like a coach, black windbreaker, you know. White leather hightops. Never seen him before and I've been to a lot of clinics 'n stuff."

"You know, there are a ton of tournaments out there for kids these days," Slaughter said. "Maybe this guy was shopping for an entirely different event."

"I guess that's possible," I mused, raising a hand to the side of my face. "But I would think somebody in the coaching community would at least have mentioned it."

"No, it's the same team," Trent said. "Same tourney."

"What makes you so sure?" Slaughter said.

"Guy 'pologized for not getting in touch with me sooner. Said he'd gotten off to a late start 'cuz the guy who was going to coach was sick with MS."

Just then, Samantha Whalen in tight cords, calf-length suede Uggs and a wet-look leather jacket that cost more than a teacher's monthly salary scooted through the doorway leading to the gym. Her makeup appeared recently refreshed.

Trent sighed, jammed his hands in his pockets, and looked the other way.

"Sorry, hon," she said to Trent. "Shitty class and it ran late. Did you win, sweetie?"

"No," he mumbled without making eye contact.

"Oh, that's too bad," she whined, catching Slaughter's gaze. He nodded.

"Trent played hard, as usual," Slaughter said. Then, after a brief hesitation, "Samantha, I'd like you to meet Coach Ernie Creekmore."

"Oh, I know all about Ernie Creekmore. Her handshake again was brief; her grip hard and tight. I detected an eyebrow tic when she assessed my scuffed desert boots and wrinkled Dockers. "You're talking about the man who's gonna put my Trent in the lights of Seattle."

She turned back to her son. "Well, I didn't have time to make anything for dinner before I left, so what about stopping at Spud for fish and chips?"

"I guess," he whispered.

"OK then, I guess we'll be going." She dug deep into the same yellow purse to check the chirping of a text message, turned up the side of her lip at the illuminated type, then dropped the Betty Boop phone to the bottom of the bag. "Did you drive, honey, or did you ride with the guys?"

"Drove," Trent said, staring at his bag on the floor.

"Well then, I'll just meet you there, hon." She smiled, raised her eyebrows, and turned to leave. "And Coach Creekmore ... you just let me know when you are ready to come by the house."

Trent waited a few moments, shouldered his bag and sauntered after her.

Fingers clutching my chin, I flicked a *What's up with that?* glimpse at Slaughter.

"Oh, I know," he said. "Go figure. He's never got much to say to her. But it looks as if she's got a lot to say to you."

I felt blood rushing to my face. "She made a point of introducing herself at the district shootaround. She's a long way from bashful."

*   *   *

On the drive home, I blinked tired eyes and cut a couple of curves in the road too tight, once bringing an unnerving lean to the boxy bus. Were there really enough days to scout, recruit, and coach these kids into a respectable unit? What I did not anticipate were the additional hours needed to vet, actually investigate, some of their backgrounds.

I parked in the driveway and trudged through the back door. The message light on the phone flashed quick reds. I stabbed the play button.

"Coach, this is Trent. Trent Whalen. Sorry how I acted tonight. Just dumb, I guess. Would like to talk, though ... about your team? Without my mom around. I have a free period tomorrow, then lunch. Maybe we could get a sandwich or somethin'. I'll be at the Calico Cupboard at eleven-thirty. Thanks. Bye."

SEVEN

I F DR. TIMOTEO Mesa called the office when I was speaking with Cookie, I'd put the boss on hold. He was that kind of guy.

The bottom line is that he rarely did, believing my time could be better spent doing other things. The unofficial trainer during most of my time as head coach, "Tim Table" never asked a favor, was the first to volunteer for the most thankless jobs, and proved to be an uncanny judge of character and basketball talent. He knew when a kid could use a mature ear or a swat on the ass, and then found the appropriate person to do it.

An all-state soccer player in southwest Washington, he became the first member of his family to graduate from college. He put himself through UW's medical school, and after his residency, he filled a vacation relief position in the Skagit County Clinic's emergency room and never left. A quiet, unassuming confidant, he had a subtle way of improving a situation or providing a pleasing surprise. He was also one of a few people who could calm me down during a game, and kept me from getting nailed with even more technical fouls and ejections from exasperated referees.

The way he chose to make me aware of Nicholas Chevalier was a perfect example. No screaming voice-mail message proclaiming "You gotta see this kid!" No open-palm appearance with expectations of payback down the road. Instead, Timoteo elected to have the player's mother contact me, which led me to believe the good doctor deliberately intended for Diane to play a major role in the calculated intro. *Dr. Smooth.*

When he did telephone, I was heading out the door to a market analysis on a well-maintained, two-bedroom cabin on an acre of Stillaguamish River waterfront before my lunch with Trent and an afternoon meeting with Harvey.

"It's a long story, and very sad," Timoteo said. "How's your time? Give you the short version?"

"Either way," I lied.

"I went to medical school with Nick's father, Anthony. Four years ago, he died in a bicycling accident on a remote road outside of Sedona. Some cowboys in a pickup had too much to drink; he didn't stand a chance. He was DOA when they got him to the hospital in Flagstaff, the same place he had worked since we got out of school."

"I'm so sorry. Were you guys close all those years?"

"Yes. His family owned a farm and small restaurant just north of Flagstaff, on the road to the Grand Canyon. The kids helped out during the summers, making sure the vegetables and eggs from the farm were ready to go in the restaurant. After school got out the first year, he invited me back. Coming from a potato farm, I knew some of the routine. But it was Anthony and his family that made the difference. They treated me like I was one of their own."

Cradling the cell phone on my ear, I recalled the kindness of the Mexican migrants when working the apricot orchards in Yakima as a teenager. Always genuine, they made my life easier under the hot summer sun.

"Did you have a chance to visit after you took the job up here?" I said, pacing across the parking lot behind the office.

"I did, and we also met in the San Juans a couple of times. Diane's a Seattle girl and had vacationed in the islands with her family. She's got a sister in Arlington who's been after her to move to the area. After a couple of tough winters in Flag, she decided to pull the trigger and give it a try. She specializes in back-end computer scheduling and billing for hospitals."

"So, how long has she been doing the computer stuff at the Skagit Valley Clinic?"

"If she wanted the contract, she had to take it by January 1. Nick was here for a couple of days after Christmas and I gave him the district's mandatory physical. I'm pretty sure he's still growing, Ernie, and you're talking about a great kid. He went back to Arizona to finish the basketball season and the winter term. He's living with Anthony's family."

"Six-nine and still growing? Man, college coaches are going to be happy to hear that. Was Anthony a big guy? Did he play anywhere?"

"Actually, Anthony was about five-ten. He and Diane couldn't have kids. Tried for years. Lots of tears, setbacks. They adopted Nick when he was still an infant in the hospital. In fact, I don't know if the Chevaliers ever met the biological father."

"Is there a timeframe for Nick moving up here?"

"The last I heard, he is set to enroll at Washington High after spring break. I get the idea Diane was looking for your opinion if you thought that was still a good place to be."

"Absolutely. The coaches do a great job and some of the honors classes are top-notch." I paused, knowing that Timoteo expected the next question without any filters. We'd known each other too long for me to beat around the bush. "Can Nick really play? I mean, have you seen the kid go?"

"Only in the driveway of his mom's place at Warm Beach a couple of weeks ago. But every shot seemed to be going down, even from twenty-five feet. Diane told me Nick was drawing some interest from the Arizona colleges, but I was not expecting somebody that big to be that accurate on a bad basket from that far out. And, the way he strides, I have no doubt he can get up and down the floor in a hurry."

I leaped into the driver's seat of the bus and tingled with the possibilities, mentally slotting players into starting positions. Even a cursory evaluation from a knowledgeable observer like Timoteo was worth more than three scouting reports from most other sources. After a late organizational start, it was exhilarating even to consider that I'd just been handed the team's centerpiece. Low-maintenance, no jerk factor. With a game no local coach has yet to see, let alone try to defend.

"I can almost hear the wheels in your head churning from here," Timoteo said. "Why so quiet? Are you concerned Nick would not be eligible because he's a recent transfer student?"

"To be honest, I don't know what the rules say about that," I said. "I would presume he would have to be a student of record by the time the tourney started. Now that you have done the physical and it's on file, we just got to make sure he's enrolled somewhere before we head to Seattle."

"I'm sure you'll be OK. I had some home-schooled kids play on my soccer teams and an address in the county was all they needed."

As I tipped the sun visor down to stow the one-page cabin description, several dusty notes fluttered to the floor.

"Tell me, Timoteo, given our long and storied history, why in the hell did you wait so long to tell me about a six-nine kid who's headed this way?"

He laughed quietly and then made me wait longer than I wanted to.

"I was fishing for an invitation to be part of the select team. Thought you might need a good trainer."

"You lyin' sack. You know there's always a place for you."

"I needed to make sure it was a done deal that he was coming here," he said. "There have been a few false starts the past two years and I wasn't sure Diane would take the job until the last minute. No reason to dangle a couple of carrots."

"A couple?"

"Well, you did meet Diane, didn't you? And the last time I looked, you were still a healthy, single male. Besides, there's something about her that reminds me of Cathy."

EIGHT

It WASN'T DIFFICULT to spot Trent Whalen among the early-special senior crowd at Calico Cupboard, one of the remaining restaurants in North Fork without a drive-thru window or a children's play area. He was one of few males in the place with hair that wasn't white or blue, and absolutely the only one who was six-foot-seven and two hundred and thirty pounds. I shot him a *Howdy* nod and walked around the front counter toward him. His booth seemed to have been made for third-graders and I waved off his attempt to slide out and greet me.

"Tight fit," I laughed.

"Yeah," he shrugged. "The lady said there were no other tables." He wore a red plaid flannel shirt that could have covered the table, khaki trousers and brown lace-up shoes. The Jesuits required a collared shirt in class.

"Like to go for the meatloaf sandwich here," Trent said. "They got great meatloaf on sourdough." He picked up the salt shaker, rotated it quickly as if winding up a toy, and dropped it back next to the pepper.

We ordered food, then blew through the usual topics such as the weather, his interests in school and the coming of Mariners spring training in Arizona. Unlike what Harvey had said about curt replies, the youngster spoke in lucid, complete sentences. We discussed high players in the state, how he prepared for games, and his need to rest during tournaments.

He asked what it was like to coach a shooter like Cheese Oliver and mentioned he had played against him but never formally met him.

After an extended silence, he said, "I really do want to play on that team, Coach." His tone bordered on desperate. He leaned back suddenly and the entire booth shook. "I hope I didn't blow my chance last night."

"You didn't blow anything," I said. "I thought you played pretty well."

"No, I meant the other thing. You know, the handshake …?"

It took me a moment to recall the incident. "Forget it, please. Not even an issue." He exhaled and extended his hands on the green vinyl bench seat. "It doesn't seem, though, that you and your mom are on the same page about basketball."

"You got that right. And now it's become a little complicated."

"What do you mean?"

"Well, when my dad was alive, he made all the decisions. She had no idea how much he'd spent on private coaches, club dues, my shoes. I guess she didn't really care until the real estate market went in the tank and my dad didn't sell any homes for a while."

I acknowledged with a nod. "He wasn't the only agent who felt the downturn. We all took a pretty big hit."

"Right. Well, all of a sudden, he's dead, I'm in a private school, and we've got no money. She'd scream when I asked her for gas money."

He stopped and glanced down at the menu when the waitress returned to take our orders. After she left, there was an awkward silence.

"Mom always seems pissed and takes it out on everybody. Even her buds, unless she's drinkin'. She doesn't have time anymore for anything."

"Are you helping her out around the house?"

"Work around the house, when I can at the Shell Station. Even pick up medicine for her oldest friend. When I can't do it, I get some of my friends to run her errands 'n stuff."

"It's great you're able to do that, with practice and all."

"Yeah, I feel sorry for the lady. She's just lonely and can't do everything by herself."

I said, "I guess I'm not really clear on why you left Everton and enrolled at Loyola," I said. "It's none of my business, but the team didn't seem that bad."

Trent shook his head. "I still don't really know. Some sort of disagreement with the coach. One day, I was gone. Dad said the academics were better at Loyola."

"It must have been difficult to leave your friends."

"Not really. What was tough was that they made me sit out a year. Said I was only transferring to play hoop. Somebody complained to the state board. Something …"

"I heard that your mom just wanted you home. Maybe she was grieving and—"

"That wasn't the case. Believe me. That was *not* the case." He dropped his chin into his palm and looked out toward the street. "I got a job at the Shell station that year after school," he mumbled, "and gave her most of the money."

I tilted my head to gain eye contact. "So when did the basketball situation become complicated?"

His eyebrows swung higher. "When she found out some guys would be willing to pay her if I played basketball for them.

Both colleges and select teams. She even sent me to see a guy at the shootaround the other day but I refused to go. She showed up there and couldn't find me and got really pissed."

"And she's not excited about you playing on my team because—"

"Loves the idea of an all-star team," Trent said. "The other guy was just her priority for me that day."

Deflated, I didn't know where to go from there. Thankfully, the waitress provided a respite, circling large platters of food in front of us. I took a bite of my sandwich, then picked at the fruit cocktail swimming in heavy syrup. Trent munched his meatloaf, wiping excess mayo from his top lip.

In between bites he said, "We'd go at it sometimes. Me and my dad. He was so stubborn. Competitive and wiry. Hell of a lot stronger than he looked, too. Couple of times I really let him have it."

I dropped my fork into the syrup and tried to cover. "Did you play guys any one-on-one in the driveway?"

"For hours. He'd stop and correct me when I didn't block out. If I didn't square up to the basket when shooting? Hell to pay."

"Like?"

"Like start running around the block and I'll tell ya when to stop. He didn't care about rain, time for dinner. Homework."

We finished our food. When the bill arrived, Trent wrestled the tray away from me and insisted that he pay his share.

"Don't take it personally, but no coach pays for me. My mom wants otherwise but that ain't happenin'. Come with me up front."

I left a tip and followed him to the cashier. As I was pulling bills from my wallet, his cell phone chirped. Trent dug the phone from his jacket pocket and stared at the name. *Paula Soijka.*

"It's my mom's friend. I gotta take this." He put the phone to his ear, opened the door and strolled down the sidewalk.

Looking down at my change, I longed for one game in the driveway. I wondered what I'd have done if my own son had not squared up.

I also wondered about Paula Soijka.

NINE

MARGIE MCGOVERN LOOKED like she'd just stepped out of a Nordstrom catalogue.

Her light brown pantsuit more than highlighted her drop-dead figure and a series of thin gold chains accentuated her considerable breasts, caringly propped beneath a dazzling beige chiffon blouse. Where she chose to button the top would spark numerous conversations inside the Skagit County Administration Building.

"Well, Ernie Creekmore," she said, rising from behind her desk. "You've made my Monday and it's not even ten a.m." She sauntered close to my side and touched me lightly on the hip. She drifted with a faint scent of roses; her lips were a glossy burgundy. "Now, tell me I'm being swept away to a long, elegant lunch."

I backed up a step. "Sad to say I've made no reservations for today, Marge. I'm in the building to look over one of Harvey's case files. But don't get me wrong. It's good to know you can be free for an early bite."

She narrowed the space between us and bumped me on my thigh with her knee. "After the sumptuous dinner we had in Seattle last week, I thought we really were in sync."

Harvey Johnston swung open the door to his inner office, his tie already relaxed from its knot and his nose deep into an overflowing file. "Marge, I would like you to call the prosecuting …" He glanced up, startled. "Oh, hello, Ernie. I didn't know you were here. Were we going to meet this morning? I'm afraid I'm not with it yet today." He shot Margie a quick frown.

"Nothing on the schedule," I said. "But I was wondering if I could talk with you a bit more about the Tim Whalen case. Maybe look at some of the notes in the file."

He stepped back, closed the file and eased it down to his side. "For the record, I can't let you do that," Harvey said. "It's an ongoing investigation and you have no official clearance. Detective Dagmar has been assigned to the case and you can certainly interview him, but he's under no obligation to say anything or show you anything. I will try to speak with him soon and inform him that you'll be in touch."

"I only want to find out where the kid has been hanging out and what questions have been covered."

Harvey stared at Margie. After a moment, she flipped her palms up and then her eyebrows.

"Call the prosecuting attorney for …?" Margie said.

"Oh, right," Harvey said. He peered back into the file just as Margie squeezed off a provocative wink my way. "Please ask her if we can move our lunch from Wednesday to Thursday."

She took her sweet time getting back to her chair, then shimmied down to a cozy place in front of a yellow legal pad. As she scribbled away, her left hand fingered the top button of her blouse.

"Coach Creekmore," she said, looking up, "would you like me to check Detective Dagmar's schedule to see when he might be able to fit you in."

"That would be helpful, Marge," I said. "Thanks for

offering. You probably have a better method for locating him than I do."

She picked up the phone receiver, scanned a plastic-coated sheet of county numbers, and quickly stabbed a series of buttons.

Harvey launched open his door. "This is just the way we must start, believe me. Please do not take the information he gives you and begin your own in-depth investigation. I will need to be kept apprised of your activities. Now, you'll have to excuse me as I have urgent matter to attend to." He disappeared behind the frosted glass.

I laughed. *Going through proper county channels*. What a waste of time.

"Ernie?" Margie whispered, cupping her hand over the phone. "Detective Dagmar says he's available now."

"Amazing. A county employee with a same-day opening on his calendar. Let me write down the day and time."

Margie scoffed, signed off with Dagmar and replaced the receiver.

"If this guy'll see me without an appointment, I need to take advantage of the opportunity."

"Before you go, how about dinner tomorrow night? Say, seven sharp at my place?"

As she gazed into my eyes, I could feel warm blood rushing to my face.

"That's quite an invitation." I peered at the floor, breaking her stare and swung my foot in a tiny arc above the vinyl squares. "I should be able to make that work."

"Wonderful," she gushed. "I'll create something special, perhaps a French spin on some fresh halibut. Maybe something spicy like curry … or me. And, remember what you said about taking advantage of opportunities."

TEN

BJARNE DAGMAR BOUNCED from behind an unmarked door, his face scowling and held high as if displeased with the contents of the file in his right hand. His gold knit tie was cut square at the bottom and about the same color as every hair on his carefully combed head. A brown alligator belt matched his tasseled loafers. Fit, tall and seemingly nimble, he looked like a youthful headmaster at an East Coast prep school.

"You want to see me right now? You must be joking. The secretary said 'Sometime today.'" He paused and rested a hand on his hip. "Look, I've got a situation to settle and it might take a while. Come back in a bit, or just hang tight." He pivoted and resumed a determined march down the hallway, heel taps clicking rhythmically on the floor.

"Right," I murmured. "No problem."

I settled into a chair.

"Excuse me," said a tiny, fiftyish woman in a casual gray jacket and a flowing, floor-length, thin-laced black skirt. She looked like a suburban gypsy. "May I help you?" She had lively blue eyes, short white hair and smooth olive skin. Her smile, charming from behind a dull green counter, probably brought visitors more good days than bad.

I started to explain about Dagrmar.

"Well, this area now is restricted to county personnel only. Our makeshift cafeteria and meeting room, thanks to the construction." The smile returned and magnified her dazzling eyes. "But you just let me know if the best coach the Washington High School Fighting Crabs ever had needs anything. You know, I nearly died when your team lost that state title game."

You nearly died. No thought still deflated me so rapidly.

"I heard your terrific player that year, you know, the Cheese Oliver fellow, is back coaching in the county."

"Right," I replied. "Linn's helping out with the freshman team over at the high school. He works during the day for his family's timber operation."

Baffled by the extent of her basketball background, I stammered my way to a combo intro and thank you. "I'm sorry. I don't think we've met."

"Maddie Kurri." Her handshake was quick yet genuine, her palm the calming texture of an aged baseball glove. "You coached one of my nephews way back when. I believe you had him as a student, too. It was probably in the first couple years you were here."

"Anthony Kurri? I remember him quite well. He was a tough young man and a great kid. He seemed to have a motor that could go all day."

"I can assure you he still can, Coach. The problem is, he sometimes likes to go all night, too." She giggled and shook her head. "He also told me on several occasions how much he enjoyed you in the classroom."

I grinned and glanced down at the celebrity magazine in my lap, which I'd opened for lack of anything better to do.

"So has Bjarne rounded up some crazy kids caught breakin' windows in one of your listings?" Maddie said. "Saw your picture on some of those homes for sale in the paper."

"No, it's a different deal," I said. "This appears to be a case that's gone a little bit cold that Harvey wanted me to kick around with Detective Dagmar. I don't know what will come out of it. I guess we'll have to do a little poking around and just see what happens."

She bent toward me and crossed her arms.

"The only thing cold around here, other than the temperature in this darn building, is the doggone Tim Whalen case," Maddie said. "Did you know the guy, Whalen? He was in the real estate business."

"I'd met him a few times, mostly at open houses. The broker in our office used to work with him at another company and said he was a top-notch agent."

Her smile faded. She took a seat on the sofa facing me. "I heard he wasn't a top-notch guy around the house. One of the gals in our garden club knows the wife. Seems the couple argued all the time and sometimes it got even worse. My gal says there were lots of bruises, especially near the end. About the time the guy started messin' around with some other woman. My gal says this Samantha is a tough little thing and probably did some damage of her own."

My neck twitched back slightly and I feel my eyebrows floating higher. Maddie nodded an affirmation.

"Do you think Detective Dagmar knows about this?" I said.

"You bet," Maddie said. "I gave him more than an earful. And you gotta think he at least checked it out. It's not as if he's got a ton of other leads to trace."

"True. But he's got other files to work besides this one. You can only spend so much time at a dead-end cul-de-sac."

"Obviously you are a real estate person."

"Candidly, Maddie, I'm surprised you're telling me all this. It's not as if I'm a cop or some sort of county employee."

"What's it going to hurt?" she said. "Maybe you can connect some dots. I understand you know more than just Xs and Os. Besides, my nephew thought he could tell you anything. He told me you didn't chew him out in class for not understanding some major American author."

"Anthony had a valid point. Ever try reading *Absalom, Absalom!*?"

I tossed the magazine on an adjacent chair. "Did your friend say anything about how Mr. and Mrs. Whalen treated their son?"

She leaned back into the sofa, her black Birkenstocks barely reaching the floor, and rested her hands in her lap.

"A few years ago, I guess the boy, Trent, got wind from his mom that his ol' dad wasn't real true blue," Maddie said. "He wasn't pleased and began acting out. Samantha took the brunt of it. According to my friend, Samantha did everything she could to calm the situation. Hired specialists, went to counselors. The dad didn't want to deal with it. He wasn't around much because the housing market was so hot. There were always weekend open houses and carting people to SeaTac Airport. You know how it goes."

I wasn't sure if I did. I'd been in heated huddles with kids before, but never with my own. How much hotter could a domestic fuse burn? Would I put family first at crunch time of my basketball season?

The hallway door opposite me swung open and Bjarne Dagmar stormed into the room as if someone had hit-and-run his car. The sleeves of his button-down shirt were now rolled to the elbow; the once-perfect tie yanked awkwardly below an unbuttoned white collar.

"Some hotshot attorney tells me to show up at two, and the guy's playing golf?" Bjarne said to nobody in particular. "Golf? In the middle of the frickin' week? Are you kidding me? Jerk's got this bevy of eye-candy assistants and nobody's got the courtesy to call?" He assessed the room and groaned. "Sorry, Maddie."

Bjarne ran a hand from his forehead to the back of his neck, every hair still in place, then angled a look my way. "So, you decided to stay?"

"I couldn't find a golf game," I said.

He sneered, tilted his head slightly, and jammed his free hand into the front pocket of his pleated wool trousers. "I heard you could be a wiseass."

Maddie smiled and flipped her hair from her forehead.

"Yes, I have been told that can happen," I said. "Now, do you have time to talk about the Whalen case or are you too steamed to switch gears?"

He exhaled deliberately. "Yeah, let's do it," Bjarne said. "I'm sorry. I got a little carried away there. Please just give me a second, then come on back." He slapped his folder against his thigh, nodded to Maddie and made his way toward his office.

Maddie excused herself and headed to a gray steel desk behind the counter. Her in-box, piled high with files and photos, would take me hours to clear. No wonder she asked if I needed help; it was a momentary diversion for her.

I looped around her workspace and wandered down the hall, figuring Bjarne found his moment to cool off. He was on the phone at his desk in a two-desk glass booth, staring out the window to the west. He pointed to a small stainless-steel stool. As I straddled it and rolled toward the window, the sun jumped around a thunderhead, tossing fleeting rays on the Skagit River two blocks away. Old brick buildings obstructed most of the view to the water, but the dead-end streets running east and west allowed for some shining spaces. Cathy had enjoyed perusing the bookshops and secondhand stores along those riverfront blocks and even talked of opening a consignment shop when our kids were grown and gone. None of it ever came to pass.

Bjarne's portion of the cubicle was spotless and orderly. When he pulled out the top desk drawer for a pen, the guy's paperclips were facing the same way. The only item on the desktop other than a sterling silver letter opener was an off-white Middlebury College coffee mug carefully placed in a far corner. Framed pictures of lacrosse players shooting, defending and celebrating dominated the only non-glass wall.

Bjarne signed off on the call, promising the female at the other end that he would take her to lunch "real soon." He plopped the receiver into the cradle, swung around in his chair and folded his arms.

"So, Harvey tells me you've got a way with kids."

An open-ended statement. Detective style.

"I don't know about that," I said. "But when you're around them long enough, sometimes you get an idea of how some of them operate."

"Got any of your own?"

I looked away and focused on a tiny dinghy making its way up river. "We wanted to, but it never happened. Maybe we waited too long. Seven years ago, my wife went into the hospital and never came out. It's a long story."

"I'm sorry," Bjarne said. "I didn't know about that."

I swiveled the stool around and faced him. "Of course you didn't, nor could I have expected you to."

After a long, awkward pause, he said, "So, what do you know about Trent Whalen?"

"Not much. Other than he's a rough-and-tumble high school basketball player who has a decent chance at getting some help from a good school."

"How much help?"

"If he has a good summer and senior season, some D-1 place that needs a rebounder would undoubtedly give him a full ride."

"You don't say," he said. "What's a full ride worth these days?'

"Depending upon where he chooses to go, a bundle. In-state public universities would be a lot less than a place like Gonzaga. However, if he heads out of state, the differences become minimal in a hurry. Coming from Loyola, he'll have a decent workload and grades. A school like Santa Clara is now forty thousand for tuition alone; tack on another twelve for room and board. Creighton's not far behind. Arizona State, San Diego State probably a little less."

Bjarne arched his eyebrows, unrolled his sleeves and buttoned them at the wrist. Despite the activity, the shirt showed surprisingly few wrinkles.

"Coach, you probably have heard that Trent's got a quick fuse. It's become more of a focus as we revisit his dad's death."

I glanced out the window. The metal grates of the Division Street Bridge opened for a tall-masted sailboat, backing up cars in both directions.

"Detective, some smart college coach, who knows nothing about your suspicions, is looking at that fuse and trying to figure out a way to harness it to help his team. If you jump in the middle of this thing and you're wrong, the kid loses a free education. At a private school, you're talking about a quarter of a million dollars over four years. Minimum. Even the perception that he was involved would nix the interest. From any school."

Bjarne guided his left ankle over his right knee, sat back in his chair and interlaced his fingers behind his head.

"As I go through this stuff, I can't help but notice a more consistent, escalated level of anger between the two of them. Players, fans, even the wife admit to witnessing more incidents. Does it add up to motive? I tend to believe so. We've also got an article of clothing that could prove very helpful."

"Listen, detective. I don't know if Trent's innocent. I also don't know if he just flat-out snapped. But I do know that adolescent fire is usually a good thing. Not enough kids have it. I've learned it's a hell of a lot better than some passive head case who's too entitled to care."

"I'm not so sure. I think we're looking at a whole different level of heat here."

"The Whalens weren't the first to the party on this," I said. "I've seen plenty of dads and sons get into it. Expectations, dreams not met. On both sides."

"But it's the first time in this county, maybe this state, where similar circumstances resulted in a homicide."

Bjarne rose and rolled open the bottom drawer of a black metal cabinet abutting his desk and snatched two thick files from a red-labeled section.

"OK, we're doing this so you have more background if Trent makes your team." He fiddled with his tie and eyed me as if ordered to reveal his girlfriend's phone number. "We've never shared this type of information with anybody outside the department. It's unprecedented, as far as I know, but you must give me your word to keep it confidential. "

I agreed. He brushed imaginary dust from the top of an immaculate manila file and began a summary which mirrored every account I'd read in the newspapers:

Tim Whalen's body was discovered nearly a year ago in an upstairs bathroom by Patrick H. Hanrahan, the owner of the riverside home for sale not far from where Skagitopia Creek meets West Tulip Road. One shot was from point-blank range to the back of the head, another to the heart. Small caliber. Investigators had been stymied by the case, and the lack of indisputable evidence, yet continued to track the killer. No forced entry, no prints, no murder weapon. A $100,000 reward and national television exposure had yet to help. According to county tax records, the two-story home was valued at $139,950, yet listed at $199,950, and had four bedrooms, three bathrooms, skylights, covered street-side porch, large cedar deck off the kitchen overlooking the Skagit River, and a two-car garage.

It was the kind of place that fit Whalen's clientele and inventory, even though the home was mostly shown to potential buyers by Cookie. Her customers seemed to display the most interest and one woman had been to see the home three times, once with a Seattle-based architect with drawings for a mother-in-law structure above the existing garage.

Bjarne and his fellow detectives found that the crime scene contained few clues. That led them to believe that it was highly unlikely that Whalen was attacked at random or that he had stumbled onto a burglary. Whalen, thirty-eight, had been an agent for more than fifteen years with Imperial National Real Estate Services, one of the largest brokerages in western Washington. The house was one of the river "palaces" that had been erected in recent years by California high-equity newcomers who elected to scrape building lots of homey, existing farm homes and start anew with impressive window walls, gleaming hardwood floors, and imported gas cooking stoves fit for a gourmet. Plus, a two-car garage to stow a drift boat and a flat-bottom sled to chase chinook salmon.

"Clearly, the epitome of a private community," Bjarne said. "When you drive down that that narrow lane, all of the neighbors scurry to the windows to see if your car is worthy enough to be there."

Bjarne said the consensus in the office was that Whalen might have been showing the home to a prospective buyer when he was shot to death. According to reports, Whalen probably gained access via a key in the lock box, which recorded his MLS serial number and the time he arrived at the house.

"So, do you think Trent somehow got Tim's code, let himself in the house, and waited for his father to show up?"

"Probably not," Bjarne said. "According to everything we've found, Mr. Whalen was already in the home when the incident occurred. In fact, without giving you a couple of details that we're still investigating, the lock-box system has actually helped track the homes Mr. Whalen had shown to prospective clients around that period of time."

"So, all agents, like me, who have a MLS code or key are potential suspects?" I said.

"We went down the lists of realtors for months," Bjarne said. "Nobody could remember anyone who ever had a beef with Tim Whalen. Not so much as an unkind word. And Tim Whalen's was the only code entered at that house the day he died."

I nodded.

"While sophisticated lock-box systems have been helpful in tracking the comings and goings of real estate professionals, there is no foolproof system that protects agents," Bjarne said. "You know that. You constantly work with strangers in unfamiliar spaces and places. And from what the neighbors say, the traffic through Mr. Whalen's open house that day was consistent, especially late in the day."

"What about the magic of DNA?" I said. "Harvey's told me it has opened a lot of doors for you guys. Especially on older cases."

"Absolutely," Bjarne said. "But not everybody in the world is in the database, usually only people who have committed a felony. There are privacy issues, too. Giving somebody your DNA is like letting somebody search your house. So, unless you're a bad guy on record, there's no way we'd be able to find a match. We couldn't match anything in that house where Mr. Whalen was found, but you never know when something might eventually turn up."

"But what about all these rumors of breakthrough investigative research coming from the national labs?"

"The advances in any kind of DNA study are not going to keep most of these people from committing crimes," Bjarne said. "Research is not something they are going to think about before acting. A lot of the situations we investigate involve crimes of passion, often unexplainable events where there isn't much reason or logic."

"So, where does Trent Whalen fit in?"

"Smack dab in the middle," Bjarne said. "He could be of the group that simply doesn't think, or part of the group that planned with passion. Look, Coach, this stuff can be a long, involved science that takes a hell of a long time. A lot of the newspapers and television people now believe we should have several suspects behind bars because the media has been conditioned to believe that DNA now provides a solution for every crime."

My mind drifted to the possible distractions at practice. The last thing I wanted were roving reporters, cameras and lights floating around the perimeter of the court, wondering if one of my players was a candidate in a homicide.

"The select tournament is at spring break," I said. "I'm not asking you to put the brakes on your investigation, but I'd appreciate a heads-up if you make a move after we choose the team. And no obvious police presence, please. We can really do without a bunch uniformed cops or sinister-looking suits hovering in the bleachers above my guys."

The detective shot up a hand like a traffic cop.

"Hey, I'm not promising anything up front. I will check in with Harvey and see how much lead time we can give you. I don't know how we will play this. It could be a while before we do anything. Or, it could be tomorrow. If it were up to me, Coach, I'd cuff the kid today. If we don't get a surprise DNA match out of the blue in the next couple of weeks, I'm betting Harvey will finally back me on the arrest."

"And what evidence could possibly lead you to do that now?"

Bjarne planted his feet on the floor, propelling his rolling chair a few more inches away from me. "Trent's red letterman's jacket was found at the crime scene. It now could be our ace in the hole. It had specks of his father's blood and tissue at the bottom of the right sleeve."

"How did Trent respond to all of this?"

"He said the last time he saw it, the jacket was with the rest of his gear in the gym. Trent told us one of the other players probably walked off with it. There were a ton of teams there. You've been there. Stuff strewn on benches everywhere."

I recalled hosting tournaments at Washington High and the mound of unclaimed clothing that our janitors hauled off to the lost-and-found closet. One weekend of games could have kept Goodwill in the black for months. "Sounds plausible to me," I said.

"Too much of a coincidence here," Bjarne said. "Anyway, the jacket somehow got by the forensic guys at first because they thought it belonged to the owner of the house. Plus, the knit cuffs are so dark that they can easily hide blood. You do know that Trent is righthanded?"

I stood briefly and stretched, and then glared down at him.

"With all due respect," I said. "Is this about nailing the right guy or pulling in a suspect to please the powers that be?"

Bjarne scoffed and slumped back in his chair. "Try this on, Coach. Let's say Trent Whalen leaves the gym after his team's first game and drives five minutes to his dad's open house. The dad wanted an update on the game and is pleased to see his son, gives him a tour of the house."

"A teenager has that much interest in rooms and furnishings?"

"Stay with me a sec. ... The dad's been standing and hosting for hours and excuses himself to take a pee. The kid follows the old man into the can and blasts a twenty-two caliber into the back of his head. The dad crumbles like a cop's marriage, and the kid lets him have another one in the chest."

I tipped my head back, pondering his theory. "Sorry, just doesn't fit for me," I said. "You're talking about aligning too many stars. An impulsive hothead methodically carries out a premeditated murder?"

"Well, the assistant DA now seems to be all ears. I'm trying to set up a meeting to see her."

"Are you telling me the kid bolts from the gym, kills his father in an open house festooned with all sorts of yard signs but devoid of any Sunday lookers, and then leaves his jacket behind as a calling card? And then goes back to play some more basketball?"

"Who knows why he left it there? Why does any high school kid leave a jacket in someone else's home? All I know is all the players we interviewed at that tournament said Trent Whalen left the gym after the last game without a coat. And, remember, you're talking about a powerful young man with a history of run-ins with his father."

ELEVEN

By THE TIME I got home and cranked up the computer to check the day's emails, my gut moaned from hunger and my head would soon revert to a vegetable state. I dialed Tony's for a large sausage and pepperoni, pulled out a Bud and loaded up the mug. Returning to the computer screen, I eliminated the spam and sorted the keepers. Topping the list were a reminder of a doctor's appointment, a bad joke forwarded from my brother-in-law that included a screen full of cc'd email names I didn't know, and another luncheon invitation from Manny Cossetti.

Much like realtors "helping" buyers find a home. I'd discovered Cossetti earned a reputation of shepherding international players to high schools and universities in the states. Some of them panned out, including a 6-foot-11 kid from Iceland who played three productive years at Washington Wesleyan before catching on with a mid-level pro team in Greece. Others got homesick, spent one semester in a dorm where nobody spoke their language, and caught a plane home before the holiday tournaments began in December.

With the influx of young Europeans into the pro leagues, guys like Cossetti were edged out by huge global management firms.

As I crafted a cryptic comeback to my brother-in-law's message, the phone rang.

"Coach Creekmore? This is Coach Bakamus from those runnin', gunnin' Rolling Bay Bulldogs."

Buster Bakamus, a successful high school coach at two high-profile schools and a member of a prominent coaching family, last summer took on the challenge of starting a new team at the county's newest and smallest school. For years, he'd used the title "Coach" in pretentious jest, not unlike Chevy Chase interacting with a team of "doctors."

"How's it going, Buster?" I said. "Thanks for returning the call. What's new and different on the Bulldog campus?"

"Just educating America's youth, my man. As you well know, an extremely rewarding and highly compensated line of work."

We both laughed. "Don't know if I'd go along with the second half of that. But, as they say, it's a tough job and some-body's got to do it."

"Hey, you're probably making as much in teacher's pension as I am working every day. If you took a job now with a private school, you'd get a good salary and your pension. Classic dou-ble-dip. But did you call just to talk about teachers' finances?"

"Actually, no. What do you know about Manny Cossetti?"

There was a long pause at the other end of the phone. Bust-er exhaled through his nose with additional purpose.

"Depends what period of time you're talking about. About ten years ago, I had a heavy-legged rebounder that Cossetti helped get some love down at USF. You probably remember him. Jud 'Stuck in the Mud' Thompson? Cossetti saw him at a tournament at Bellevue Community College, and a few days later an assistant's in my office wanting to know about the kid's grades. Stuck in the Mud gets a partial ride his first year; full-meal deal the second."

The deal made me queasy. Kind of like watching a long-time hoop parent buy a drink for gorgeous stranger in an out-of-town bar. "What was the connection between USF and Cossetti?" I said.

"The USF assistant was an old frat brother of Cossetti's. I checked it out. Manny was simply doing the guy a favor. A little 'accidental scouting' while taking in a tourney. You know that a lot of school grads, boosters, buddies pass along tips when they think a kid can make it. Makes the booster feel important. Most of the time, they are such awful judges of talent that it becomes a big waste of time. Even worse when the booster makes statements to the kid's family like '*I know Coach McMahon is very interested in Joey because I just had lunch with Coach yesterday.*' Most of the time, the Coach doesn't know the kid exists."

I felt naïve and ignorant at the same time. The other sneaker had to drop and I scrambled for the words to keep it from falling on my head. "Mister Butt-In Booster has always been a challenge. I'm told guys like Manny have been dancing around the perimeter of the sport for a few years. What has changed?"

"The money," Buster said. "Some bright jerks found out that the services guys like Manny provided for freebie tickets and dinners were worth real cash. When Manny found out, I'm told he lobbed a few subtle inquiries to several colleges. A few specific D-1 schools. It turned out that if Manny delivered a kid, some coaches were more than happy to pay."

I paused and pondered the COD concept. My thoughts flashed back to my meeting with Cossetti.

"You still there, Ernie?"

"Yeah, sorry. Say, Manny told me he doesn't take money

from schools."

Bakamus's laugh turned to a brief cough. He momentarily muted the receiver, then returned. "Well, he takes money from parents. Parents who will pay to get a kid on a team like yours. Then, some guys who *coach* a team like yours, get a part of that action. Some guys in your position, Ernie, can make a lot of coin in a lot of ways."

I snickered, trying to absorb the complexities and the preponderance of options of players and coaches.

"When Eastern Michigan recruited me out of high school, all it offered was an apple and a road map. Of course, I was no crown jewel, but it's a long way from Yakima to Ypsilanti."

"Yeah, the backroom shenanigans have really changed. This might hurt a little Ernie, but the days of slow six-four white guys getting full rides to D-1 schools is over."

"Ouch! I wasn't *that* slow. At least, not every day."

We both laughed a long while until he had to excuse himself for a deeper cough. I'd forgotten how easy it was to speak with him and how quickly we reconnected. So many men in the coaching community were the same way.

"As I was sayin', all was good for a time until Manny started to leverage his relationships. You know, *Sully is willing to pay me five grand so why would I steer him to you for nothing ...?*

"I remember hearing some of the rumors, but there are plenty of coaches who say he's a stand-up guy."

"Problem is, you don't know who's paying the fiddler," Buster said. "Some of those guys are conductors on the big under-the-table gravy train. They certainly don't want to get sideways with guys like Cossetti."

"I thought Cossetti was mainly known for taking cash from

international parents, promising to get their kid a look at a U.S. school."

"True. And that compounded the problem and the guy's reputation. Cossetti may have been taking cash on both ends, from both the parent and from the college coach. If the player's a teenager, maybe the coach gets him placed with a friendly booster in a great school district. Booster just wants to help out; maybe the coach comps him some tickets."

"I'm getting the picture there are a lot of pieces to this," I said. "And I'm sure kids going straight from high school to the pros didn't help."

"It was a zoo, Ernie," Buster said. "And it's dirty, nasty stuff. Started to steamroll about the time you got out of coaching. The one-and-done deal helped, but only for a while. That's because at least you knew most kids were headed to a school for at least one year. Now, the kid signs a deal for a school *and* anything that happens after that. So you still don't know if a guy like Cossetti is working for a professional management company, a shoe manufacturer, a university, or all of the above. I've seen agents come to blows with college recruiters at concession stands over who owned what 'client.'"

"What?" I returned to the computer desk, I balanced the phone against my cheek and shoulder, rolled out the high-back oak chair, and took a seat.

"Anyway," Buster said, "long story on a topic we could talk about all night. Last thing I heard about Manny Cossetti, he was trying to shop Loyola's Trent Whalen to some smaller D-1 schools. Now that I think of it, maybe it was another guy. But there's a kid who can rebound. He on your select list?"

"He is," I said. "And I certainly liked what I saw from him

on the court."

"Roger that. There's a lot to like."

I thanked Buster for the call, hung up the phone, and stared at the email from Manny Cossetti.

TWELVE

THE LINE CLICKED twice during my conversation with Buster Bakamus so I dialed my voice mail to pick up the messages. As I punched in the last numeral, somebody slammed the not-so gleaming brass knocker on my front door.

"Got your pizza, Coach," said a red-haired, freckled-face kid too short to be anything but a point guard yet a shoe-in for a Norman Rockwell cover. "George, er ... I mean Mr. Berrettoni, said he'd put it on your tab."

Staggered by the mouth-watering aroma of spicy meats and fresh pesto sauce, I balanced the warm, grease-stained cardboard square in my right hand. The kid blushed, wiped his nose with the back of his hand and looked down at the front deck.

"OK. I'm giving you the last five bucks in this house," I said, reaching into my cords, "if you can name a major American author and one of his famous works."

"Herman Melville. *Moby-Dick*."

I smiled, knowing the fix was in. "Very good. And fast."

He sheepishly looked down the street. "Mr. Berrettoni told me to plan on a Steinbeck or Melville question if I expected a tip."

"Well, you can tell him I've greatly expanded my circle of candidates."

I folded the fin and slapped it into his hand via a

congratulatory low-five.

"So if you see me begging down by the river, you can tell people you knew me when I had money."

The kid's big-league grin flashed a full set of silver braces. "Thanks, Coach! You rock!"

More like creak, limp, or sag.

As he spun away and jogged to his car, the phone rang. Like a snooty waiter, I lofted the pizza box to my fingertips, transported it toward the kitchen and lifted the wall-mounted phone next to the refrigerator.

"Buona sera."

"Bona, who? I'm lookin' for Creekmore, Ernie Creekmore."

"You got him."

"Good," the caller said. "Just wanted to make sure you got the donation in the name of my man Elmo." The voice sounded coated with years of cigars, and probably, bourbon.

"I did get it, and I wasn't happy about it. You want to give me an address to mail it back or should it just be an anonymous donation to the Fighting Crabs Booster Club at Washington High?"

"Don't be like that," the caller cackled. From the background shouting and loud music, I guessed he was calling from a tavern's pay phone. "Thought you might be able to use some nice new threads when the club hits the road."

I could feel my eyes narrowing at the suggestion. I slide the pizza box onto the kitchen counter and nearly bowled a dirty beer mug into the sink.

"It appears your Phi Beta Kappa courier dropped his loot on the wrong person," I said. "The only road we're hitting is Interstate 5 south to Seattle for one tourney. Thirty minutes;

max forty-five."

"Well, I hate to break this to you, Coach," the caller said. He covered the receiver momentarily and barked at someone to get him another 7 and 7. "But the powers that be want you to lead a North Counties touring team next year. Kids from Edmonds north to the border. They're talking stops in Vegas, L.A., Miami, maybe even Puerto Rico. Looks like a couple of the cities already have committed."

Despite my record and connections, there would be no way the state association would send a first-time touring coach to those high-profile events. But then again, this job came as a complete surprise, too.

"For your information, I'm already one of the snazziest dressers on the sideline, and I don't take money, be it gift-wrapped in a Brooks Brothers box or crammed into a greasy hamburger bag."

The caller choked a laugh.

"Seen you dress, man. You could use some wardrobe assistance. You really need a tailored coat, maybe a nice pocket square. And, hey, I could care less about the spring break games in Seattle. Plan on riding you for the long run. Big lights down in L.A., baby."

My head began to throb, and the pizza no longer appeared enticing. I gripped the tile lining on the front of the sink with my left hand and nearly strangled the phone with my right.

"Listen, slick," I snarled. "Why don't you just ride on out of town? Please take your slush fund to a Reno sports book and bet on all the teams and horses you want. But stay away from me and my kids."

"Excuse me if I'm not scared, tiger," he whispered. "But

this ain't my first rodeo. You really don't want to screw with me. 'Cause if you do, you won't be screwin' Harvey Johnston's secretary, at least not the way she looks now. And she does look, man. Nice 'n heavy up top; one of the finer fannies in the county. I believe you're aware, Coach, that the cute young thing lives alone. Ya know her house is off in a corner, away from the streetlights? Can get pretty dark at night."

Short of breath, I stepped away from the sink to digest what had just been said. I curled a hand across my forehead and felt more sweat than I expected.

"You lay a hand on her, or anybody else ..."

A light snicker. Then the line went dead.

THIRTEEN

BOBBY BEVACQUA'S POPPED polo collar appeared more suited to an upscale Seattle dance club than the chilly Everton High School gym. As he directed lay-in drills at half court in razor-creased khaki shorts, I wondered if his wavy brown hair would remain perfectly in place when practice was over. Perhaps he had the same stylist as Bjarne Dagmar.

Bobby, bannered to be "the answer" to the Seahawks' hoop mediocrity, now found himself on a fairly warm seat after only two-plus seasons. He'd won fewer games in that period than his once-revered predecessor, and his innovative run-and-gun offense often misfired, thanks to a lack of consistent rebounders. Trent Whalen's transfer didn't help, yet Bobby insisted he could succeed with an inner-city offense executed by rather slow white kids who had to make three-point baskets to stay close in games. The athletes still appeared to be the same size and makeup. However, like many districts, the attitudes within their homes seemed to have evolved from play hard to privilege.

Everton gets about half as much rain as Seattle. Once Southern Californians figured all this out, they showed up in droves, buying mainland and island properties for a pittance of what they would cost back home. In doing so, they changed the face of towns like Everton. They poured cash into the new high school.

With growing crowds came growing expectations. High

school athletics often become the lightning rod of the entire community. Three years ago, Virgil McCrossin, a smiling, passionate coach four years removed from the school's last playoff appearance, landed on a hot skewer guided by a nucleus of influential parents. The group persuaded the rest of the team parents that ol' Virg's method of a slow-down, slam-it-inside offense should have been abandoned with low-cut Converse. The school's booster board jumped onboard and pressured the administration to oust McCrossin and begin an intergalactic search for an up-tempo leader who could take the Seahawks to the magical next level.

Virg was my vintage, a respected peer, and I hurt for him. McCrossin reluctantly moved on to a private school where he became extremely happy teaching Math and Driver's Education, while drawing a comparable salary plus a full public-school-district pension. He also plays golf after school and takes his wife to the movies on Friday night, far from the critical screams of all-knowing fans.

As I slouched against the wall under the newly painted Seahawk logo, a youngster with a clipboard jogged toward me.

"Coach wants to know if you checked in at the principal's office," the young man said as he swiped his nose with the sleeve of his navy nylon windbreaker.

"No, but I will if that's necessary."

"Yeah, any outsiders are supposed to have permission to be on campus. You're an outsider."

"I see. Well, I will take care of that right now."

"Thanks. Coach likes to know who's watchin' practice. Doesn't like any other schools findin' out about our stuff."

I sidestepped out of the gym and onto the playground.

Before applying for my official campus clearance, I returned to my VW bus, grabbed my cell and reviewed messages while I approached the administration building. Two retired fishermen had inquired about the same waterfront cabin, and Diane Chevalier called to say she was back in town. I wondered what that meant.

Moments later, properly signed in, I shunned any stealth scouting notion and grabbed a seat near the foul line about four rows above the gym floor. Bevacqua directed individuals to each side of the midcourt line, dividing his troops for a scrimmage.

Bevacqua stepped back and admired his work.

"That looks pretty even to me," he said, just loud enough for me to hear. "Both teams have scorers. Now let's see who can rebound and play some defense. Call your own fouls, but no ticky-tack stuff." He pivoted and began walking toward me, head down. "Call out the screens," he turned and yelled. "If your teammate is about to get picked, let him know about it. Not like the other night when one of our guys got decked."

Bobby blew his whistle, and a shrimpy guard inbounded to a slick six-foot-two kid in white wristbands who nonchalantly dribbled the ball between his legs in the backcourt. The scoreboard clock ticked backward from eight minutes.

"We don't have all day, Howard," the coach shouted. "Are you stalling for some reason? Blue team, pick up at halfcourt." He waved an arm, prompting the Blues to advance. "Come get 'em at halfcourt!" One hand under his chin, he watched for a moment before turning to me and briefly making eye contact.

"Ernie Creekmore," I said, reaching my hand down a few rows. "I don't think we've ever met."

He responded with a quick grip that caught only three of my fingers.

"Bobby Bevacqua." His eyes darted back to the basketball action on the floor, head moving side to side. I sat down and spread my arms across the row behind me. "And I know who you are. But frankly, I'm surprised you are here. I wouldn't say we had any viable candidates who really should be considered for your all-star team."

I sat up and turned in my seat to face him. He didn't budge, a stone profile sited in another direction.

"I actually came to speak with you about one of your former players," I said.

Slowly, he swung toward me, one hand cupping his elbow while the other hand tugged at his chin, a thinker's pose. "Really?" he said. "Off the top of my ... Wait, you mean Trent Whalen?"

"That's right. I know you understand the value of rebounders, especially aircraft carriers who can run the floor."

"And he's gotten a lot bigger since he left here," Bobby said. "I saw him down in town at a Seattle U game, and it looks like he's really put in his time on the weights at the gym. I just wish his father would have given us more than one year to turn this thing around. God knows we could use him. Just look out there."

I got up and stood beside him and surveyed the action. A scrappy forward with long hair lunged to the floor for a loose ball, then flipped the ball from his knees to Mr. Wristbands racing to the basket.

"Way to give up your body, Myles!" Bobby shouted. "I can see there's at least one guy who came to play today. C'mon, guys! Who else is ready to step up?"

The players responded to the challenge, cranking up the tempo the next trip down the floor.

"I was hoping to get your opinion as to what type of teammate Trent would make," I said. "Obviously, there have been some things in the past that were questionable. You coached him, so you would ..."

"The only thing wrong with that kid was his father," he said, finally turning to face me. "I know it's not kosher to speak this way about the dead, but Tim Whalen was an absolute pain in the ass to me, other team parents and, most of all, to his son. When they decided to leave, some parents thought losing Trent's talents was going to be a disaster, but then they realized they no longer had to put up with Tim. It turned out to be a wash for them. The guy was just so distracting. I mean, I heard about him from other coaches, players, and even the refs. They had to run him out of more than one gym because he'd become so irritating."

"That couldn't have been easy," I said. Then, after letting his comments settle, I added: "If you were in my shoes and Trent earned a spot on the team, would you have any reservations about keeping him on the squad?"

Bobby swiped at the gym floor with his shoe. "You know, you look back and wish kids would've handled situations differently. But they are kids, and they make mistakes. I don't think Trent was any different in that regard."

"That doesn't sound like a resounding yes," I said.

After a long pause, Bobby said, "Trent had these enormous eruptions of anger. You probably heard all about them. Maybe you even saw it once or twice yourself. Hell, he even took a swing at me one time, and thank God he didn't land the thing or I'd probably be six feet under."

I scoffed and looked away. "You make it sound as if all kids have those kinds of anger issues. They don't, and you know it."

"Look, a lot of kids pull chippy-shit stuff on the floor. But Trent let players get under his skin far too easily. Often, we couldn't see any reason for the explosion. He became easy pickings, and other coaches were smart enough to exploit it. They knew they stood a better chance of winning with him in foul trouble or kicked out of the game. He would go off, and that was it. We were sunk."

The trusty team manager who busted me earlier scooted over with a slip for Bobby to sign. The coach yanked a pen from the kid's pocket protector and scribbled blindly at the bottom. The youngster drifted away, head down.

"I've actually seen Trent play recently and was actually quite impressed with him," I said. "Both on and off the court."

Bobby nodded, as if expecting the statement. "The thing is, once his father was gone, I think Trent got better in a hurry. I just wish the kid would have stayed around here a little bit longer."

A wayward pass bounced my way. A lanky forward sporting a tie-dyed do-rag strutted over casually, scooped the ball from my palm and inbounded to his buddy.

"Keep it moving, Boop," Bobby said. "Everybody gets a blow at the quarter, but everybody hustles until you hear that horn. Now, let's go!"

The teams increased their defensive intensity, shutting down drives in the lane. Two long-range jumpers followed with shooters at both ends squaring up to the basket, feet, shoulders, and hands in perfect position. Play suddenly deteriorated, including a no-look pass that found the first row of seats.

"Excuse me, Coach Creekmore, but I need to get my head back into this."

"Right, right. One last question. What was the reason Tim Whalen gave for pulling his son and seeking a transfer? I mean, you brought in a new look, different system. I would have thought the Whalens would have been thrilled to give it a shot."

"Tell me about it," Bobby said. "That shot lasted exactly one season. Our go-go style seemed right in the Whalens' wheelhouse, but just as Trent was getting comfortable in our offense, Tim pulled the plug. The next thing I know, Trent's playing summer ball over at Loyola."

"You mean you didn't know about the transfer until school got out in June?"

"You got that right. Later that year, Tim was found dead and Trent sits out the season. Samantha said she just wanted him at home."

FOURTEEN

SLEEP HAD NOT come easy, nor was it renewing. The number of restless nights the past two weeks far outnumbered the restful ones, yet I felt the lingering lack of magnetism with Margie, my newfound fascination for Diane, and the enigma that appeared to be Trent Whalen failed to reach the center of my uneasiness.

And the apprehension no longer was restricted to nights. A newer, sharper nail had emerged in my foundation, and it pierced my focus and concentration at all hours of the day.

Any glow of success in player discovery or selection for my all-star team now mingled in the echoes of the conversation with Augustine Coatsworth regarding the confusing, eye-opening avalanche of adolescent player recruitment and representation. I'd known during my coaching years at Washington High that competition for top athletes had passed the intense level and entered the fierce bracket, but the pool of possible candidates had become deeper and wider for no logical reason. I'd experienced relentless college assistants and understood they were simply trying to out-work and out-guess their peers. It was their job to get the best possible athletes signed and enrolled before another school snagged the star.

But the bothersome word that kept beeping on my radar was "booster," and the most active one during my tenure was serving a seventy-three-year prison term for the murders of two people and the attempted murder of a third. What other possible roles had the booster, Mitchell "Wide Load" Moore, played as treasurer of the Washington High School Fighting Crabs Booster Club?

When I first considered visiting Mitch Moore at the Clallam Bay Corrections Center, I felt reluctant to ask for company. After five years away from full-time coaching, I now selfishly wondered only if "my program" had been tainted, with little regard to the idea that our school could have gained a negative reputation—let alone negatively impacting an individual's growth and psyche? Was I really more concerned about containment and possible damage control, or assisting the young people who could have been severely damaged and confused?

Perhaps I had lost more from being away from the bench than I knew.

That third person, Linnbert "Cheese" Oliver, is the son I never had. Assaulted with a baseball bat, he was left bound and gagged and near starvation in a remote shack near Lake Wilhelmina by Mitch Moore. Linn's crime? Missing the critical shot in the school's only appearance in a state championship game.

Since that day, I wished the victim had been me. I could have called a timeout late in that title game and set up a better play. Instead, I saddled the dreams of a one-high school community on the back of a hometown hero secretly hiding the limitations of a knee injury brought on by an off-season logging accident. In the end, Linn was labeled as the kid who missed "the shot" and, despite some healing, he's still paying the price seven years later. In the eyes of some people, he will never be forgiven.

I'd spent considerable time with Linn and his longtime girlfriend Barbara Sylanski, discussing physical and emotional therapies and treatments. Linn said the assault and successful recovery had provided him the second-chance spark to live life bigger and fuller. He also said that he had forgiven Wide Load and moved on long ago.

While I mentioned I'd felt the same way about life since being diagnosed with MS eight years ago, my forgiveness had not come as easily.

On Wednesday night, as Linn and Barbara finished up their lasagna dinners with pistachio gelatos at a surprisingly crowded Tony's Place, I sauntered over to their table and explained what I had in mind.

Tall and athletic, Barbara always downplayed an impressive figure. Her perpetual smile invited fun and creativity and typically succeeded in pulling Linn out of his dour moments. A classic bob haircut swirled above her midnight-blue cable sweater.

"Actually, I'd kinda like to hear what he has to say," Linn said as Barbara sagged against the back of her chair and glared at him. "I'd also like to see what the guy looks like. See what some real time in the slammer has done to the man—"

Barbara's smile vanished. "The man who nearly killed you?" she blurted. "I mean, c'mon! Please remember, he did manage to murder two other people ..."

"Barb, listen. It's just—"

"It's just what, Linn? What could it possibly be?" She glanced at me, then back to Linn, her mouth open. "I'm sorry, but I see absolutely no benefit to this." She dropped her forehead into her hands, blonde hair falling around her forearms.

A little girl at a nearby table eyed Barbara, frowned and turned to a twenty-something woman opposite her. "Mommy, is that lady crying?"

"Just great," Barbara muttered, her head still down. "You think we're the center of attention now? Just wait until this gets out in the community. I can't even imagine …"

I waited a moment. "I didn't come up with this idea on a whim. I've thought long and hard about heading over there."

"I hope so, Coach," Barbara said. "I really do. I must say you've shown better judgment in just about everything else since I've known you. But this … this …"

As the mother and daughter headed for the door, I said, "I've got this need to know—just ask the guy—what went on at Washington High when I was there. Maybe I was clueless and all hell was breaking loose, but at least I'll know. Knowing what I do now about recruiting, I need to ask the questions. I'd be upset with myself if I just let it go."

"Why can't you let it go, Coach?" Barbara said. "Linn let it go and he's the one who got clobbered, in more ways than one. Now you want to drag him back into it, bring back those awful times …? Tell me something … what if one of those guards over there craves a deep-throat reputation and just happens to call Greg Smithson at *The Trib* and says, 'Guess who's over here visiting Mitchell Moore'? Maybe snaps a quick pic of you and Linn cruising to the visitation room? Would it be worth making the trip then?"

"Greg would always call Coach first if—"

"No, Greg's a reporter first!" Barbara snapped. "He's not going to clear this with anybody before he jumps all over it. You guys sound like you've forgotten how big of a story that whole mess was. Every small-town paper in the country ran the wire service story of the over-the-top fan who strapped a naked player in a chair and forced him to watch a video of the last-second shot he missed! Then *ESPN, Deadspin.* Then *Fox Sports …*" Her voice sunk to faltering whisper. "Over and over …"

Her tears came quickly. Linn reached across the table and held her hand. I waited while she dabbed her cheeks with a napkin and then touched around her nose with a tissue from her purse.

"You're right, Barbara. I'll handle this on my own. It's my issue, my problem. There's no need to involve Linn."

"There's no need to involve Linn," Linn replied. "But he'd like to be involved, anyway." Barbara's chin dipped to her chest. The tissue disappeared in her fist. "If the offer is still on the table, I'd like to ride out there with you. Give us time to catch up, talk about some players."

From behind, I felt a lingering stroke along my upper back and shoulders, the kind of introductory touch my wife used to signal her arrival outside the locker room after a game. The accompanying aroma reminded me of lemon-scented fabric softener.

"If it isn't the big, strong basketball coach," a woman slurred. I twisted toward the voice. Every one of Samantha Whalen's fingers was ringed in ornate silver. One sip of red wine remained in a glass half the size of a basketball. Her blonde hair curled flat against concave cheeks and ended in gold razor-wire tips. A tie-dyed halter top, questionable even in July, accentuated her breasts.

"Now who are these nice young people that I haven't met?" Her hand came to rest at the back of my neck. Linn cleared his throat. Barbara's weary eyes grew wider. Startled, I half-stood, partly in surprise, plus I wasn't eager to give up my seat and invite her to linger. More importantly, I didn't want to submit Linn and Barbara to her.

Before I could speak, she began drifting toward the bar, then turned and tipped her glass and head while gliding away. "Why don't you just meet me over there and buy this girl a drink?"

She didn't wait for a reply.

"Ernie, come on over to the bar and say helllooo," crooned Samantha while curling an index finger my way.

"How can you turn down that deal?" said Barbara, her voice laced with sarcasm. "Candidly, Coach, I've always wanted you to play the field, but that particular woman might be in an entirely different league."

Attempting to remain cool, I passed a fist under my nose. "She's just a player's parent. The mom of one of the kids I am considering for the North Counties team."

Barbara responded with a *That's your business* shoulder hike. Linn smiled and shook his head.

"I don't really know her at all. Just met her once, briefly, after a game."

Linn sat up and slid his dessert cup to the edge of the table. "Local kid?"

"He is, and you've probably heard of him," I said. "Trent Whalen over at Loyola High."

Linn nodded. I was pleased but not surprised. "Played with him. A couple of times at open gym at Stanwood. Smart and he won't back down from a bigger guy."

"Ernie," Samantha called again. "There's someone here

who wants to meet you."

I made eye contact with her and nodded, not sure if it registered.

"Oh, Ernie, we've been waiting ..."

Samantha's, rowdy sing-song invitations now drew the stares and snickers of other patrons. Their eyes and directional nods darted from her to me, and attempts at screening my face now felt comical. Given my lengthy stint as coach and teacher, I was an obvious target. Such was life in a one-high-school community.

"Excuse me," I said to Linn and Barbara. "But I need to put out this fire."

FIFTEEN

"PAULA, THIS IS the coach I was telling you about that's gonna make my Trent a star," Samantha announced as she slowly worked a palm and forearm from the top of my shoulders to my lower back.

"Trent's already a star," Paula muttered.

"Ernie, I'd like you meet somebody from back home who now lives damn near 'round the corner. We even sold lemonade and cookies on the corner as little girls. Smilin' for cute boys with money!"

"And that ain't all," Paula giggled.

Samantha laughed so hard that her forehead nearly bounced on the bar. Paula grinned and raised a triumphant fist.

"Say hi to Paula Soijka," Samantha said.

"Oh, he's cuter than you said." Paula's words came fast and almost curt, not unlike her handshake. She could pass as Samantha's slimmer older sister, but I doubted if there was any age difference. She was the type of woman whose deep crow's feet on the sides of her face came from squinting rather than smiling.

Samantha's arm remained on my back. With her other hand, she jerked a barstool away from the rail, attempting to provide space for me to stand between the two women. The stool teetered and crashed to the floor, bringing a *What's up?* glare from Scooter Hannegan, George's substitute bartender.

I righted the stool, and Samantha slid on.

I eased my hands on the bar and dipped lower, trying to reduce my six-four frame. Paula powered down the remainder of her cocktail, then quickly shook the ice-filled glass toward Scooter for a refill. Scooter pointed at me, and I shook my head, indicating I wanted nothing. That is, other than to be at home and looking at basketball film.

I finally offered, "You two look quite a bit alike."

"Lotta people say that," Paula said, digging through her purse. Given the yellow tint of her teeth, I figured she soon would be heading to the parking lot for a smoke. Her black mock-turtle sweater accentuated a dry, weathered face that makeup failed to hide, cowgirl skin minus any bronze coloring from the sun.

"Now, why don't you tell us all about what you are going to do for Trent," Samantha said, her hand slowly moving along the back of my belt. "A guy like you probably has a long list of influential people for him, and me, to meet." She halted her hand movements and hooked a thumb inside the waistband of my pants. I reached behind me, gently grabbed her wrist, and moved it away.

"My role is strictly coaching," I said. "Until we finish the tournament in Seattle, all players selected for our team will not be meeting with anybody. At least, not if I can help it."

Paula picked up her cocktail as soon as Scooter delivered it and took a big swig. She smugly waved her pile of bills on the bar.

"I got Samantha covered," Paula said. "In more ways than one."

Scooter waded through the money, plucked a ten-spot and

quickly returned to slap down the change.

"Wait," Paula said. "You need to take something for yourself this time." She tried to slide him a fiver, but the bill drowned in water rings left by her glass. Scooter peeled the bill free and fanned it through the air.

"Much obliged, ma'am."

Samantha clutched the stem of her glass and swirled her wine, mesmerized by waves flung high on the sides. I cherished the conversation break as her wine breath had pushed me close to the gag line. The break didn't last long.

"Oh, come on, Ernie," Samantha moaned. "We all know there's a lot more to being a select team coach than just coaching." Her massage resumed, this time starting at mid-back before beginning a circular motion on my butt. Startled, I grabbed her hand and halted the action before she could hit the six o'clock marker.

"Yeah, Samantha tells me you probably know a lot of money guys," Paula said. "Investor types." A light sheen of perspiration now glowed on her forehead. "Maybe these guys' interests go to things other than basketball."

Startled, I began grappling for a reply while disconnecting Samantha's craving hands from my body. Diane Chevalier gleefully emerged from the banquet room, chatting with a man and a woman I'd never seen. The women clutched notebooks to their chests while the man carried a brown briefcase. She caught my eye before I could look away. Diane smiled and waved hurriedly and continued her conversation. They walked and talked to the front door opposite me where Diane shook hands with them all and said goodbye. She turned, beamed, and began to approach.

Her eyebrows rose when Samantha's hand returned to my backside.

"Ah, hello, Ernie," Diane said. The ubiquitous snappy white blouse emphasized a winter tan and a tiny gold necklace. "I was hoping to see you sooner than later, but I can see your hands are full right now."

"Got that right, honey," Samantha giggled.

Dangling somewhere between anger and embarrassment, I stammered toward an intro. "Ah, Diane, this is another player parent. I'd like you to meet Samantha Whalen and her friend, Paula ... I'm sorry, Paula, how do you pronounce your last name?"

"It's Soy-ka," she snapped. "You know, like soy sauce?"

Oddly, I thought she smelled about the same. Fragrance by association.

"And, I'll tell ya what, she sure likes her sauce," Samantha laughed. "And other shit, too." She roared at her comment but had no other takers.

"Well, it's nice to meet you both," Diane said, shooting me a *Really?* look.

"Sit down and have a drink with us, girl," Samantha said.

"Thank you, but I really can't stay," Diane said. "I'm just waiting for Nick's takeout. I know he's famished."

"Plenty of time for a cocktail," Samantha said. "Scooter, bring—"

"Really, I don't care for one," Diane said. "But thank you nonetheless."

I tapped a swizzle stick on the bar, praying for the to-go order to arrive.

"Diane's son is a post player that just fell in our lap for the select team," I said. "Not only does he move well, but he gives us a surprise factor that will catch some teams off guard."

"Where's home?" Samantha slurred.

"Here, now," Diane said. "We've relocated from Arizona, where I have a technology consulting business. My husband went to medical school with Timoteo Mesa and we've stayed close for years."

"Tell me about this Timmy guy," Paula chimed in. "Make my day by saying he's single and a pharmacist."

Diane's eyebrows arched higher, and her eyes drilled right through me. Squirming, I ended the extended silence. "So it looks as if you got some sun recently. You certainly didn't get it around here."

Samantha's head bobbed lower toward the bar. She jerked back quickly, like one of my former students caught napping when called on in class.

"I had to scoot down to Phoenix at the last minute on a business deal," Diane said. "From there, I drove up to Flagstaff to sign the closing papers on our home sale. With those funds, we can actively look to buy in this area. Does anyone know a good real estate agent?"

"Yeah, right," Samantha mumbled. "Why don't you scoot on out of here, bitch."

Diane tossed her notebook and purse on the bar, spilling Samantha's wine. The glass spun off the bar and shattered at Scooter's feet.

"Excuse me," Diane seethed, stepping toward Samantha. "What did you say?"

I leaped between the two women, facing Diane, my back to Samantha. "Look, it's obvious she's had too much—"

"Whoa-K," Scooter declared. "Everybody just take a deep breath at this end of the bar. We want everybody to leave in one piece, nice and cozy-like."

"I ain't going anywhere," Samantha babbled.

A perky waitress arrived with a white paper sack and a foam container the size of a hardbound *War and Peace* that smelled like warm treats from heaven. Diane lunged for her purse, rifled through her wallet, and handed the waitress a twenty-dollar bill. "Thanks. That's yours."

"Wow," the waitress said. "Thanks so much!"

Diane glared at me. "And I'm gone." Arms full, she backed out the door.

"Good riddance," Samantha chirped over her shoulder.

As I began to follow Diane out, Bobby Bevacqua entered from the outside and held the door open for Diane. He barely acknowledged me before dashing toward the bar, his blue nylon warmups swooshing as he walked. He stopped where I had stood, between the two well-oiled buxom blondes. I stared open-mouthed.

"I told you, not tonight," Samantha snarled. "And I meant it."

"Shsssh! Keep your voice down for once, will you?" Bobby said. "You said you had work to do but I don't think this qualifies."

Paula appeared puzzled yet managed a moon-like smile. She waved at Scooter for another round.

"Don't you fucking tell me what's work and what's not," Samantha said. "Did you call those people I told you to call? The Cossetti guy?"

Bobby looked at me and lowered his voice. "Look, this is

not the place."

"I'll take that as a 'no,'" Samantha said. "Shit, you can't do anything right. Except screw."

"Not here!" he hissed.

"You'd better step it up, buster. You're gonna find yourself in second place real fast."

The exchange zapped me out of a fog and out the door in pursuit of Diane. The red tails lights of her white Lexus glowed at an intersection one block away. I slipped back into the restaurant and used the pay phone to call information. The operator refused to divulge the address listed under Diane's or Nick's name, but I telephoned the number and left a rambling message that the evening "was not as it seemed."

Replacing the receiver, I tried to digest the last fifteen minutes, then noticed Linn and Barbara rising from their table. I staggered their way.

"My word, Coach, what was that business at the bar all about?" Barbara said. "I nearly sent Linn over to rescue you."

"Believe me, you don't want to know," I said.

"OK, then. I guess we better keep moving. Tomorrow's a workday. Besides, if we stay here any longer, I'm sure Margie McGovern will show up and snuggle up to Coach. Seems to be the night for this babe magnet."

I scoffed and looked away. "Well, if she shows before I leave, I'm not going to flag her down."

"Really," Barbara said. "Why's that?"

"I need to tell her we're going to slow that train down."

"Interesting," Barbara smiled. "All of a sudden, there seem to be a lot of cars on that train."

SIXTEEN

GETTING A HIGH school player to buy into a "defense first" goal on an all-star team is nearly impossible. In my years as a select-team assistant, I'd witnessed full-scale player mutinies when the head coach refused to turn the squad loose and employ a playground run-and-gun. Bring up the D concept and a candidate typically rolls his eyes, indicating it is in direct conflict with his expectations.

"Defense" and "all-star" have become contradictory terms. And I can't blame the kids. They tune in to the NBA All-Star Game and see monster dunks and jumpers from the parking lot get rewarded with replays on *SportsCenter*. Pro defenders tend to merely get out of the way, allowing offensive bling to shine for the TV audience. As a result, many high-schoolers seek to one-up the latest showstopper and earn a coveted place on an agent's human highlight reel for distribution to college coaches.

I could tell from the first time I saw Eddie McGann that he was not the typical young man, or select-team candidate.

Immediately apparent was his impressive wingspan, flexibility and dexterity. In the pregame layup line, Eddie bent over and flapped his wings like Michael Phelps on the starting block, arms wrapped an improbable distance around his back. As the game progressed, Eddie demonstrated an uncanny ability to know *when* to help on defense, a quality nearly as striking as his physical attributes. In my years of coaching I've found that too many kids help a fellow defender, or try to stop the ball at the wrong time, allowing an opponent an easy basket. Remarkably, Eddie was the first man back on defense, never allowing his man to beat him down the floor.

"You got help left, Bobby," Eddie said. No screams. No barks. Just confident, audible messages. Later, "I'm back." Then, "Here if you need." Or simply, "With you."

"Talk about a coach on the floor." I recognized the voice, clear and strong from over my right shoulder.

"Bosco Bossenmaier." I laughed as I spotted the speaker five rows behind me. "A blast from the past. The last of the near-sighted referees."

"Old School Ernie Creekmore," Stuart Bossenmaier countered. "Still not giving hard-working officials the respect they are due."

"That's because your organization failed to respond to my request that all members receive annual eye examinations. You guys missed so many calls, you now need three individuals to do the job of two."

Stu Bossenmaier grinned, picked up his clipboard and slowly began shuffling toward me. Given the amount of tonnage plopped over the front of his brown braided belt, he hadn't missed many meals. He offered a fist-bump hello, yet I simultaneously submitted an open-palm handshake.

"Ah, still shakin' regular," Bosco muttered. "Old-school at its best. Probably still playin' that badass man-to-man defense all the time."

"That would be correct, my friend."

In trimmer times, Bosco called games with an understated

confidence, lending effusive coaches the attentive ear they de-
manded but never allowing their antics to upstage the game.
Unlike some of his control-freak colleagues, Bosco blended
with the ebb and flow on the court. Most of the time, he let
the kids play. His charging or blocking calls were restrained
decisions rather than major theatrical presentations. When his
third knee surgery sidelined him for good, it left a huge hole
in the referee pool. Bosco was one of the best on the floor for
nearly three decades, but coaches waited until he retired to tell
him so.

"Most kids only like to take the reins on offense," Bosco
said as he plopped down next to me. "This guy really cares
about defense. Kinda refreshing."

"Here's what his coach wrote," I said, flipping to my notes.
"Edward Patrick McGann. Steady Eddie. Legit six-four. Keeps
his mouth shut. Junior. Long arms. He'll stalk ya on defense
as if you stole his girlfriend. Great parents. Never miss a game."

Bosco's rough whiskers had worked the collar of his blue
shirt into a series of tiny polyester balls. Beige patches on the
elbows of his corduroy coat matched his Hush Puppies. He
looked like an overweight architect taking a break from a drafting table.

"Don't tell me you're at this game scouting lock-down defenders," I said, still surveying the floor.

"Nah. Bunch of leagues hired me to review and critique prep
officials. I will be turning in my evals on these two guys next
week, the last of a big group of pairs on my list. They've been
pretty good other than that one foul at the three-point line. You
see it? The younger ref reacted as if it were a murder indictment.
Just call the foul, fella, and get the hell out of the way."

"Never foul a jump shooter at the buzzer," I said. "Especially anywhere near the arc. Saves coaches a lot of gray hair."

"Refs, too," Bosco said.

We reminisced about this and that as our heads swung back and forth with the action on the floor. "How is Mabel?" I said.

"I wouldn't know," Bosco said. "She left me eighteen months ago. Eighteen months and six days, to be exact. Said I loved basketball more than I loved her. I said that might be true, but I loved her more than softball. That didn't help at all. Still, I missed her not being in the bleachers. You know. In her usual seat."

"I know all about that feeling."

He touched me lightly on my arm with the edge of his clipboard. "I'm sorry, Ernie. Your losing Cathy and my Mabel leaving are totally different ballgames."

For years after my wife died, I continued look to the same row, the same seat for inspiration from that fabulous face. Always upbeat, Cathy glided to her seat in the bleachers above our bench for every home game and most of the away contests. With pursed lips and a clenched fist, she encouraged me to hang in there when things got tough.

I shook my head for a second, then massaged my watery eyes.

"Tell me, Bosco," I said, stretching my arms over my head. "Did you catch Loyola this year while grading your zebras?"

"Seen Loyola a coupla times. Kids did a decent job despite the coach. Guy kinda gets frazzled at crunch time. Hell of a recruiter, though. Those Catholic schools don't have to worry about school district boundaries or if a kid is moving just to play sports. I'll tell ya, they make the most of it."

"Well, they now have the Whalen kid from Everton, and he's a force inside."

"Used to have more than a mean streak, Ernie," Bosco said. "That big fella might well have had some anger issues. I've seen him go off like you would not believe. And not just on the court."

"What do you mean, used to?"

"I think he's been better about his temper this year. He's been rough and aggressive but not out of control like he was up at Everton."

Eddie McGann drove his defender to the foul line then found a teammate cutting backdoor with a belt-high bounced pass for an easy lay-in.

"Coaches can talk all they want about Xs and Os," Bosco said. "But this game is won by the Jimmys and the Joes. And I'll tell you what. This McGann kid is no ordinary Joe. Did you check that pass? How many players his age would be looking to dish at that spot on the floor? Most would have swung it around to the wing."

"Give the cutter some credit, too," I replied. "See how he acknowledged the pass after scoring?"

We both examined the floor action for a few minutes. A husky forward sealed off the basket from other rebounders, forcefully boxing out early as every shot headed toward the rim. A younger, heavier Dennis Rodman without the tats but slower than molasses.

I placed my paperwork on the bench in front of me, arched my back to ease a tired shoulder, and turned to Bossenmaier. He scratched above his ear, sending a few white flakes toward the ground.

"Why do you think Trent Whalen might be behaving differently this year?" I said.

As Bosco plopped his stubby legs across the row below, a few inches of hair and skin showed above his white socks. He stared off toward the far scoreboard. He paused for a long moment and then said, "Might have something to do with his dad not being around. Crappy thing to say, but the old man was always in that kid's grill. It looked to me like Trent was afraid to make his own decisions. It was as if his father was running him with a remote control."

I stayed a few more minutes, then headed to the parking lot. On my way out, I noticed Trent Whalen a few steps from the restroom door.

"Hey, Coach. Didn't see you there. How ya doin'?"

"Good, Trent." We stepped out into the hallway. "Rather surprising to see you here."

"We're off tonight 'cuz of that non-leaguer against Rainier Vista. Needed to get out of the house."

"Well, I know you're not scouting because these schools aren't even in your division."

He plopped his hands to his hips and looked down at the floor. "'Member that agent guy I told you about, the one my mom wanted me to talk to? Well, she says he's helpin' a guard here tonight. Eddie McGann. Says I could be part of some package."

We both looked away as the scoreboard buzzer announced the start of the fourth quarter.

"It sure would be great to play with Eddie," Trent said. "Knows when to shoot it, dish it. Great quicks."

"I'll wait for you here. Then we'll talk."

Moments later, Trent strolled back out with a stocky man dressed all in nylon: black snap-off warmups that drooped over untied, scruffy white high-tops, and an orange windbreaker top with no pockets tightly gathered at the neck. Mr. Nylon nonchalantly spun and angled his thick black shades as if he had eyes in the back of his head. I identified him as the observer high in the bleachers who drew Augustine Coatsworth's ire at the all-comers clinic.

He extended his hand ten feet from where I stood, which gave me more time to decide whether or not to shake it when he reached me. His appearance, history and most recent stop entered into the equation. Also, I recalled Trent's handshake reluctance when we first met.

"Howie Blackwell." The voice seemed vaguely familiar. He took my outstretched hand but made no attempt to squeeze or move it. His palm felt spongy.

"Ernie Creekmore."

Blackwell's smooth cheeks held a few random whiskers and reminded me of my former high school juniors. The stubble on his upper lip appeared to be in early cultivation.

"It's good to meet you, Coach," Blackwell said. "I'm sure we can do a lot for this young man."

"Is that so?" I said, taking a wider stance. "Do you work with Manny Cossetti?"

Blackwell scoffed as if I'd brought cheap tenny-runners to a full-court scrimmage. "Let's just say he's the competition." He looked down the hall and smiled. "If you could even call the dude a competitor."

"I see," I said. "Well, let me tell you what I have in mind, Mr. Blackwell. I'm going to coach, and the players are going to play. It's going to be strictly business."

Blackwell sneered and looked at Trent. "I'm about business, too. And so is this guy's mom." He cranked a thumb toward Trent.

"Does Samantha know that you were offering her son your services in a public restroom?"

Blackwell twitched and shuffled his sneakers.

"Trent, give us a second, will you," Blackwell said. The youngster waved a *You-got-it* gesture and headed down the hallway.

Blackwell shook his head and stepped toward me, too close for my comfort, and looked up. I figured I had him by at least five inches and twenty-five pounds.

"Look, old man," he whispered. "You've been gone too long. You'll be cutting yourself off at the knees. Get with the program. There's a ton of guys out there who would kill for your job."

I carefully folded my paperwork and slipped it into my hip pocket. I then rocked back on my heels and blasted both palms into Blackwell's chest, sending him reeling backward. I followed with two more jolts until he was pinned against a pale-yellow wall that appeared to have once been swabbed with wallpaper glue and then abandoned.

"Listen, you jerkball," I said, wedging a forearm under his chin. "You stay the hell away from me, any player that I pick, and any assistant I happen to select."

Blackwell smirked. "You're making a big fuckin' mistake, man. You don't think we'll find a way to get around your ass to your kids?" He flicked his chin up higher. "Fuckin' think again."

I forced my arm deeper into his throat, bringing a groan followed by a wry smile.

"Just so we're clear, Howie, my man. If I so much as—"

"Hey, wait a minute!" Trent yelled, jogging back toward us. "What is goin' on here?"

I released my arm from Blackwell, who shook out his feet and arms like a track star preparing to sprint.

"No problem here, Trent," Blackwell smiled. "Just gettin' a few things square with Coach."

Turning down the hall, I stopped close to Trent's shoulder. "It's him or me, son. The choice is yours."

SEVENTEEN

I PAIRED MY THIRD cup of coffee with a bowl of Cheerios and spread out *The Herald* on the kitchen table.

The rivers continued to rise, much to the dismay of winter steelheaders, but there was no mention of a flood-stage warning. A campaign for a new school levy drew a bold headline. Parents and administrators pushed the need for more computers in the elementary school classrooms, while seniors on fixed incomes, their children grown and gone, opposed any tax increase.

In all my years with the district, I never met anybody over the age of sixty-five excited about shelling out cash for schools, unless the funds were dedicated to a new gym, baseball diamond or football field. They'd write big checks to the booster club, but elementary schools never made it to the state tournament. Sports headlines held a special place in household budgets. Ask any former player if he's got a few extra bucks to help print this year's programs.

Then, leading off the Northwest section, I was stunned to find a four-column picture and thirty-inch feature on Eddie McGann, headlined THE BEST PLAYER YOU NEVER HEARD OF. Clearly written before last night's game, I was curious why the package landed in Northwest and not Sports. Quotes from Eddie's father, siblings, and teammates praised the player's dedication, skill and selflessness. Oddly, his coach was not mentioned. At the bottom of the article was a two-column box summary of last night's game. McGann finished with nineteen points, twelve rebounds, and eight assists in the team's victory.

I tossed on a tattered Santa Clara sweatshirt, a faded-red gift from my brother, a former Bronco point guard. Finding a clean pair of jeans in the laundry room, I stuffed my feet in old Brooks running shoes and headed for the office. The VW's heater had yet to kick in by the time I reached the parking lot of the agency.

Cookie crammed the one upstairs room with promotional fliers and signs, extra office furniture, and metal cabinets filled with old transactions. On a rainy day, it was a semi-secret retreat for confidential calls, which, for me, usually involved basketball.

Before I got two steps through the back door, Cookie scooted down the hall, waving a fistful of papers in one hand. At five-foot-two and an intriguingly long stride, she always appeared to have rollers on her shoes.

"I thought you or your dad knew every damn fisherman in this county," she sneered, pushing the papers into my chest. I juggled them awkwardly and caught most before they hit the carpet.

"Well, we do," I said, squinting to speed-read the top sheet on an angle. "What's up with this, and with you?"

She curled her lip and looked around as if I'd stolen the last Snickers from her purse, then asked for a bigger commission split on my property deals.

"What's up with me is that my fanny is fryin'. These two prime riverfront listings went to some hick office in

Burlington"—her voice soared from alto to soprano— "and not to the hard-working folks right here at Big River Realty. I mean, those bozos up there can't even be considered competitors. Now help me understand that, Coach, because I am rarely stupid!"

The multiple listing service printouts showed that one of the cabins was an estate sale. The document showed that the present owners, probably the children of the last occupant, lived in the Eastern Washington town of Colfax.

"Looks like the kids didn't want the place," I said, perusing the pages. "They probably located the real estate office closest to the cabin, then called the Burlington guys. Besides, you can't expect me to land *every* riverfront listing. Some of them don't even fish. Some, like this one, we've never heard of and are five hours away."

Cookie's eyes narrowed. "Maybe if you were out shaking the bushes a little bit more for customers, you'd meet the people when they're on this side of the mountains! Pay 'em a visit when you see a car in front of the cabin, for crissakes." She jerked the bottom two pages from my hand. "So, what about this one?"

When my eyes caught the name opposite the *Occ Nm* line in the listing agreement, I immediately understood why the owner avoided our office.

"The father had twin boys he thought would be the next Van Arsdales. Get full rides and then on to the NBA. We beat them three consecutive years in the districts, keeping them from going to state. When the twins were seniors, the dad was quoted in *The Herald* that we deliberately ran up the score. That didn't happen."

"Nor did it *happen* that we got to list his riverfront home!" Cookie roared. "For frick's sake, Ernie, I thought I hired you because you were a *popular* coach who everybody loved. Any estimates on how many other noses you whacked out of joint?"

I flexed my fingers trying to ease the numbness, anchored a wider stance, and glanced both ways down the hall. "Look. When you win games over a long period of time, not everybody's going to join your fan club. That is especially true of parents from other schools. More important to me is that we've landed every property owned by any coach and administrator in the area. Including my fiercest rivals. But there's no way in hell we can expect to get every parcel that's a stone's throw away from every lake or river."

Cookie stared at the floor and toed the beige berber with her tiny white Reeboks.

"Yeah, I know. Sorry to chew you out like that, but not that sorry. Having two go to a place like that on the same winter day just bit my ass. Our in-office listings are down. We need to get on both sides of these deals, not just the selling side. Everybody loses sight that we get paid at closing for listing the thing as well."

I reached out and touched her arm, then began heading for my desk. "We've got the word out, believe me. I'm seeing people all the time and my dad mentions it when the old boys meet to talk about tying flies."

"Hey, Ernie," Cookie said. "Is that guard featured in the paper as good as the story says? I haven't seen the paper devote as much space to a high school kid since Cheese Oliver. What do you think they had to pay for that?"

"Writing a check for a story? Is that what are you talking

about?"

"The paper's been hurting, Ernie. For months. The new publisher is not above a little pay-for-play. Believe me. They've come after us several times since Labor Day wanting to know if we'd be willing to pay for a feature. You know, a detailed history of the office and some of its top producers. That's how most of the national real-estate mags survive. Anyway, said thanks, but no thanks. Some retailers, restaurants took them up on the deal, though."

"But a high-school athlete? C'mon. From what I know about the coach, he probably sent an early-season message to parents to always promote the team and never a particular player."

"Yeah, well, it might be somebody other than the family. There might be someone else who just might want to make that happen."

The possibilities dropped me into a mild funk as I picked up a surprising stack of orange WHILE YOU WERE OUT messages on the top shelf of the metal basket on the corner of my desk.

"Oh, yeah," Cookie shouted from down the hall. "We're overhauling the voice-mail system. Those dunces should be done by noon tomorrow. You talk about clueless ... Anyway, Peggy had to take all the calls and handwrite those messages. So be nice to her."

My funk took a deeper dive when the first slip was from Manny Cossetti "looking to nail down a time for lunch." Three of the notes were from area coaches wanting to know if they were too late to submit candidates for the select team. I separated two others that were potential property customers, making a mental note to call them ASAP, especially in light of Cookie's latest outburst. Near the bottom of the stack was a zinger from Margie McGovern "Where have you been?" that, knowing our lovely and nosy receptionist Peggy Metzger, already had been merrily broadcast throughout the building.

I kept the receiver in my hand and dialed one of the two inquiries about real estate, an out-of-area number. A real person failed to answer. Instead, the generic, robotic response.

"Hello, I'm sorry I missed you. Please leave a message, and I will return your call as soon as possible."

"Uh, this is Ernie Creekmore. I'm not quite sure what—"

"Hello, Hello? Coach Creekmore? Is that you?"

Male voice. Upbeat and, I guessed, rather young. Clearly not a retired coach, but not an adolescent.

Then, out of the blue, "How 'bout them Hurons?"

Baffled, I slid the receiver from my ear and stared down at the hard black handset, digesting the message. After a moment, I tucked the phone between my ear and shoulder and reached for a pencil and notepad.

"Eastern Michigan changed its mascot in 1991," I said. "The team's now known as the Eagles. I'm sorry, have we met?"

"Say, I've heard a lot about you, but didn't know you were selling real estate now."

"Have been for quite some time. How can I help you?"

"There are a couple of listings up at Lake Wilhelmina, a little east of your office. I was hoping there might be a time I could see them."

"Sure. I get up there quite often. But there are more than a couple of homes for sale up there. What two did you have in mind?"

There was a muffled response at the other end, as if the

speaker held the phone close to his body and dropped it on a hard surface. Then, after a long moment:

"Sorry about that. There was a newer place, a three-bedroom on Bamboo Lane, listed in an ad in a Marysville flier. The other one looks more like a tear-down on South Shore."

"Well, you're talking about the two ends of the spectrum," I said. "And, I'm not sure I caught your name."

"It's Scott. Scott Hazelton."

I recalled the baggy calypso shirt, its back filling with air like a bellowing body spinnaker as he strutted down the breezy hallway with Gene Slaughter. A curious clothing choice on a crisp winter night.

"OK. Well, I don't know how much you know about the lake, but both of those places are on no-bank waterfront. Flat lots, very good sun exposure, but the cabin on South Shore would be strictly for summer only. No insulation. You'd freeze there in the winter. Were you planning on using it other than Memorial Day through Labor Day?"

"Well, we hope so, but it would depend on my job and new responsibilities. Some to be determined; I'm unsure of my new territory. Waiting for clarity on that this week from my boss."

"I see," I said.

"Let me call you back with some days and times in the next week when I can get up there. I should be able to get back to you in the next forty-eight hours."

"Then I'll just wait to hear from you?"

"Right, Coach. Really looking forward to visiting with you. Say, if I need to call you back, should I call the office again? What's your direct line there? Better yet, what's your cell?"

My admission that I'd misplaced my cellular phone,

because I rarely used it, because I was probably the last person on the planet without total dependency on a cell phone, brought a response somewhere between a chuckle and a snort. Plus, for about the next twenty-four hours, my direct line was the main line to the office.

"Just call the same number you originally called."

After hanging up the phone, I eased back into my chair and shook my head, doubting any meeting would ever take place. While Hazelton probably didn't fit under Cookie's mantra ("a lot of buyers are liars") he sounded more like the friend of a friend always promising to have lunch but never firming up the time and place.

Like a frazzled waitress in a noontime diner, Peggy Metzger zigzagged around three cluttered desks and handed me small slips of paper. Shiny black hair nearly hid her black headset oval, except for the tiny microphone opposite her thin pink lips. When she spoke, the whitest teeth in the county highlighted the mic. A light brown cotton sweater drooped with stylish bulk but I thought her green cords were a bit tight for the office. At twenty-three, she'd "stopped out" at Seattle University for lack of funds, yet planned to re-enroll.

"I appreciate you taking my calls. I know you have a lot of boyfriends' calls to return."

"No sweat," she said, smiling down the hall at the couple milling around her desk. "A cutie phone guy is supposed to have the system squared away by tomorrow. That guy could stay all year as far as I'm concerned. Great pecs. Hey, nice sweatshirt. You're looking as sharp as ever."

She darted off, rapidly snapping *I'm coming* nods to the two elderly walk-ins at the front desk.

I slipped the remaining interesting slips into the front pocket of my jeans, eyeballed my desk, and turned for the hallway leading to the back door.

EIGHTEEN

By THE TIME I showered and responded to the messages on my home machine, most of them tips from the basketball community about "deserving" kids and "the best" cell number to reach me, I had just enough time to change clothes and head to Margie's for dinner.

Even though I'd decided on a navy blazer fresh from the cleaners, I'd also decided dinner was all that the evening was going to be. While Margie was a stunner, and available, her only child grown and gone, it was time to cast a broader net for single women. It had taken me years since Cathy died to get back in the dating game, but Margie simply made the first step too easy; she was geographically desirable. She'd lulled me into complacency, and I'd become lazy in my search for female company.

The MS diagnosis had simply jolted me into doing more, expecting more of every day I woke up healthy. The disease rekindled my love for basketball and clarified how I truly wanted to spend my time. It was time to carry that clarity through to relationships, which meant being honest with Margie.

Realistically, I knew there would probably never be another Cathy, another woman who would understand my curious affinity for high school buckets, let alone classical musicians, major American writers, and West Coast history, yet I needed to put forth a better effort. Particular, but shy of picky, and a long way from passive.

And now there was Diane, who never called back. Go visit? Call? Text? I felt like a kid hoping the new girl in school had a crush on me. Could she have wondered the same about me? The bright brick Tudor tucked away on half an acre off a *Leave It to Beaver* street came with a weekly gardener and no mortgage, thanks to a hefty settlement that Margie received when her ex, an executive with a prominent import-export firm, decided to stay with a young Asian associate in the company's Hong Kong office.

The gray-trimmed, slate-roofed home, one of the first built in the neighborhood, sat on a gentle knoll and was accessed via a long, narrow weedless driveway between two Craftsman houses built closer to the street.

Margie greeted me in the arched alcove with a peck on the cheek. I presented her a bottle of Reynvaan Family Vineyards' Syrah, one of the stellar Washington wines produced in the booming Walla Walla region east of the Cascades.

"Oh, Ernie." She smiled, reading the golden label. "You really shouldn't have."

"Blame it on my mom. She never let me go anywhere empty-handed. Anyway, this wine is supposed to go with anything."

"Please come in. Make yourself comfortable while I open this."

"Why not save it for a special occasion? It's a gift."

"This is a special occasion," she declared. "And it should pour very well with our entrée. I'll be right back."

The kink in my shoulder returned. Trying to stay loose, I whirled and rotated my arm like a quarterback before the first series of game. Plus, I felt a curious need to remain busy rather than cozy. The atmosphere didn't help.

Five spruce logs crackled in the fireplace and formed a perfect pyramid beneath a blue Italian tile border. Expensive, thick magazines featuring architectural design in a variety of foreign countries properly overlapped each other on a dark cherry cocktail table. The ornate oriental rugs over the oak floors in the living room led to a plush white dining room carpet with distinct, carefully vacuumed rows, just waiting for a guest to spill red wine. The delightful notes of a familiar jazz pianist floated through well-hidden speakers.

"Thelonious Monk?" I said, as she meandered between rooms, tying a Pike Place Market apron around her waist and lighting candles while checking the china and silver on the white linen tablecloth.

"Correct. I remembered the tape. You had it playing one night in the VW bus when you drove me home."

Thoughtful, but somehow, it didn't sit right. Another example of trying to please me while offering very little about what she preferred. I'd asked about different likes and dislikes, wants and needs on several occasions, but the response always came back close to "Whatever you decide will be fine with me."

"Actually, I saw The Monk one night in a tiny dive in Detroit when I was in college," I said. "We were in town for a tournament. I played the first game of a doubleheader, then headed out with a couple of guys who had grown up in the area. Somebody got us in a back door. I remember a dark, smoky, special place with only about fifteen tables."

"Well, dinner will be ready any second. I tried to make the halibut just the way you like it. Lemon, butter, a little garlic."

She moved in closer and fingered a silver button on my

coat.

"Since we *both* will be having garlic, I'm sure it won't make any difference when we're close later."

"I'm sure the fish will be terrific," I said, underwhelmed with the lack of creativity and feeling guilty for it. The woman was bending over backward to try to please me but even the exquisite "same-olds" no longer hit my hot buttons.

I found myself trying to carry the dinner conversation, yet received mostly one-word answers about the upcoming school levy, her choice for Academy Award winners, and the national debt. We quickly moved to idle chitchat about the office, county pensions, and clothing allowances for senior female Wall Street executives.

She lifted the napkin from her lap and set it beside a gold-etched plate. Reaching for my hand, I wondered how her bronze skin got so dark in the dead of winter. It seemed to magnify the gems in her gleaming silver rings. As she began to speak, her fingers dug deeper into the center of my hand. Her eyelids looked to be at half-mast.

"Ernie, I simply can't wait any longer to be with you." She shifted in her seat and rested her other hand on my wrist.

"I am with you," I said, attempting to be as clueless as possible. "I'm sitting right here."

"No, you know what I mean." She smiled slyly as she blew out the candles. "I say we leave these dishes right here and—"

At first, I thought a lightning bolt had found the side of the chimney.

But when I turned to discover the shattered picture window in the living room, I realized the message had not come from Mother Nature. While I leaped for the front door, Margie remained wide-eyed and open-mouthed at the table.

"Go in the kitchen and call the cops," I yelled. "Then get down and stay out of sight."

Opening the heavy wooden door a crack, I saw no figure or motion of any kind in the front yard. The floodlights above the garage glowed down on my bus in the driveway and beyond. I flung the door open and sprinted toward the street, the soles of my shoes on the concrete making the only detectable sound. No brake lights, headlights or turn signals in either direction.

Jogging back toward the house, I grabbed a flashlight from the VW's glove box and scanned the shrubs on both sides of the driveway, then scoured the perimeter of the property. Nothing. Not even a footprint in the grass.

From the front yard, the window appeared to be a huge, shimmering spider web, its tentacles splaying out from a nucleus in the lower right corner. All of the glass remained in the frame except for a dusting of crystals that coated the top of the wood sill.

In the cedar planter box under the sill rested an object the size of an orange wrapped in white butcher paper and secured with a wide rubber band. As a black-and-white unit glided up the driveway, I unrolled the paper to find a billiard-ball-size stone and read a message scribbled in red ink:

Choose Your Players Carefully

*   *   *

Margie remained frazzled and anxious after the cops left, so I took her down to Weller's for some coffee before checking her into a room at the Cranberry Tree Motel. She urged me to stay, and I nearly did. But one bed in the room coupled with a splitting headache provided ample ammunition for me to begin my easing away from her.

Maybe I was a selfish jerk for not holding her all night, but I could now live with that. I needed the comfort of my own home, for a variety of reasons. Before leaving, I slipped the night desk person a twenty-dollar bill and told him to call me immediately if there was any activity outside Margie's room.

As the bus revved and rattled through its low gears in the deserted downtown streets toward my neighborhood, it reminded me of the new muffler I'd ordered three years ago when Linn Oliver worked part-time at Petty's Shell Service. It straddled two trusses in my unfinished garage, ready for installation.

The clamor allowed me to concentrate on images other than the commotion at Margie's house or her teary cheeks inside the desolate hotel room. The farther I drove, the bigger the selfish asshole I became. Thankfully, I then flashed to a jam-packed basketball arena and a hoped-for highlight film of my hand-picked all-star team in the Seattle tournament, each member delivering a delicious piece of his individual game to benefit the team.

I coasted into the garage, grabbed a Corona from the outside fridge and ambled toward the back door.

A swooshing sound and a chilling "Ugh!" arrived a split second before a crushing blow just above my right kidney sent the beer bottle flying and left me upright writhing in pain.

"What the hell?" I groaned.

"Ugh!" Another whack, this time to my left hamstring, brought me to my knees. I turned and tried to throw a blind punch, and a jab like a piercing hot poker exploded into the base of my spine, numbing my entire lower body. My vision seemed mired in uneven black frames, punctuated with periodic bursts of flowering gold fireworks.

"Ahhh!" I flopped onto all fours. The neighbor's upstairs light went on just as my head began to spin and my elbows angled down to the wet lawn. The sound of what I guessed to be a garden tool striking my home's concrete foundation broke endless seconds of a sinister silence.

"What's going on out there?" yelled my neighbor, Marty Spring. "Ernie, are you all right?"

Muffled grunts and groans continued behind me. Two gloved hands gripped the back of my collar and propelled me like a battering ram into the cedar siding on the rear wall. Somehow I managed to turn my head and splay my hands and forearms, reducing the impact on my face before falling back to my knees. Woozy and disoriented, lights flickered in the other neighbor's yard as my face skidded lower on the wood planks.

A knee dug in below my shoulder blades, paralyzing my arms and forcing my torso backward. At the same moment, I felt a glove clutch the hair on the back of my head, driving my chin toward the sky. As I sensed a wire loop slide into place against the front of my neck and crisscross down behind me, I felt my ticket had been punched. I envisioned walking down the aisle with Cathy on our wedding day and then flashed to her cheering in the high school gym, fists in the air, behind our bench. The scene faded to her silhouetted on a deserted beach, wind in her hair, and water rushing around her feet and out to sea.

Then, everything went dark.

NINETEEN

HARVEY JOHNSTON PACED across the emergency room and took a slug of coffee from a foam cup. He wore a corduroy sport coat over what appeared to be a pajama top.

"Nice threads," I said. Inwardly, I thanked my lucky stars I could even see.

"Do you know where you are?" he said, amid lights bright enough to light a movie set. "You are at the clinic. It's three a.m. Somebody tried to wrap you up with a phone cord after taking a few shots with a shovel. If it hadn't had been for Marty, we might have been shoveling you into the ground. I guess when he shined the spotlight over the fence, the guy took off down the driveway before closing your deal."

"The way I feel, maybe he should have closed it. And, how can you be so sure it was a guy? It seems like there's a lot of feisty women out there lately."

Harvey scoffed and sat on the side of the bed.

"You have no broken bones but the docs want to wait a few hours to see how you pee. It's about that nasty bruise around the kidney area." He hesitated and looked deep into my eyes, probably sizing up my pupils. "Do you want to go over what happened now or would you rather wait until later? You were keeping my officers busy in more than one location last night."

"Nah, let's start and see what we can get done."

"Roger that. Now, did you see the guy at all? Recall any

clothing, appearance?"

"I pretty much got blindsided, so I didn't see much, and it was dark to begin with. Rubber-work type gloves on both hands, not dishwasher rubber. Hurt like hell when he yanked my hair. When he slammed me into the house, I thought I saw a stocking mask out of the corner of my eye. I was looking down most of the time."

"Were you able to see if he was wearing boots, maybe shoes?" Harvey said.

"White high-tops. Leather, not canvas." My eyes felt heavy, and I got the feeling this session was going to be shorter than hoped for.

"This really perplexes me," Harvey said. "I thought you'd be about the only person in this whole mess who didn't stand a chance of getting hurt. Think about it. Why in the hell would someone want to harm the guy making the decisions that might bring somebody headlines and interviews? Maybe even fame and fortune?"

"Maybe someone who wanted more control over those decisions."

"OK," Harvey said. "Before I let you rest, let me jump quickly to what happened earlier in the evening." He turned a palm to the sky. He looked like a priest eliciting a responsorial psalm from a Sunday congregation. "What kind of preposterous message does this kind of note send?" He fluttered the sheet of paper. "Of course you're going to choose your players carefully."

I was uncertain if he expected a response. "What did your cops have to say about my lovely evening?"

"It was probably the same dialogue you heard from the

officers at the house," Harvey said. "They turned up no trace of any prowler and all of the windows and doors were secure. They assume whoever hurled that rock at the window did so from the driveway and then quickly departed on foot. As you can surmise, it is difficult to locate evidence of a footprint on dry payment. Let me offer this, however: Had our pitcher thrown a strike down the middle and not hit the outside corner, that package would have been in Marge's front room with glass everywhere. She would have been finding shards in the carpet months from now."

I tried to prop myself up on my forearms, cringed at the pain, and fell back down.

"Well, whoever pulled the stunt at her place, their beef is with me, not her. It all started when I accepted the offer to coach this select team and she just happened to get in the middle of it. Man, did I hear about that."

Harvey placed his cup on my bedside tray and raised his eyebrows. I knew I had gone one step beyond and would have to pay the price.

"Excuse me? What, exactly, did you hear?"

"Some jackass called. He would not give his name. It sounded like he was in a bar somewhere."

"And?" His eyes grew wide and his arms flew open.

"And he said he knew I was seeing Margie. Also said he knew where she lived and if I didn't play ball with him she wouldn't look the way she looks now."

Harvey shook then lowered his head like a pitcher who gave up a game-winning homer. "Ernie, when were you going to communicate this to me?"

I don't weasel well. I tried to casually clear my throat but failed, even in my condition. "I figured I could find out who the guy was on my own, set him straight, and be done with it. He's probably some agent trying to get a piece of a kid. Either for a school or some payola from a minor league contract."

"Now, we've talked about this before. You are not a professional investigator, especially when threats to my employees are involved! This goes way beyond talking to kids and parents about joining teams."

"Slow down, Harvey. Some of this is on you."

"On me? What are you talking about?"

"Seems everything was fine and dandy until *you approached me* about snuggling up to Trent Whalen and trying to find out where he was and what he knows about his father's death."

"And have you?"

"Indeed. I've even seen him play. What I also know is that simply asking around the basketball community about the kid has produced a rock to a window and two bizarre notes."

Harvey gripped the metal armrest on the bed.

"What do you mean, *two* notes?"

I coughed nervously and swallowed hard. Then I closed my eyes and tried to hide behind a thumb and forefinger.

"Ernie!"

"Earlier in the week I got a note in a hamburger bag that was left on the floor of my car at the office."

"What did it say?"

"*To insure excellent service.* Blue ink, not red like last night."

"Insure or ensure …? I or E?" Harvey asked. "Anyway, sounds like Mr. Elmo Service is in play here. I'm wondering what this mysterious notewriter planned to insure it with. Big Macs?"

I took a deep breath but let it out too hard.

"What?"

"Harvey, there was a thousand bucks in the bag. Ten crisp Franklins."

"I absolutely cannot believe what I am hearing," Harvey mumbled. "What other secrets are you keeping from me, Mister Detective? You might be talking about a string of workable clues here, but, thanks to you, we might be so far behind that we'll never catch up."

"I dropped the cash off at Washington High and told them to give it to the Fighting Crabs Booster Club. The girls' freshman and JV teams could use some new warmups."

Harvey rolled his eyes, then rested his forehead in his palm

"A gentleman can live through anything," I said, hoping to sidetrack his attention.

"I know that's a William Faulkner line," he said, "yet I am a bit chagrined that you bring it up now. *As I Lay Dying?*"

"*The Reivers.*"

"Hmmm ... Would never have gone there."

After a moment, he refocused. "Did you ever think that I might want to see the bag, the note, and the cash?" When he got to "cash," he was upright and shouting, bringing glares from the nurses. "Damn it, Ernie. I've warned you time and again. Your instincts and communication skills with young people are not to be confused with collecting and evaluating legal evidence. You may have just accepted a bribe from a person who could now be linked to a murder investigation."

"I didn't *accept* anything. Some jerk left cash in my bus. And I was about as surprised at finding it as I am at you telling me I took a bribe."

"How in the hell are we supposed to know what you did

with it? Osmosis? You are supposed to report any and all activities of this kind to the local authorities. And, hello! I'm the local authority."

Harvey opened his arms as if he'd just discovered a room full of treasures. Gray chest hair curled out from his coat and top, giving him a clown-like look. I grinned. Harvey peered down at his chest and frowned.

"Mr. Creekmore, it appears you are in the middle of a mess now and someone's found a lot of methods of getting to you and pushing your proverbial buttons. Given what happened last night, officers will be patrolling your home for the near future. More importantly, how do you plan to protect Margie in all of this? Lord knows your all-knowing brain already has come up with several solutions, I'm sure."

"It's reassuring to know that you are putting her well-being way above mine."

Harvey glared and folded his arms across his chest.

"What if I send a subtle message to the community that we're no longer seeing each other?" I said. "It may be a good idea to take other women to games, public places. If I'm less predictable, maybe we can keep more rocks from going through windows."

Harvey hiked his shoulders as if to indicate that he didn't know. "Have you actually talked with her about this? You know, she's pretty goofy over you right now. I'd say the chances of you breaking her heart are pretty good with this ingenious plan."

"Better that than somebody breaking her neck," I said. "Actually, I'd planned to tell her last night that I needed to see other women, but I never got the chance to do it. And, I'd appreciate you not mentioning what transpired after I left her at the motel last night."

Head down, Harvey strolled for a moment and circled away, two fingers curled over his lips.

"Thank God you're two single people and not dragging any oblivious spouses into a dark hole," he sighed, returning to the bedside. "Please speak with Margie the first chance you get. And be gentle, damn it. Wrap your message in some empathy as if you're breaking bad news to a player who's been cut from your team. I'll make sure we're covered at the office in case there's a ton of tears and she misses some desk time. Then make sure you tell the Berrettonis down at Tony's that you two are kaput. Especially George. I love him dearly but the guy gossips like a woman in a quilting club."

"He does have a way of spreading the word, particularly on this topic. I'll spend some time there ASAP. And, you don't need to tell Cookie about tonight. For that matter, don't tell anybody."

"Hmmm, I see," Harvey mused. "Are there other orders, sir, or is that it for now?" He saluted like a weary soldier. "This might surprise you, but I would like to get a few hours of sleep. Is there anything else I need to know about the past few days?"

Harvey cringed and stared at the ceiling.

"The Skagit and the Stillaguamish are still running too high," I said.

"Tell me something I didn't know."

"Unfishable. In fact, it'll be weeks before we can get put in on the Stilly, then it'll be up near Oso."

"I am leaving now," he groaned. "Don't be surprised by the number of police vehicles circling your block."

"Remember," I said. "This was all your idea."

TWENTY

THE CLINIC TURNED me loose at dawn, and Timoteo drove me home. My head hurt, my side burned and the reality of my situation grabbed me by the neck. He glanced over twice before I broke the silence.

"Man, I love coaching but I sure as hell didn't sign up for this," I mumbled. "I mean, I can handle the clueless parents and questions about playing time. That all comes with the territory. But the threatening calls, the jerks always wanting a piece of the kids ... And now this? We haven't even been on the court yet."

Timoteo lifted his chin and bounced his head high against the headrest. "Say, why don't you come and stay at our place for a few days? We've got that apartment over the garage, and nobody's using it. You can park the bus back there and nobody will even see it."

When I crossed my arms across my chest, I flinched in pain.

"Thanks for the offer," I said, "but I need to get to my own bed for right now. I'll get some rest and hopefully look at all this stuff with a clearer set of eyes."

Timoteo pulled into the driveway, helped me inside, and checked every room.

"Ernie, there are a lot of people in this town who would miss you more than you think. Just for a second, remove hoops entirely from the picture. I'm certain there are other things you want to do that don't threaten your life."

"You overestimate my interests."

"If you weren't around … well, I'd lose my chance to get you out on a bike. That'll be my life after basketball and it'll save your knees. It's certainly a better cardio workout than golf, and it doesn't take as long."

"I'll ride, but not in the rain." I tried to laugh, but it hurt.

"Think about it. If you weren't around, George wouldn't have an audience, and Harvey would be forced to find a new fishing partner."

"I've thought of all that. Believe me. It does hit home. And then there's a part of me that refuses to give in to these clowns."

He turned and opened the front door. "Ernie, there's stubborn and then there's stupid. Please consider making a change, somewhere. Maybe give up the semi-Sherlock role." He pointed to the bedroom. "Now get in there and try to sleep. Call me if you need anything."

After Timoteo left, I snatched the extra key from the garage, locked the doors, and slept until noon. Sore and groggy, I gingerly swung out of bed en route to the bathroom and nearly crumbled to the floor in pain, thanks to the knot in my lower back. Using the bed, dresser, desk chair, and doorknobs as props and crutches, I shuffled to the shower for thirty minutes of hot water therapy. I dressed, scrambled some eggs, and found that I was better off on the move.

My energy restored and my limbs on the way back, the short drive through town further boosted my outlook. When the sun begins to break up the fog suspended above the Skagit River, I often envision teams of native canoes negotiating the big bend just south of North Fork, their trusted guides

paddling gold-seeking prospectors to the once-popular panning banks and remote mines northeast of this pioneer outpost
more than a century ago. Not only did the dreaming bring joy
and wonderment, but the region also produced a sense of pride
and privilege.

The thought of all that coming to a halt, along with never
again witnessing a speckled steelhead rising in the afternoon
sun of the Stillaguamish River, sent me a message to curb my
cavalier outlook on safety.

The lines at the Gas 'N Go's three pumps were longer than
usual, mainly because the shrewd Korean owner had reduced
his gas price two cents on his plastic marquee within thirty
minutes of the new price posted at the I-5 Chevron. I steered
the bus to the shortest line, turned off the engine, and delicate-
ly burrowed through the glove box and side pockets in search
of my cell phone. After a battered blue GMC Jimmy pulled
away from the pump, I pulled forward and returned to the cell
phone search. Finding an old Stanwood Holiday Tournament
program proved to be a surprise bonus, and I began paging
through it for player data.

A tap on the window startled me.

"Hey, did you know the car in front of you isn't even hooked
up the hose?" a blue-haired lady barked. "I'm behind you and
I've got to get to the beauty parlor."

Tossing the program to the floor, I groaned down out of
my seat. The heavy metal nozzle still rested on the side of the
pump. A midnight blue, four-door Dodge Avenger with a
VANCOUVER RODEO bumper sticker and no driver in sight
sat in first position in our four-car line. Tiny paw tracks meandered over the dusty trunk. Two open Kleenex boxes sat in an

L on the shotgun seat.

"I'll check the store," I said, waddling toward the minimart at the far end of the lot. When I swung the glass door open, the cashier was scanning several items that Paula Soijka had scattered across the counter.

"Excuse me," I said. "Ah, Paula ... we're all waiting to get gas and your car is blocking us."

She glanced up, squinting. She yanked the sleeves of an ISSAQUAH SALMON DAYS t-shirt on to her forearms. Baggy pink cotton sweatpants fell atop pink flip flops highlighted by a gold-glitter flower.

"Is it done?"

"I don't think it ever started."

"Ohmygod! I can't believe ... Coach, right? Hey, hang right here a minute while I fill 'er up."

Paula tried to jog out the door but the effort lapsed to a hobble. Her purchases included a six-pack of Schmidt's beer, three boxes of Sudafed, two large Benadryl bottles and a pack of spearmint gum.

After several minutes, she made her way back. I nodded to her as I passed, but she stopped me with a wrist grab.

"Coach, that Timmy guy? Weren't you going to have him get in touch with me?"

Dr. Timoteo Mesa was not a person I'd send Paula's way unless she needed immediate medical attention.

"I'm sorry, I don't recall that."

"Really? I thought that's what you said at the bar. Anyway, let me know what I can do for your team. I'd like to help the kids if I can. I always have errands and odd jobs that need to be done, and I'm sure they can use the extra cash. Trent's been a great helper in the past. Besides, Samantha says not all the kids will be getting help like Trent."

"Oh ... well," I stammered. "Thanks for the offer. I'll give that some thought."

"Yeah, you do that. Say, maybe I'll take a shot at designing some shirts for you. I'll get Trent to model one that next time he's over. Who knows? Maybe they'll become the rage in town. We'd get all the stores on Division to stick 'em in their front windows. I can write a story for the paper about the fundraiser, too."

"I'd hate to go to the well too often and ask people—"

"Hell, they'll love it. We can get the kids in the schools to help. I know some of Gene Slaughter's kids over at Loyola, and I could get them to pitch in. Don't worry about the cost. I'll get somebody to front the money." She pointed toward the store. "I gotta go pay for this. Don't worry, I'm all over those shirts."

The time between the Gas 'N Go and the office flew by fast and fuzzy. If I hadn't pocketed the gas receipt, I'd have no clue how many gallons the bus had consumed.

"Blue jeans?" Edith snarled as I strolled through the back door. "You come to work in blue jeans?"

"Rough night," I said. "But what about this colorful flannel shirt. Whaddaya think?" I yanked open my down vest so she could have a full-on view of the wool-print Pendleton. "And don't forget the rather new hiking boots. In fact, I believe I dress just like a majority of my customers dress. You might not believe it, but I actually spent a lot of time debating whether I should have worn my dinner jacket this morning. Since there were no high-rise execs on my agenda, again, I decided this ensemble was absolutely appropriate."

"Don't you raise your voice with me, young man," she huffed. "You look like you've been in a bar fight."

"Close, and thanks. It's a relief to know I'm still young and can look forward to years of clothing consultations from you."

"Young as in child. Make that an immature child. And ..." She angled closer to my chest. "Is that a huge hickey on your neck? How absolutely disgusting!"

When she concluded her glare and swooshed off down the hallway, Cookie posted up against her office door, eyes squinted, cranking a crooked come-here index finger.

"What?" I said.

"Get your butt in here, now. You look awful, worse than usual."

As I passed in front of her in the doorway, the edges of her mouth sank down and away, hiding most of her lips. The familiar leather armchair in front of her desk was cold to the touch, and to my bottom.

"Why aren't you using that gorgeous new cell phone I bought you last year?" Cookie said. "That model has more frills than a whore's dream."

"I can never remember to take it off the charger in the kitchen. Besides, the thing went off in an old coaches' dinner one night. Everybody laughed at me when I didn't know how to turn it off. I actually haven't really used it much since."

"Tell me about it. All my calls ring out. You don't even have a recorded message! Why don't you just keep the phone in your car?"

"Then it'll just run out of juice before I want to use it."

She shook her head as if not believing how I operated. "You know, one of the many things that worry me about you is the number of telephone calls you get *here at the office* from the chief crime inspector in this county. These"—she fanned out a fistful of orange slips—"lead me to believe you are off pretending to be Sherlock while I provide you with a desk, secretarial services, plus a mammoth amount of tender love and care so that you will list and sell residential real estate. Now, if you elicited an equal number of telephone messages *for the job for which you were hired,* perhaps I would be feeling differently this morning!"

"I went to see Trent Whalen play basketball, and I'm sure Harvey and his guys are extremely anxious to hear what I have to say."

"Oh, really? And why is that important right this second?"

"Well, I can't spell everything out for you right now, but believe me when I say I will have to take time out to talk with Harvey very soon."

"Time *out?* For frick's sake! When are you going to have some consistent time *in?*"

For a long, awkward moment, I considered the countless hours I would need to block in the next few weeks to mesh a dozen individual skills and personalities, schedules and distances, into a workable chemistry that might become a successful basketball team. When the mental tally became colossal, I decided to save the conversation for another time.

"Now, don't be zoning out on me," Cookie steamed. "It's too early in the day to be daydreaming. Go get said what you need to say to Harvey, and then bring me some positive ammo on the property front."

She rocked back and forth. I could almost hear her reloading.

"But let me tell you, Coach. If the help you are giving him now takes as much time as the Cheese Oliver case, I might have to get another warm body in here to take some floor time. I can't have walk-ins driving up the freeway from Seattle and nobody in the office to show them our listings." She lowered her voice, opened her top desk drawer and began pushing pens and paper clips aside with both hands.

She patted an open palm with the ruler. "Say, Margie has been leaving some of Harvey's messages for you. While I know *she is* his assistant, doesn't he usually try to reach out to you himself?"

I shifted in the chair and felt it had warmed considerably.

"The guy's workload continues to pile up," I said. "I mean, you should see his desk. It's way worse than this one. He's probably got a million things going on, and she's making a number of his calls."

"What the hell's wrong with my desk?"

*   *   *

Margie McGovern answered my call to Harvey Johnston's office on the first ring.

"That was quick," I said, expecting a few more moments to clear the expired listing flyers from the top of my desk.

"Well, I saw the Big River Realty caller ID and was hoping it would be you."

"Yup, it is. I guess the boss has been trying to track me down."

"Yes, he is, but I also wanted to reconnect with you. We kind of left our business unfinished the other night and I was hoping to get back on your schedule. Soon."

"We might be able to do that," I muttered, thinking about basketball and wondering how she might feel if "soon" turned out to be June or July.

"That's wonderful, Ernie. Thank you. And Harvey wants to see you in person, so I'll look at the calendar and give you a few alternate dates by the time you get here. I'm assuming you are coming here?"

"Yeah, sure. No problem. Is one time better for him than another?"

"He has appointments for the remainder of the morning but his afternoon appears to be wide open. Shall we say two p.m.? I'll telephone you immediately if that happens to change."

"OK, two it is. I'll be there."

"And I'll be waiting."

I hung up the receiver, pivoted my chair away from the desk and interlaced my hands behind my head. While it became clear that the prep tournament would top my priority list for at least the next four weeks, it would wonderful to catch a couple of new listings to take the edge off at the office. A solid sale would float a lot of boats.

The main problem was the season: February was an awful month to sell second homes, and everybody knew it. Including my boss.

Peggy Metzger be-bopped by, heavy metal rock escaping from her shell-shaped ear buds. She popped one into her hand and delivered a quick message while snapping a wad of Juicy Fruit. The smell gave the flavor away as she was poised to load another yellow-wrapped stick.

"I'm in the lunch room, but only if somebody really needs

me. Martina's covering my phones. Left you one right there." She pointed to my wire inbox and didn't stick around for a reply.

Under the morning edition of the *Bellingham Herald* was a phone slip not included in Cookie's earlier stack. I didn't recognize the area code. The letters "SH" were scribbled in the *Name* line.

"Maybe it's the president of S&H Sugar wanting me to come to Hawaii to assess his holdings," I said to nobody in particular.

"It's C&H," said Ted, a retired Army officer and the newest member of the staff, unseen and working in the cubicle behind mine. "And it's not a good sign when you start talking to yourself."

"Right." I laughed. "Sorry, but this just may be the start of it."

I punched in the phone numbers and waited through more than a half-dozen rings. The tones were broken and inconsistent, as the call was apparently being forwarded, re-routed or bumped by call waiting. As I moved to end the call, a breathless voice came on the line.

"Who's this?"

"I'm sorry," I said, startled by the surly tone. "To whom am I speaking?"

"Who'd you wanna talk to?"

"Look, man, I was returning a message I received from SH, so I'm not quite certain."

"This is Scott."

"Oh, OK. Well, this is Ernie Creekmore, and I sell and list mostly vacation properties."

"Coach Creekmore! So good of you to call back. This is Scott Hazelton."

"Right. Now, if I recall, you were interested in some property up at Lake Wilhelmina."

"Yes, well, that's correct, but I'd listen to any other recommendations you have to offer. I'm not dead-set on anything. I've heard that Wilhelmina is quiet during the week, has terrific waterskiing, and is not a bad commute from SeaTac Airport."

"Correct on all counts, but the traffic on I-5 can be brutal through Everett just about any time of the day."

"That's what I've heard. But if things go according to plan, I'll be able to pick and choose my travel times. In fact, another reason Lake Wilhelmina is so attractive to me is that it's about midway between Seattle and the border. I'm working right now to lock down some interesting new Canadian clients, so I could be spending a lot of time up there."

I said, "Certainly no traffic issues from the lake to Blaine, other than the occasional deer on the lake road. The lake road is paved all the way to North Fork and the locals keep it clear in the winter for the school bus. So, when you get closer, give me a holler, and we can run up there and take a look. Right now, there's a diverse inventory, and a few properties got beat up pretty good by the weather. Some of the homes have waterfront, others have waterfront access, and still others have views."

"I happen to be in the area now. Finally, I get to slow down for a few days in one place. Actually, I was hoping maybe you would have some time for me this afternoon."

I spun around in my desk chair like a kid on a park carousel, wondering how this guy would spin his in-person pitch.

"Well, I've got a two o'clock meeting in North Fork that I

can't miss. It'll probably go at least an hour. That doesn't give us much daylight to look at homes. Why don't we just postpone until we can block a few hours?"

"But it would at least give me a chance to meet you. Press the flesh. Get an idea of the lay of the lake. I've got a chunk of cash I need to find a home for soon, and I can't think of a better place than a nice lakefront cabin with a dock."

"Understand. You're coming out of a 1031 exchange and need a replacement property. What's your deadline?"

"A what? No, I just need to move some money I received from another opportunity. That's all."

I could smell the fishiness through the phone. But if he did have the wherewithal to buy, and soon, the sale would get Cookie off my back and provide a bit of a buffer for the hoops time I would need away from the office.

"Tell you what," I said. "Meet me up at the lake's fire hall at three forty-five. If you're coming from the south, drive to the Possum Store and follow the signs. From the north, head east on the highway out of North Fork and stay on it for about twelve miles until it becomes South Shore Drive. The fire hall will be on your right, opposite the boat launch and the Mountain Market."

"Got it," Hazelton said. "If I get lost, I'll just call you from my cell phone."

"No cell service up at the lake. There's a pay phone outside the Mountain Market. It's the only phone around for miles."

"I'm sure I'll be OK. If for some reason I'm early, I'll just grab some coffee at the market and hang out. See you up there."

He rang off before I could mention that the Mountain Market had closed for the season. I also avoided giving him my cell number, which might make a difference if and when I eventually locate the phone.

Press the flesh?

TWENTY-ONE

B JARNE DAGMAR SHIFTED apprehensively on Harvey Johnston's county-issued vinyl couch.

"Can't image why they'd call this darn thing a love seat," the detective said, gripping a chrome armrest with his "good" hand. "Be like makin' love on a slick concrete driveway."

Harvey scowled.

"Sorry, sir."

"Oh, Ernie," Harvey groused. "I'm *supposed* to tell you that I sent Margie to the post office but she should return momentarily."

Feeling a twinge of relief, I tilted my head back as Bjarne angled me a *Really?* look.

"So, Ernie," Harvey said. "What was your impression of young Mr. Whalen?"

"He's a lot smarter, and stronger, than I thought he'd be," I said.

"Sounds like somebody I'd like to see play," said Harvey. "He's basketball-smart, street-smart, intellectual-smart?"

"Maybe all of the above, but hoop-smart for sure. He's got the knack of recognizing mismatches immediately, and then he can orchestrate where movement should flow. All of this in a split second from down low, near the bucket, without even having the ball."

"How strong is the kid?" Bjarne said, slumping into the seat next to me.

"Trent's upper body is very developed for a high schooler. He's put in more than his share of hours at the gym. The guy sets screens as wide as an oak wall unit. Man, what a good shooter could do coming off picks like that."

"So, does he have any help on that team?" Harvey asked.

"Not really. Certainly no other D-1 kid. There might be a guy or two who could play at an NAIA school."

Bjarne cleared his throat and frowned my way. "Can we return the focus to the crime and his possible participation?"

"I have to say, I actually enjoyed watching the kid play and speaking with him," I said, and went on to explain that Trent asked intelligent questions regarding the select team, received a glowing recommendation from his coach and inquired about other potential team members, including Elmo "Excellent" Service.

"God," Bjarne said. "Who gave him that nickname?"

"The ladies," Harvey mimicked in a deep, impressive Elmo tone. "See what I'm sayin'?"

Bjarne shrugged and shook his head. "Let me cut to the chase. Did Trent Whalen show any sign, maybe use any words that would make you suspicious that he murdered his father?"

"No, none at all. But I've never had a son, let alone one that I pushed to the edge for years in a row. It sounds as if Tim Whalen's continuous hounding might have shoved him over the edge. Would some kid snap because of it? Maybe so. Some run away, others take drugs, throw punches."

"Or fire a gun. Twice," Bjarne said.

"Look, we don't know what life was like in their home," Harvey said. "Is he capable? Under certain circumstances, I think some people would be capable of anything. There are spur-of-the-moment decisions made all the time that people end up regretting. From what Ernie says, Trent has more strength than most men, but obviously it doesn't take much to shoot a gun. It's not as if the kid would have had to break into the home and overtake his father. Tim would've welcomed him with open arms."

"We still don't have any hard evidence," Bjarne said. "No murder weapon, no indisputable knowledge that Trent was anywhere near the crime scene. But we really didn't expect all that to change just because Ernie had one conversation with the guy. Did we?"

"No, the plan was to get Coach Creekmore close to Trent over an extended period of time. On and off the court. That's still the plan. If Trent gives up some old stories, plus maybe some personal experiences, tendencies, we might accumulate enough ammo to charge him. But right now, we're obviously a long way from anywhere."

I stood, wrapped my hands on the back of the chair and stretched my legs, bending one knee at a time. "I'll tell you something that *was* curious and disturbing that night," I said. Harvey and Bjarne stared straight through me.

"Yes?" Harvey said.

"There was a professional agent in the gym who seemed to have more than a passing relationship with the Loyola coach. The guy was even in the locker room at the half."

"Are you saying Trent Whalen is good enough to play professionally?" Harvey said.

"No, not now. But I've recently learned there are a lot of teams outside of the NBA and elsewhere who are interested in players down the road. If a guy like Trent does eventually sign a contract, the guy who brings him to the table gets a piece of the pie."

"Wait a minute," Bjarne said, leaning forward. "Aren't most of these kids concerned about catching the eye of some college assistant? I thought the real competition was among relentless young coaches who try to babysit talented athletes until they sign on the dotted line."

"Yes and yes," I said. "College coaches usually are assigned regions where they recruit the best players. They lob telephone calls, write letters and make personal visits during specific times of the recruiting season. During the precious weeks known as the 'contact' period, a lot of these coaches camp out in their designated regions, constantly seek face time with their targeted athletes, and don't make it home to see their families for days.

"But guess what? Do you think for a minute these fiercely competitive coaches plan to leave their prize players alone during the dead period? Hell no. They hire a rep, somebody with no known ties to their school, to craftily continue the recruiting process in their place."

"And these reps are paid?" Bjarne said. "Or are they college-color-wearing car dealers who simply want to touch the cape of the next local Superman?"

"Good question. This person has evolved and adapted like crazy the past few years, a recruiting survival of the fittest. For a long time, the guys keeping the fires burning were grads who got their jollies out of helping the ol' alma mater. They're still out there, slapping big green bills in kids' palms at restaurants, wining and dining them on sunset cruises, making sure Mom finally gets that trip to Universal Studios to see King Kong crunch the bus."

"The what?" Harvey said.

"A trip," I said. "Anywhere. Make it Disneyland, I don't care. Regardless, now there are real professionals chasing these kids, and there's no way to tell who they are representing. These 'runners' dance from kid to kid, school to school, and now, agent to agent."

"So, one of these clowns could get a little sugar from Bucksnort State if a player enrolls there, and then a piece of a professional contract when he eventually signs with *Vaya con Dios* in a European league."

"Exactly," I said. "And you never really know the runner's true relationship at any given time. A kid could say 'no' to Bucksnort State. Five minutes later, the runner brokers a deal to Cornball Tech and the kid accepts. Cha-ching for the runner. Plus, he's still got the possible European league deal down the road."

"I wish I could say it's illegal," Harvey said. "But it's definitely not right."

Looking at my watch, I began guessing how long it would take me to get through town and up to the lake to meet Scott Hazelton.

"It used to be so easy," Bjarne said. "If a high school senior was driving around town in a new convertible, chances were that somehow, some way the school that signed him was behind that car. The locals played it like a bogus caper involving a part-time job. None of them wanted to cop to it because they all knew the designated booster with the big bucks."

A light rap on the door halted the brief laughter. Margie

McGovern entered before Harvey could speak.

"Oh, hello, everyone," she said, panning the room. "Coach, Cookie just called to inform you that you had an appointment at the lake."

"Really?"

"I guess a man called the office to make sure about the time. Cookie talked to him and said the guy, her words, not mine, 'is as ready as a Girl Scout'. Actually, in this case, I guess that would be Boy Scout."

"Right. That's OK. I got it." Margie pivoted, hid her wink from Harvey and Bjarne, then swayed back to the outer office.

"What's this about meeting a Boy Scout at the lake?" Harvey chuckled. "Kind of an odd time of year to be meeting anybody in the middle of nowhere, but perhaps this is some sort of offseason training."

"I got a feeling he will be anything but a Boy Scout," I said. "The guy who says he wants to see cabins up at Wilhelmina is the agent-runner-whatever who was in the Loyola High locker room last night. The same person who seemed so buddy-buddy with the coach. It seemed a bit strange because the coach appeared to be a very bright guy, somebody who could see a flim-flam man from a mile away."

I leaped to my feet, knowing I'd allowed too much time to slip by. "As much as I'd like to stay in this warm, cozy office and continue this stimulating conversation, it's time for me to hit the road."

"Look, Ernie," Bjarne said. "Bottom line? I'm still liking Trent Whalen for his dad's murder. That kid's a walkin', talkin' explosive charge."

Before I could respond, Harvey jumped in.

"OK, keep your eyes open with this guy at the lake," Harvey said. "I'll be asking you to rate his demeanor so pick up your home phone if it rings, and for crying out loud, try to find your cell."

I was in no hurry to locate the cellular phone. Not only was the first month's bill more than my mortgage, but I also had no desire to learn how to properly use it. That would take time away from basketball.

"If I see your name on the caller ID, I might pick it up," I said. "Depends how I'm feeling at the time." Harvey scowled. "And remember, there's no cell service at Lake Wilhelmina anyway, so even if I did find the dumb thing, I'd still be out of range for the next couple of hours."

I was hoping Bjarne would follow me out of Harvey's office, thereby allowing for a superficial conversation in the reception area that we could continue into the hallway. That would avoid a one-on-one with Margie. Another candlelight evening most likely would top her list, yet I secretly preferred another encounter with Diane Chevalier, and soon. *Geez, what did that say about me?*

When Bjarne lobbed Harvey a question about county pensions, I opened the door and peeked into the outer office. Empty. "Later, guys," I muttered over my shoulder, then closed Harvey's door behind me.

Margie's desk sat tidy and deserted, its matching chair pulled back close to the wall. Steam rose from a purple University of Washington mug resting on a cork coaster near her phone, a tiny square tea tag dangling on a string from the rim.

Relieved, I darted for the hallway door and collided head-on into Margie, her eyes perusing a brown legal file open like an oversized magazine in her hands. When we bumped, the file flipped backward into her face, and I instinctively reached out to steady her motion. Her white blouse was somehow crisp yet soft. She smelled like honeysuckle, and it was a long way to summer.

"Well, we can forget about fancy intros for today," she laughed. I dropped to my hands and knees and began gathering the papers scattered on the unappealing commercial tile.

"You OK?"

"Of course. I'm fine. I'm also glad I didn't miss you before you left."

Attempting to straighten and tap the pieces into a package with both palms, I caught myself admiring her muscular, curvy calves before rising and delivering the still-uneven clump of paper.

"Thank you so much, Ernie. Maybe you would allow me to make you dinner tonight. We never really got to visit the other night. It seems like we both have been running with our heads down ever since. In fact, I think what happened just now is a good example."

She smiled so brightly that I expected a star to magically burst from her Vanna White teeth.

"You know, Margie, this appointment at the lake might take a while. There's really no saying how long I might be stuck up there. If the guy is serious and wants to write up an offer, I might have to hustle back to the office and continue with the paperwork, get ahold of the listing agent—"

"Well, you are going to have to eat sometime," Margie said. "And what are the realistic chances that you'll get a first-look deal? You've said for a long time that people are taking two, three, sometimes four visits to a place before they go down on paper."

"A lot of these out-of-town guys are different. They know their time here is short, find something they absolutely love and fall head over heels for it before they get back on the plane to go home."

"They sound similar to the people who buy timeshares in Mexico. They leave their brains at the border and become helpless in the hands of a handsome salesman. When they get back home, they wonder why they signed on the bottom line."

"That's not exactly what I meant," I frowned. "People do have a tendency to weigh the pros and cons of different properties for hours after they see them. That type of debate has ruined a lot of dinners over the years, and I just thought I would eliminate the possibility tonight. Especially given the last time I was at your place."

She nudged me in a resigned agreement, laid the stack of papers on her spotless desk blotter and scooted back her chair.

"Well, if something happens and things wrap up faster that you expected, call me from the Mountain Market or when you get down the hill and into cell range."

"Will do," I nodded, and then made my way out the door and down the hall, wondering if I would find my phone under the car seat, and if it would have any power left in it to call anybody.

TWENTY-TWO

HIGHWAY 9 MEANDERS southeast of North Fork toward
Lake Wilhelmina and features a jumble of primary residenc-
es and second-home retreats: stately brick Tudors topped with
gorgeous gray slate and wrapped with freshly painted fences
or squared-off hedges; peeling doublewides flanked by abandoned pickups; and one-floor ranch houses, white smoke swirl-
ing from kitchen woodstoves, overlooking a twisting creek
tumbling west from Big Lake.

A scattering of FOR SALE signs, ranging from coarse, mis-
spelled announcements spray-painted on sheet metal to the
stoutly posted "premier" placards of national firms, tended to
mirror the condition of the home behind it. None of the signs,
however, carried a Big River Realty logo, a fact that Elinor Cutter drilled home to her agents as often as possible.

A major portion of the road, once the main south supply
line to town traveled by horseback farmers and ranchers, hosted one of the first north-south freight lines linking Seattle with
British Columbia before giving way to the present two-lane
blacktop. As more noisy big rigs downshifted into the turns
and spewed dark diesel exhaust on this pastoral detour just east
of I-5, more homeowners fled, leaving their roadside acreage
to neighboring dairy farmers. They gladly paid low dollar for a
little extra room for their unconcerned cows.

The highway zigzagged past the Big Lake Bar & Grill,

skirted a community golf course and briefly bordered a few acres of lake marshland before slanting south toward Arlington and Marysville. At the widest portion of the marsh, across the road from the damp peninsula where a slippery California developer attempted to build a community of "pole houses" before the county shut him down, the Lake Wilhelmina cutoff snaked away to the east. It started with ten miles of blind curves, gorgeous creek vistas, and legions of oblivious deer before forming an eight-mile loop around Wilhelmina.

I've always told my core group of retired teachers, coaches and administrators that the best time to buy a vacation property was in the dead of winter. Especially for a buyer with a fat wallet. Owners don't want to leave the comfort of their cozy den, jump in their car and drive in the dark to wrestle with broken pipes or track down a dock section that floated away in the last storm. When a client is on the fence about selling, want/ need of money usually trumps the pleasures of winter maintenance. Cash talks at a shrieking pitch when there's ice on the roads, fallen trees and limbs in a cabin's driveway, and the county assessor is demanding another year's taxes.

As I drove by a cluster of winterized, deserted cottages on South Shore Drive, I couldn't help but think that the owners of 'Casa Costalotta,' 'Larsens' Looneybin,' 'Paradise Found' and 'Hodges' Podge Lodge' would listen to an all-cash offer with a twenty-day closing.

As I rumbled in third gear toward my agreed-upon meeting place with Scott Hazelton, a squatty figure in a plaid wool jacket emerged from a sunken driveway on the lake side of the road. I recognized the choppy waddle and the faded Fighting Crabs baseball cap, and cranked the handle on the driver's side window.

Startled, Warren Gustaffson turned, removed his cap and ran a palm over his freckled, bald head. Approaching seventy, Warren was a Washington High booster, tried and true. Retired from the State Patrol's ballistics unit, he stuck by me during the early years when I was finding my way as the new coach at a new school. Two of his sons played for me, and they were as tough as nails. Just like the old man.

"Didn't recognize you there, Coach," Warren said. "How ya doin'?"

"Great, sir. I'm on my way to the fire hall to meet a possible customer."

"Well, I think your people have been tooling around in a rented Ford," Warren said. "You can tell the tourists this time of year from a mile away."

"People? Did you see more than one person in the car?"

Warren looked away for a moment and rubbed his chin. "Now that you mention it, I can't say for sure. I was down on the dock checking my pilings when the car slowed down here at the top of the driveway." He turned and waved a backhand toward the pavement behind him. "It's a maroon four-door I saw through the trees as it looped around the lake. The type they'll likely return to Sea-Tac, then jump on a plane."

"I know what you mean ... So, what's otherwise new and different up here?"

"The wind and rain last night slammed us pretty good," Warren said. "An alder nearly conked somebody's car in Henry Bevacqua's driveway. Black Chevy Tahoe. Nice one, too."

"Sounds like a close call. Say, does Henry have children?"

"No, just Henry and Helen. H and H around here. His

brother's got a slew of them."

I rolled back my jacket cuff in the door's window and checked the time.

"I've got to keep moving because I'm supposed to meet the guy in a minute down at the fire hall."

"Listen to you," Warren said. "Man, how you've changed. You used to be late for everything. If the world ended tomorrow, Coach would always have another week."

"Yeah, well, I guess I've cleaned some things up a bit."

I nodded, urged the clutch to the floor, and guided the bus down the road. The core gathering district for the Lake Wilhelmina community centers are three parcels at the southeast end of the lake, the chuck-holed boat launch, the seasonal Mountain Market and the volunteer fire department. The fire hall, officially Skagit County Fire District Number Sixty-Nine, featured a dank, dark meeting room with restrooms and kitchen facilities plus three metal-sided bays housing two ancient pump trucks and an aid car. The car, considered a coup by lake residents, was donated by the North Fork private ambulance service. The company upgraded its two-vehicle fleet after both broke down on winter runs to Seattle's Harborview Medical Center in the same six-week period.

An off-red Ford Fusion fitting Warren's description sat in front of the garage door sheltering the aid car, a no-no move in the event of an emergency. All non-department vehicles were to be parked clear of any driveway or door, or so read the instructions on the emergency siren switch adjacent to the main entry. As I banked the bus onto the slope just off the black-topped lot, Scott Hazelton appeared to be snoozing behind the wheel, a purple baseball cap pulled low over his eyes.

I slipped between the two front seats and hunched over the bus's back bench, sorting listing sheets in the order we would be visiting each property. Rolling the sliding door open, I stuffed one arm into a windbreaker, gathered the pages with my free hand and sauntered toward the Ford while slipping on the rest of the jacket.

"It's a great day to buy lakefront real estate," I shouted half-heartedly, a few paces from the car. Hazelton didn't move. I bobbed and peered through the windows' tinted glare. The interior seemed immaculate except for a black briefcase resting in the middle of the backseat. I knuckle-tapped the glass.

"Scott, time to blast off. It's going to be dark up here before we know it." Hazelton still didn't budge. Perhaps a few late nights, coupled with lingering jet lag, had tossed him into the zonked-out zone. I rapped on the window, this time firm and fast.

"C'mon, Scott. We've got houses to see."

Not even a slight stir.

I stepped back, folded my arms and snorted a half-cough. "I can't believe this." Annoyed by the non-response, I stepped toward the rear of the car, rested my palms on the trunk, lifted a foot on to the bumper and rocked the rear axle up and down. Hazelton's head move slightly toward the driver's side door.

"Man, were you out," I said, now outside his door. "I didn't think …"

The left side of his head, mostly covered by the hat, was propped against the window. I tried the door handle. Locked. Slapping the glass with an open hand, I leaned down and screamed.

"Scott!"

A trickle of blood emerged from beneath the hat, slowly moving in the space between his freshly trimmed sideburn and the front of his left ear.

"Scott! Can you hear me? Scott!"

Sprinting around the hood to the passenger door, I stopped, stunned at the surreal view through the windshield. The right side of Hazelton's head was nearly blanketed in red; bright, thick pinstripes streaming through his matted hair and painting his cheek. Wet stains on the shoulder of his blue cotton sweater expanded down his sleeve.

"Jesus Christ!" I whispered.

The shotgun door refused to open, as did the two rear passenger doors. I raced to the emergency alarm at the fire hall's main entry, flipped open the all-weather cover, and threw the switch.

TWENTY-THREE

Fewer THAN NINETY seconds after the siren built to its crescendo, a battered Jeep Cherokee roared into the parking lot and skidded to a stop in the dirt ten yards from the bus. A heavyset man who looked vaguely familiar swung up and out in a hurry.

"Coach? Is that you?" he said, slamming his door. "It's Toby Rockwell, but it's been awhile. Tough selling summer homes in the winter, but at least it ain't rainin'."

"We got a guy here who's in tough," I yelled. "The car is locked up tight, and I can't get him out."

The former football player broke into a jog, his massive stomach bouncing with each step. "Why can't he just unlock ..."

When Toby reached the car and got a glimpse of what was inside, he recoiled, whiplashing his neck. "You gotta be shitting me. Coach, hit that switch again and cut the siren. I think I've got something to open this door."

As Toby lumbered to his Jeep, two other volunteer firemen leaped from a just- arrived Toyota Land Cruiser. "What truck are we taking?" one yelled as he strutted toward the building. "I've got an extra set of keys right here to Number Three."

"No, no, Johnny! The situation's right here in that car," Toby screamed, pointing to the Ford. "Talk to Coach. He was the first guy to find him."

I gave the pair from the Land Cruiser a thirty-second version of my scheduled meeting with Scott Hazelton.

Johnny cringed as he circled the car, scratching his head. "How in the hell?"

"Let me give this thing a shot," said Toby, swinging a tire iron as if slashing tall grass with a machete. He raced around the hood and crashed the bar into the shotgun window shattering the tinted glass. Using the tapered end of the steel rod, he battered a hole into the middle of the tempered web, sending hundreds of tiny glass shards on to the passenger seat and floor below. Three more swings enlarged the opening. Toby reached in and opened the passenger door, then stretched across Hazelton and released the lock on the driver's side.

When Johnny pulled the door open, Hazelton's cap floated to the pavement, revealing a horseshoe-shaped valley the size of a tennis ball at the hairline just above his forehead.

"Jesus frickin' Christ," Toby muttered. "Somebody bashed the shit out of this guy's head."

The third man, a portly guy in coveralls and a black beard, searched for a pulse by placing his fingers at the carotid artery on the side of Hazelton's bloody neck. After probing two locations, he pivoted and began pulling Hazelton from the car, his huge hands grasping the man's armpits.

"I can't get a pulse, and he's not breathing," Black Beard said. "Let's get him flat on the pavement so I can work on him. Johnny, fire up the aid car and radio the guys at the ER."

A cold blast from the north flapped my jacket and persuaded Toby, now on one knee hovering above Hazelton, to duck lower and briefly close his eyes. As I tipped my head down out of the wind and watched Black Beard pump on Scott Hazelton's chest, I gave way to an all-out shiver, knowing Hazelton probably would never be warm again.

TWENTY-FOUR

A HEAVY, BLUNT OBJECT," said Dr. Burton Brownell, the Skagit County Medical Examiner. He pointed to chairs in a corner of the clinic's waiting area. I plopped into an uncomfortable high-back cane piece suitable for Goodwill. Harvey remained standing. "Technically causing a crushed skull with avulsion of the cranium and brain."

"You're thinkin' baseball bat?" Harvey said, turning to see who was within earshot.

"Sure, that's possible," Dr. Brownell said. "A lot of times they are the instrument of choice in this type of injury. Why do you ask? Did you find any Louisville Sluggers near the scene with blood on them?"

"No, Burt, we didn't. But the last case I had that involved basketball also included a baseball bat. You remember, Cheese Oliver? The boy took a big-time blow from a crazy booster."

"My guys just taped off the parking lot at dusk and are up there now with flood lamps and flashlights," Harvey continued. "As of right now, we're starting from scratch, and we don't have squat. I'll head up there with Ernie in the morning and have a thorough look around. I doubt if the few lake residents up there this time of year will be able to shed any light, but we will be talking to everyone we can possibly find."

We thanked Dr. Brownell and stepped into the hall. Harvey turned the conversation back toward Trent Whalen. "Where are you getting with him?" he asked. "Does it look like he's going to make the team?"

"It looks as if that is going to happen, if he wants it. The guy's tougher than nails, doesn't need the ball to positively impact the game and can score just about any time he feels like it. Plus, he's got an Einstein basketball IQ that you might see a couple of times in a decade. I just happen to like the kid."

"Have you spoken to his mother about the all-star time commitment?" Harvey asked. "Being a big, strong only child, I'm wondering how much she needs him around the house." He pointed toward the exit. "Let's take this outside." We stepped down the hallway.

"No idea, but it's curious how she goes hot and cold about basketball. A lot of parents are savvy enough to know those four years of free tuition could be on the line. That's cash money that few families have the opportunity to nail down. Think of the hours the average couple would have to work to save an extra forty grand a year. That's after taxes, Harvey."

"Oh, I know," Harvey nodded. "We had to take out a big fat home equity loan to put our youngest daughter through Seattle U. We still haven't paid that sucker off, but are chipping away at it every month."

"Frankly, I've spoken to only a couple of parents because I'm still scouting kids and time is getting short. I haven't promised or offered anybody anything. When I do, I will put a list together and you can be the first to see it, if you wish."

"Thanks. I'd appreciate that. As you probably know, what happened today changed things considerably. We'll need to check commonalities, tendencies, cross-reference kids with all sorts of sources and people. The only two unsolved murders in this county just happen to involve basketball and you are now in a primary place to gather information about both."

"Does that mean I'll be able to ask questions of professional business people?"

He narrowed his eyes. "I don't like it when you are a wise guy."

I pushed open the lone mechanical glass door to the clinic's main entry. Harvey waited for the electronic pair to swing out, then trudged outside.

"Correct me if I'm wrong," I said, turning to face him. "But what you are asking now means a hell of a lot more than talking to high school kids, one in particular, about what makes them tick and their relationships with agents, assistant coaches ..."

"And their parents."

"Great. Toss in the folks, too!" I shouted. An ambulance driver shot me a *What's up?* glower and jogged toward his waiting vehicle. "How do you expect me to twist very personal and private information from people, sometimes angry people, who see me as an old geezer who only knows about Xs and Os?"

"For every minute you remain angry you give up sixty seconds of peace of mind."

"Ralph Waldo Emerson," I said.

"See? You often underestimate your recall and wisdom. Use it to elicit intel from adults just like you extracted answers from kids in the classroom. Hell, I bet a lot of those kids didn't even know they were giving up information when they did."

"Adults are different."

"The hell they are. Think about the number of times an angry parent chewed you out for not giving the kid enough playing time. You knew how to handle it. Probably brought out that velvet hammer of yours that gets you what you want and pacifies them at the same time. Besides, we really don't have much choice. I need you to tell me everything that you can, but I cannot take any responsibility for your actions. Everything you do regarding these matters must be off the record."

"Talk about blunt. You've really cranked up the expectations without supplying any official backup."

Hands on his hips, Harvey cocked his head to one side and closed the distance between us. "Two dead guys, Ernie. Two! And the district attorney wants to know when basketball became a questionable pursuit."

"I've just begun to wonder about that myself."

"Well, I better mosey. Martha baked a pot roast, and I'm going to hear about it if I'm much later. You want to swing by for a bite?"

"Thanks for the offer, but I'm about cooked on both sides. Margie asked me for dinner earlier, but I'm going to call her now and beg off. After what I saw this afternoon, I don't think I'd be very good company."

"OK," Harvey nodded and began heading for his car. "You be careful out there. You're my star researcher, and I can't afford to lose you."

"I'm getting that drift. What if I deliberately withhold information that might be useful in your analysis?"

He stopped in his tracks. "What? Well, among other things, I would never take you steelheading again, and it's my turn to choose the river."

"You'd better make that a priority soon or we're going to miss the winter run and have to wait for the spring chinook."

"Speaking of priorities," Harvey said, with an upward nod,

"try to find out where in the hell Trent Whalen was about the same time Scott Hazelton got his brains bashed in at the lake. And Ernie? Do it soon."

Harvey tugged up his trousers and cleared his shirt cuff to check his watch.

"I guess I better tell you now. I don't want you to get blindsided."

"What?"

"Detective Dagmar wants to question you about Hazelton's murder."

"I already gave my statement to the cops and—"

"He thinks there might be more to it than that, and he's got an assistant DA in his corner."

"What? Harvey, you have to be bullshitting me."

"I know, I know. But somehow he's got this crazy idea in his head that you stand to make more money with Hazelton out of the way."

"Money? From what? Tell me you're going to run a little interference here and set that bastard straight."

"I absolutely will for as long as I can but I'm letting you know it's probably going to happen. The DA has already accused me of allowing you too much—"

"I cannot believe what I am hearing!"

"Look at it from behind the DA's desk. There are two basketball murders, you were the last one to see the victim, your prints will be on the car ..."

"You go to hell, Harvey! And take Dagmar with you!"

TWENTY-FIVE

"HOLY MOLY," GEORGE Berrettoni said as I slid into a chair in the first row of restaurant tables behind the bar. "Look what the freakin' cat dragged in. Not like the ol' Coach to show up at this hour. Must have been some sort of goofy day."

Tell me about it. The early evening slot was not my sweet spot. When Cathy was alive, we'd come in for beers after work and maybe grab a pizza to go, or hold court in a back booth to dissect the night's Fighting Crabs basketball game. Now, the seniors seeking the midweek earlybird special had cleared, as had the flannel-shirt bar crowd from the MacTavish & Oliver lumber yard.

"Long day," I said. "It began early in the office, then cold afternoon up at the lake then an even colder meeting down here."

"Really?" George said. "Did you get any snow up there? Man, was a northerly come through here that looked to be carrying some serious weather up that way." He waved me up to the bar and pointed to a corner seat. "I'll feed you up here. Scooter had to run a few errands, get to Costco before it closes, so I've got to work the register for a while."

I lifted my coat from the back of the chair, shuffled to the end of the bar and looped the windbreaker over an adjacent stool. Two older gentlemen with buzz cuts and down vests chatted at mid-bar. When I settled in, one of them nodded my way and swirled the ice cubes in his glass with a crooked finger.

"Coach."

"How you fellas doin' tonight?"

"Still breathin' and drinkin'," the man said. "Not every-body's as lucky."

"You've got that right," I said.

George made sure I was watching and then slid a full schooner of beer down the bar, the frosty glass circling to a stop at my left elbow. He brushed his knuckles across his chest, polishing the invisible star atop his white apron.

"Man, you still got it," I said. "Just like in the TV commercials."

"Damn right. They could film 'em right here. Just like the guys at the Pike Place Market throw the fish. I could be the guy that slides the beer."

George ducked into the kitchen and returned with a mammoth slab of sausage and onion pizza, all corners of the cut triangle flopping over the edge of a dinner plate. He dipped lower behind the bar and located a fork and napkin.

"I was just about ready to ask you what I should be ordering," I said. "I thought the gang in the kitchen might have made too much of something."

"Tonight yours comes compliments of Jimbo Lambert," George laughed. "I love the guy to death, but sometimes his Alzheimer's kicks in, and he forgets what he ordered. Our delivery kid gets to his house, and the old boy just stands there, says he didn't order a thing."

I winced, then waved to an older couple headed for the door. "Hey, don't laugh," I said. "We may end up in the same boat one day."

"Yeah, but if I do, my Evelyn would row me out in the boat

and use me for crab bait. You're going to be OK because the big brains are going to find a cure for MS, and there's no way the big guy at the scorer's table upstairs is going to hit you with both."

"I see." I looked away, knowing that many people wanted to express their concerns about my disease. Other than George, they almost never did so. The right words rarely surfaced, and I understood completely. For years I felt awkward verbalizing my concern for friends with cancer and kidney disease. Multiple sclerosis gave me a new outlook on life and a new vocabulary, but MS is not cancer. It didn't belong on the same sympathy scale. I preferred that my friends be informed rather than worried.

As was his way, George checked the room before imparting information he deemed critical. In his lowest possible tone, he passed along the latest basketball news: La Conner High had hired a new girls' coach from out of the district, and a mutual friend and referee needed a new kidney. Too much information about catheters, urine and dialysis.

The big man's mouth often was in motion before his brain was engaged. Prime George's pump, and get ready for the flood. The data transfer occurred even faster if I lobbed a juicy morsel of information into his hopper. Since I went to work in real estate, I learned that anything negatively related to my office always tweaked a tender nerve.

When he finally took a breath, I jumped his sentence by declaring, "I went all the way up to the lake to show property and didn't look at one cabin."

He grabbed the bar and braced himself as if it might move. "And why the hell's that?" George said, black eyebrows flaring.

"Somebody die or somethin'? Getting shut out doesn't pay the bills, you know." Had Scott Hazelton purchased a lakefront cabin, George would've pocketed a few extra bucks. "Remember, me 'n Pop floated Cookie the dough to open the doors at Big River Realty. Even helped her name the place."

I leaned over the bar and whispered, "Actually, somebody did die."

I explained the afternoon's events, minus Bjarne's inquiry about me. When finished, George looked as casual as Tony Soprano after another day at the office.

"Sounds like you got stiffed by a stiff," George said. "But didn't you say you thought the guy was kind of slippery? Not a confirmed asshole, but maybe heading toward that category?"

Elbows on the bar top, I rested my chin in an open hand and recalled Hazelton's phone calls. "He knew too much about me, like the former mascot of my university, to be just a cold-calling real-estate looker. I'm certain this had some hoop connections. The guy wanted something, just had to. Maybe he was pushing a player in his pocket, a kid nobody'd heard of. Perhaps a type-A rich daddy put up some bucks to get little Johnny under the spotlight.

"Or there's always the chance that Hazelton was fronting for a sponsor who wanted some sort of influence over the team. Sneakers, jerseys, maybe an energy drink."

"Or the schedule," George said. "A lot of these clowns are now pimping new events all over the country. You know, if they can guarantee they will deliver a hotshot team from the Pacific Northwest to a tournament on a certain date, they get paid big-time."

"No, I had no idea the size of the cesspool. I'm just beginning to learn all this crap, and high school basketball has been my entire life. How the hell are you so well versed in all this stuff?"

"I own a bar that just happens to be frequented by most of the major sports movers and shakers in the county. Including your own bad self. I keep my ear to the ground, baby."

"Really? I didn't know we had any headline-makers this far north of Seattle."

"You'd be surprised how much junior-varsity coaches hear at clinics and grade-school tournaments. Seems they're coming after younger kids like they used to scout high-school kids. Had a group of them here last month. Some guy in a fancy linen shirt, like something Ricky Martin would wear, was doing some serious schmoozing."

I pushed away the pizza plate and shook my head at the state of recruiting.

"A beer for your thoughts," George said. He dumped my empty glass into the sudsy sink water, filled another chilled one from a line of brass-plated taps, and set it in front of me. "You want a little salad or something?"

"Nah, thanks. But another hunk of that pizza would be nice … You know, the guy, Hazelton, said he'd recently arrived in town, but I have no idea how much time he'd spent here in the past. He was obviously dialed in on property at the lake, but that all could have been an excuse just to meet me someplace in private. "

"Hold that thought. I'll fire up another slice."

My perceptions of Scott Hazelton tilted toward the toxic, but what could I truly glean from two brief phone conversations and the glimpse of him emerging from the Loyola High locker room with Coach Slaughter? I'd already pigeonholed the guy without ever meeting him face-to-face, much like some people did with my MS. What did that say about me? Maybe it was just that damn shirt. Plus the too-crafty grin that bordered on cunning.

"This sucker is steamin'," George said as he placed the plate on the bar, using his apron as a potholder. "Got a little carried away with that new oven." The mozzarella bubbled momentarily, a hissing series of tiny circles.

"Do you remember who was with the guy in the snazzy linen shirt when he was here last month?" With a fork, I sawed away the tip of the pizza and quickly needed a swig of beer to counter the heat.

"Well, let's see," George said, his thick, stubby fingers gripping a bar rag. "Bunch of Catholic parents. Father Fogerty was with them for a while. One of the Jebbies from Loyola, too. Pretty big group, because I remember we pushed a couple of tables together in the back room."

"Sounds like a recruiting session," I said, mouth half full. "A lot of those eighth-graders at St. Brendan move on over to Loyola. Parents set up carpools. The Jesuit was probably putting his best foot forward, trying to impress future freshman parents. And it's not easy. The tuition there is as much as a good used car."

"And you've lost some good athletes over the years, too. Not much a public school can do when a kid from the local parish wants to stay in a private."

I took another bite of the pie, savoring its homemade crust. After washing it down with a swig of beer, I continued. "You never really know, George. All hell can happen. You get goofy injuries, poor chemistry you never see coming. Some players mature early, stop growing, and then can't match up physically as juniors and seniors. But, yeah, I figure I lost one good kid, maybe two, a year to the privates. And it was more than players. I lost a great group of parents, too. People who really get involved, volunteer, help out. Very few become a hindrance and hover above your every move."

George poured a drink down the way, suspending a bourbon bottle high above the bar in a showy production as the amber liquid streamed perfectly into the lowball glass below. He swirled a swizzle stick into the ice and sauntered back.

"Yeah, but a lot of rich kids tend to come with an attitude," he continued. "I've seen it here in the bar. They think their cash should bring them a different standard of care … Anyway, I'll tell you who else was here that night. Trent Whalen's mother. Man, you're talking about one attractive little bundle right there. Might be the best-lookin' little woman around. Lot of small broads got that female Napoleon thing going, but Samantha Whalen's the freaking captain. Brassy and sassy but, jeezus, what a package."

He glanced to his left, more of an excited twitch, and went on. "She used to come in here sometimes with a cougar named Paula, who's also got a rack I'd like to roll around on. Bad teeth, though. Don't see them together anymore, though. I've got a feelin' ol' Paula likes to visit the nose-candy shop, if you know what I mean. No disrespect, really. I mean, I know Samantha's husband's only been in the ground a few months, but good gawd. Makes me wonder where Trent got his size. The dad was fairly tall I guess, but I'm tellin' ya, if my Evelyn weren't …"

I raised a forefinger, attempting to slow his pace. "Did she seem to be paying any particular attention to any individual?

Perhaps our friend in the Harry Belafonte shirt?"

"Ricky Martin shirt," he laughed. "You know, the Puerto Rican Elvis guy? Chicks dig him and I don't get it ... Anyway I don't remember. Two servers were out sick that day, another big bunch came in unannounced, and we were hustling just to get food on the table. It was a madhouse."

I picked up the pizza with both hands and began munching the remainder.

"I can see the ol' Coach's brain churning," George said. "You're thinking the mysterious Mr. Ricky Martin could have been a big hard-on for little Samantha."

"Take it easy, George," I hissed, hoping no patrons were listening. "We don't even know for certain if the guy who was here after the elementary school jamboree was Scott Hazelton." Arms on the bar, I angled closer. "Please get it into your head that I am merely trying to find out if and when the man I saw with *his* brains bashed this afternoon spent much time in this area. And, if so, how much."

George stepped back, palms up. "How many clowns do you know dress like that? Freaking long-sleeve bowling shirts ... I think it would be safe to say the dots will soon be connected. And Harvey's gonna be a whole lotta pissed if he finds out you brought the pencil and eraser to connect 'em. Remember what happened when you put on your investigator's hat when Cheese Oliver disappeared? Frickin' shitstorm. And other than me, of course, Harvey's probably your best friend."

Glancing toward the window, I pondered how much to expose. I decided to lay it out, allowing George the chance to help me connect the dots. "Harvey's essentially asked me to gather information but not let anybody know," I said. "He told me to dig, but make sure nobody sees the holes, and then hand him the dirt. The DA is already down his throat, and the murder just occurred this afternoon. But I'll tell you what. It's also intensified the heat to solve the Tim Whalen case."

The big man nodded. "That's a helluva switch, but it makes sense. Two hoop-related guys get whacked; why not employ the most knowledgeable buckets guy in the area? Other than me, of course."

"That's what would piss Harvey off," I said. "The use of the word 'employ' as it relates to yours truly."

One of the oldsters in the middle of the bar caught George's eye and nodded at the lonely ice at the bottom of a glass he balanced between a raised thumb and forefinger. George pointed down the bar. "Bourbon and soda?"

As he strutted away, I started wondering where Hazelton fit. Was he the engineer driving the gravy train or merely the conductor punching the tickets? Perhaps he'd broken away from the old norm and begun a new pitch. The notion that Hazelton had grown tired of being a bag man for a big-time corporation and was trying to play with his own funds didn't feel right, even though he'd oozed the fresh, edgy energy of a self-staked sole proprietor.

And, clearly, somebody had wanted him dead.

"So," George bellowed, coming back my way. He toned it down considerably when he reached a spot directly across from me behind the bar. He whirled in closer, elbows landing atop the glossy mahogany. "You came in here at this hour tonight to begin the basketball category of your comprehensive investigation?" The man could flip a switch and sound official faster than a one-term politician. He'd easily make a living voicing reverse-mortgage commercials.

"Actually, I didn't think about asking you any questions until I got here and had my first sip," I said. "To tell you the truth, I didn't want to go home to a cold house, and God knows I'd be lousy company to anybody else."

"So, you just assumed you could bring your lousy company in here. See, that's a great example of what I put up with living the prestigious life of a bartender. Bring on your down-in-the-dump days, awful attitudes and cheating spouses. Lay it all out there for the poor ol' barkeep."

"Give it a rest, George," I chuckled. "I brought you none of the above tonight. Besides, you eat up all the sleuthing-type stuff. Think about it. You'd probably explode if you had no one to unload about what you see or hear in the bar. For instance, the next time I see Harvey? I'm sure he'll know that I was lousy company tonight."

"C'mon, Coach! I ain't that bad." He scowled and stared over my shoulder, toward the entry. "But, if I were to venture a guess," he tapped the side of his nose, then examined a marinara spot on his apron, "somebody *probably* requested your company tonight. And, for some insane reason, you decided that just wasn't going to happen."

I ran a hand behind my head, knowing it would do nothing to eliminate his interest or my need to reply.

"You're right," I exhaled. "Margie did ask me to come over tonight, but I didn't feel like gearing up to be a scintillating conversationalist. You know, I just can't go over there, be a complete dud, eat and run. After what happened today, I just didn't have the bandwidth to keep up with her tonight."

"Man, I'm tellin' you. What I would give just to try to keep up with her for one night. Wouldn't take a lot of bandwidth, either, my friend. If my Evelyn weren't around, I'd be drafting that babe in the first round and signing her to a long-term contract and a huge bonus. Life is all about give and take, Ernie, and this could have been one of those nights when you could have easily dipped into the take column. Lordy lord, Coach, it's clear as day she's got that giving look in her eye."

"Not the way I want to play it, George." He groaned and shook his head. "Look, she's the first woman I've seen since Cathy died, and I just don't know how far I want to take this down the road. They are totally different people and I'm not yet sold on the exclusivity factor."

"Hey, play the field, man! You are one single, very eligible guy. What's to stop you, for crissake? I'd just keep in play what's already in play. Goodness, what a body." He cranked his eyebrows way up on his forehead.

"Not my M.O. to date a bunch of different women at the same time. Could never do it in a town like this, anyway. Would never go over. Especially for a coach, or teacher. But the one-and-only thing is just not sitting right. Yet."

"Ever think about those online dating groups? You get to put down everything you want. Kinda like a huge online menu, a create-your-own pizza. But this is babes."

I coughed out a laugh so powerful that it caught me by surprise and nearly brought tears to my eyes. "Right, it's *just* like that." I twisted back and forth on the bar stool, shifting my weight. "I'm not there yet, George. Hell, I may never be there. I'm a long way from taking a picture of myself and sticking it out there with a capsule summary of what I am seeking, feeling, and hope to accomplish."

"You may not have to," George said. "If word gets out that you plan, much to my amazement, mind you, to cool it with Margie, I'd be willing to bet you Pop's finest gelato that a bevy of beauties would be beating a path to your door in no time. You are too much a freakin' stud to be a free agent for very long."

The stifled tune, an old Jimmy Buffett-Coral Reefers instrumental version I hadn't heard in months, was too muted to be floating from the antique jukebox in the corner.

"That's your cell," George said. "I stuck in the custom ring when we were playing with your speed dial a couple of weeks ago. Guess you don't take many calls, do you?"

I wheeled around and randomly patted the pockets of my jacket, slapping and rummaging for the miniature device instigating the methodical steel-drum rhythm of "Banana Wind." Finally, I unzipped the lapel pouch and palmed the phone above the bar.

"Geez. Speaking of the devil," I said. "It's Margie. Her ears must have been burning."

"Sure as hell would give her a chance to burn mine," George smiled. "Let me know if you need back up."

Looking down, I waited for the tune to stop. The digits on the phone faded.

TWENTY-SIX

THE CLALLAM BAY Corrections Center answered society's desire to put bad guys in the middle of nowhere. The place isn't on the way to anything, unless you scored one of the precious few salmon-fishing cabins at Sekiu or up at the end of the line on Highway 112 and the northwestern-most landmarks of the United States, Neah Bay, Cape Flattery, and the Makah Reservation. The Clallam locals joke that if you miss weekend-only visiting hours, you can always go catch a huge Chinook in the serene saltwater bay two miles away. ("Why drive all this way for nothin'?")

Kids seeking *Twilight* roots and memorabilia blow past the Clallam turnoff on 101 and slice through a remarkable piece of Olympic National Park to the town of Forks, an hour south of the prison. White-haired tourists focused on the gorgeous gardens of Victoria, BC, and kayakers bound for the rugged coastline of Vancouver Island stop an hour east at Port Angeles and hop the Black Ball ferry across the Strait of Juan de Fuca.

The Clallam Bay compound can handle eight hundred and fifty offenders, more than three quarters of whom are of the violent variety. That majority includes Mitchell "Wide Load" Moore, whom prosecutors believe will serve most of his seventy-three-year sentence for brutally clubbing both a prominent Lake Wilhelmina resident and a wayward recluse, then chopping them up and depositing their remains in a waterfront septic tank.

Not to mention what he did to Linn Oliver.

Linn's timber schedule called for him to appraise several tracts west of Port Townsend, so we planned the trip to Clallam Bay with one of his Westside Fridays. I drove toward Everton, then south over Deception Pass to the Keystone ferry dock. After the 35-minute crossing to Port Townsend, I met Linn for lunch at The 3 Crabs in the tiny community of Dungeness, outside Sequim. He bounced from his green company truck, offering to buy, to celebrate his landing two bargain properties.

We sat at the counter and ordered our meals. I recalled my last time this far out on the Olympic Peninsula. It was the weekend Cathy and I camped at Olson's Resort in Sekiu more than a decade ago. She nailed a twenty-pound king, and I could still see her parading it down the pier to the cheers of the other boaters. I hadn't been back since.

A short time later, our food arrived. "Just because we got clearance to visit doesn't mean we have to go," I said, cracking into the orange-red midsection of a crab the size of a bar stool. "Are you sure you want to do this? I certainly don't want the visit to throw you into some deep dark funk. Who knows? That guy might just go off and start screaming how we screwed up the school's only chance for a title in sixty-seven years."

"I'm not worried," Linn said. "Besides, there's a nice thick piece of glass between us and him. We do the phone deal, right?"

"On the wall, just like on television? Nope, I'm told we'll be in a room with a table. Mitch Moore will be sitting directly across from us. Because you are a victim, who applied and was then approved for visitation, there will probably be a prison guard in the room. I can make a request to do it another way if—"

"No, no. It's all good. Really, it'll be better this way."

We took my VW bus so Linn could stretch away his day. The ride was pleasant and featured expansive views across the strait to the north and countless tree farms to the south. We discussed my choices for the North Counties select roster plus some of the players who stood out on Linn's freshman team at Washington High. For miles on end we sat in silence, comfortable with the quiet.

As the distance to Clallam Bay dipped under twenty miles, my crab lunch seemed to crawl around the bottom of my stomach, and I began wonder about the visitors' restroom at the jail, and if I could make it there in time. Dryness coated my throat, and swallowing no longer was an involuntary reflex. I spoke, attempting to conceal my discomfort.

"Do you remember when that assistant coach from some school in the south approached you after your sophomore year?" I said, glancing toward Linn. "The guy who did little to hide that he was willing to fly you home at any time if you chose his school?"

"Clancy Wannamaker," Linn laughed. "Hard to forget. Southeast Trinity. Great name for a coach wanting to make anything happen for any recruit. I think he got wind right away that Barbara and I were tight and there was a good chance for homesickness. Told me he got 'the hometown honey thing.'"

"Were there others after that? Maybe offers that bounced on the borderline or were clearly under the table?"

Linn locked his knees and pushed his shoulders into the seatback. "There were, but I wanted to be a Husky all my life and made up my mind early. Most everybody knew my feelings. Saw no reason to make a bunch of recruiting trips although I think we got six visits back then. I pretty much became immune to the BS."

I took a deep breath, let it out, and peeked his way. "Did Wide Load ever bring you a deal? A situation that might have made you think he was a middle man? Sort of like a broker?"

"Maybe once. He wanted me to join a club team down in Lynnwood. Had a couple of tourneys out of state. Saw him talking to the main sponsor after one of our booster dinners. I got the feeling if I showed up there'd be something in it for him."

"You mean Moore was wheeling and dealing at Washington High events?"

Linn looked out the window and pointed to the turnoff for Eagle Crest Way. "I can't say for sure. I would've told you if I could. It just seemed he had a lot of friends I'd never seen before in town."

The prison did not exactly blend in amongst the evergreens, its two-, three-, and four-story white rectangular buildings looking like a botched attempt to create a massive, multi-cornered igloo. A sign indicated visitors' hours ended at 7:15 p.m.

The representative at the other end of the main-gate intercom asked if we had completed and submitted visitation forms. After the voice said he'd located our approvals, we were instructed where to park and enter the complex. A guard tower loomed overhead, which did little for my queasy gut. The short walk from the car in the chilly air provided some relief.

At the door, we were asked to state our names and the inmate we requested to visit.

"Ernest Creekmore and Linnbert Oliver," I replied. "We're here to see ..." I hesitated, unable to mouth Moore's name.

"And the inmate, sir?" I couldn't speak. "Sir? I'm sorry, the name—"

"Mitchell Moore!" Linn blurted. "Mitchell 'Wide Load' Moore!"

* * *

The visiting room was boring beige and smelled like fast food and sour milk, not unlike a high school homeroom after lunch break on a rainy day. A large formica-topped rectangular table and four metal chairs took up most of the space. Two cameras bolted to walls near the ceiling pointed down at the table.

A door opened, and a guard held it so a handcuffed Mitchell Moore could shuffle through. Unshaven, his straggly hair showed more gray than black and fell over his shoulders. He'd lost weight yet was still more than pudgy. Jerry Garcia on the decline. The guard helped him to his seat. Moore nodded and the guard stepped back against the wall.

"Fuckin' Cheese Oliver," Moore sneered. "I thought I could smell you from the other building." He glared at me and curled his lip. "And his loser coach. Tell me, what did I do lately to deserve such assholes?"

"We won't stay long," I said, holding the side of the table. Linn leaned back and folded his arms across his chest.

"Stay as long as you like," Moore whispered, feeling his stubby whiskers. "I sure as hell ain't going anywhere."

I straightened up and glared at him. "I need to know if you were paying Washington High kids to look at schools, to play on club teams. Were you the intermediary between college coaches and parents?"

"Who the hell wants to know?" Moore said. "The state board call you on the carpet, Coach?" His orange prison jumpsuit appeared clean, yet he smelled like a newspaper press operator who hadn't washed in a week.

"When I said 'I need,' that's what I meant," I said. "This is all for my information only. It's important to me to find out if—"

"Your teams, your guys, weren't fucking good enough," Moore barked. "Don't even flatter yourself. Plus, your parents were too damn cheap. If I did line them up with a deal, they wouldn't have paid the fiddler."

I leaned in closer. "You're saying Linn wasn't good enough? You must be joking."

Wide Load shook his head and looked away. "He was the best fucking player in the state. Shit, I could have made more money by telling people to stay away. Don't spend your recruiting cash on a plane fare and a hotel room for a hard-headed kid headed to the Huskies."

I sat back and considered his statement. Linn didn't move a muscle. "Now, you've got me confused."

"That's always been easy to do," he snickered.

"You're telling me when Linn committed, all the interest in him stopped?"

"Not all, but it slowed down. I still could have made a buttload of money until the day he graduated from high school. You have to understand something, jerkoff, I'd been promoting this kid nationally since the seventh grade. I told a lot of schools I could serve him up on a silver platter."

"Somehow I don't believe you just got out of the way," I

said.

"You just don't follow, do ya? Hey, I was offered a ton of under-the-table cash that you never knew about. My problem was THAT KID"—he stabbed a finger toward Linn—"was too fucking close to his goody-two-shoes coach!"

Moore went on to say basketball reps make money only in the inner city, and that football was king for colleges because income from games in mammoth stadiums paid the bills for all other sports combined. He mentioned he "made a couple of nickels" for steering baseball prospects away from the professional draft to four-year schools and that their parents "had no clue" what was going on behind the scenes.

Linn glared at Moore, his fingers steepled under his chin.

"You can get big dough for sending a football kid to a school," Moore continued, "but there are no club football teams. None that travel to tournaments in Vegas, San Diego, Miami where there are scouts, agents ... That's where the cash is in basketball nowadays. Probably more there now than from college recruiters. But I wouldn't know now, would I? I mean, I'm in here. Thanks to you fuckers."

After an extended quiet moment I said, "And we're out of here. I think I got what I needed."

"Sounds great to me," Moore said. "Please don't feel the 'need' to come back."

"If you feel that way, why did you allow us to visit? You could have easily taken us off the list."

"Just wanted to see if the famous Cheese still has that unique stink I so dearly remember. It's a real treat to the ol' nose."

Linn wheeled around and clenched his teeth. "What if I would have made it?" he said. "What if that final shot had gone down?"

Moore grinned as his eyes danced between Linn and me. "I would have collected on all my bets, moved to a little town outside Guadalajara, and never laid eyes on you fuckers again."

Linn made a move to get up, and the guard stepped toward him from his post near the door. Moore snickered as Linn settled back in his seat and pointed at Moore.

"I missed ONE basket," Linn snarled, "and you, you asshole, you left me to die!"

I slid my chair back, then stood behind it. "Linn, it's time," I said.

"Ah, don't be like that, Coach," Moore said. "Since you're here, let's talk about those young Crabs. I remember about the time they stuck me in here reading about a superstar eighth-grader." Moore glanced down to the table and rubbed his chin. "I even think he was mentioned in a couple of national recruiting mags. Anyway, did the kid turn out to be something special, play on the high-school varsity as a freshman?"

Astonished, I turned and looked at Linn. He stood, curled his lips and puffed out a silent whistle.

"Ah, c'mon you guys," Moore said. "I don't get that many visitors, let alone people who know anything about high school buckets. What players does Washington have coming back? Any good transfers that you know about?"

As we turned to leave, Moore sat open-mouthed. "What?" he said.

I opened the door. Linn walked out, and I followed him.

TWENTY-SEVEN

We DROPPED LINN'S truck at the timber company's annex near Sequim and rode most of the long way home in silence, catching the 8:30 p.m. ferry from Port Townsend to Keystone on Whidbey Island. We agreed to review the day at another time, yet I could not get Moore's play-for-pay words out of my mind. How could I have been so focused on coaching and not suspect even an inkling of the peripheral activity? My gut rumbled, knowing the extracurriculars would be front and center for my all-star squad. And my head ached, realizing I could do nothing about it.

Linn remained in the bus for the thirty-five minute crossing while I went topside to stretch my legs and call Tony's for takeout food upon my arrival back in North Fork. By the time we drove up the island over Deception Pass and across the Skagit Flats, it was nearly 10 p.m. I slapped him two twenties, then kept the bus running while he darted in and out of the restaurant to pick up the food.

"How'd it go?" I said.

"Good. Barbara called and added artichokes to our pizza. Scooter said you also got a call from a person wanting to know if you were in the restaurant. He didn't say who it was but that he expected you before ten thirty."

"Well, let's get you home. She's probably starving."

I dropped Linn at the couple's small farm south of town

and hopped on the levee road for the return. I dreamed of the select team and pictured Eddie McGann floating to the left wing, his long arms glistening with sweat under the bright lights, caressing a bounce pass in his huge hands, then immediately leaping and launching a long-range jumper with picture-perfect extension, his feet, hips and shoulders expertly squared toward the basket. There was Nick Chevalier setting a textbook screen at the foul line, head up, hands crossed over his crotch, feet anchored, knees slightly bent. Then, after picking off the defender, rolling to the basket at precisely the right moment to lay the ball softly off the glass for an easy two.

A car behind me seemed a bit close so I slowed to allow it to pass. The driver seemed content to stay put on the two-lane road, perhaps waiting to clear the Silvana curve and cutoff before making a move.

"C'mon, man," I said. "What do you want to do?"

My thoughts returned to hoop and Trent Whalen's skills. Double-teamed down low, Whalen calling for and receiving a pass at eye level, wheeling to his left and lofting a soft jumper from the baseline that finds the rim and lazily swirls into the hoop. Hustling back on defense, the always intense Whalen fires a thank-you index finger to the point guard, gratefully acknowledging the dish. But who ...?

I realized that not only did I need to land a do-it-all point guard who could get my scorers the ball, but I also had to fill several more spots on the roster, schedule practices, and determine what type of team this could be. Up-tempo all the time, or slow it up and cram it inside?

Time was not on my side. More importantly, I was particularly amazed how quickly my mind defaulted to coaching basketball. When in doubt or chaos, it became my cozy retreat. Today's events proved it again. When push comes to shove, some guys say they invoke their wives, kids, an exotic vacation or what life could have been like with an old girlfriend. I visualize hoops.

I became confused by the actions of the car behind me. Maybe the guy knows me and wants me to pull over? It blinked its lights after we'd passed the Silvana cutoff. I raised my hands in a *What do you want?* gesture and again slowed below the speed limit.

"Dammit, man!" I yelled. "Figure it out!"

Truth be told, basketball took up more of my brain than anything else. I pondered Xs and Os constantly, much more so than anything flowers, candy, or a sexy negligee might get me. Now, after so many years away from daily practices and player management, I still retained an instinctive understanding of what was required, and when. Like riding a bike. The basics remained alive and well, but I'd yet to test the contemporary high-performance components that are now critical pieces to today's coaching package.

The car—a dark four-door with privacy windows—bolted alongside me just as a set of headlights moved toward us. Rather than pull ahead and pass, the car maintained its speed.

I honked. "Make up your freaking mind!"

I glanced left, but the tinted windows allowed no chance to identify even the slightest shape. The driver cranked his car hard right and sideswiped the bus, shoving me onto the shoulder gravel, precariously close to the edge.

"You asshole!" I summoned all of my strength to balance the oversized steering wheel but my big box swerved uncontrollably, tires screeching, its two left wheels briefly leaving the payment. When I maneuvered it back on all fours, it brushed the car again as the looming lights bore down on us.

"Move it," I yelled. "Move it, now!"

The oncoming car's horn became a consistent blare; its emergency flashers blazing. I slammed on the brakes. The phantom car copied my move, turned into my lane and cut me off, narrowly avoiding the oncoming car, and sending me careening off the road.

*   *   *

"This is déjà vu all over again, Yogi," Harvey said, attempting to eke out a smile in the Skagit County Clinic's emergency room.

I motioned for him to come closer. "Your suspect in the Hazelton murder nearly died?" I whispered.

"I probably deserved that, but don't be a jerk right now. I am concerned about you and what's going on in North Fork. Incredibly, nothing big was broken, but you cracked two ribs. The bus needs a lot of work. These guys—" he spoke louder and pointed to Dr. Timoteo Mesa and Dr. Elmer Crehan "—want to hear more about how you got in that ditch."

I'd learned from the aid-car driver that Mesa was on-call in the ER. Crehan was a neurologist and my multiple sclerosis physician.

I told the story. Timoteo stepped around the bed toward me.

"Coach, we're a bit concerned because you apparently have suffered two blackouts in a short period of time."

"Blackouts or conked unconscious?" I said. "I mean, I could have passed out both times for understandable reasons. It looks like somebody tried to kill me, maybe twice. Doesn't that qualify for special consideration?"

"It does," Dr. Crehan said. "Yet, we want to find out as much information as we can in order to help you get better."

An attendant wheeled in a young girl in a soccer uniform. The girl wiped away tears with the back of her hand while holding her left knee.

Crehan pulled a floor-to-ceiling curtain that enclosed my party in a semicircle.

"Ernie, do you remember feeling dizzy before tumbling down the bank last night into the field?"

"You think this might be MS-related?"

"We don't know, but it's best to ask the question. So far, most of your issues have involved your hands and feet. Your bus had several blue-black paint scrapings, but we don't know if you slammed another vehicle or somebody hit you."

"I wasn't dizzy, bleary ... whatever you want to call it. Somebody ran me off the road and I bumped my noggin. Period."

Harvey sauntered closer and looked down at his notepad. "Excuse us, doctors, if you would." Both white coats nodded and slipped through the curtain.

"This is about all we know," Harvey uttered.

"You mean that Bjarne Dagmar is an asshole?"

"Save it a minute, will you? Now, a woman driving by found you at about twelve thirty a.m. She was the one with the flashlight who called 911. The bus came to a stop in a huge irrigation ditch and probably flipped four or five times before it got there. Your back axle was stuck in the water. You're quite fortunate you didn't drown."

I planted my palms on the mattress and shifted my weight from side to side. My head began to pound. "Do we know if anybody saw anything at all?"

"A dairyman called the office late last night about the incident, but the man had to run out of town this morning for supplies. Anyway, the message mentioned some possible plate numbers. I talked with his son but he hadn't heard anything about it. I'll have to wait until the old man gets back."

My ribs stung, slightly worse than after the shovel slam. The tight bandages restricted my breathing more than I expected. A lingering tautness accompanied by a mild sweat stretched far beyond my physical woes. For the first time I felt afraid. If I bailed on everything, could I return to a normal life?

"Harvey," I said, "I can see your wheels churning. You think all of this is connected."

"Just like you, I get more wary about coincidences. And tell me, do you know where Trent Whalen was last night?"

"I don't, but I do know the Shovel Man was not six-foot-seven. Besides, couldn't the road incident have been a drunk or stoned driver?"

Harvey stashed his notes. "Possibly, but not probably. Dr. Mesa said you're healthy enough to continue coaching this team and that's what I need right now. My department will simply have to keep a closer eye on you."

"That's exactly what I wanted to hear," I lied.

At that moment, I could've cared less about what he needed. I wanted to pick my team, coach the tournament, and stay alive. I prayed I could pull off all three.

TWENTY-EIGHT

THE ELEMENT OF surprise in high school hoops went out the door with year-round tournaments, elite traveling squads, and full-time paid recruiters armed with cell phones ready to film the cold-crossover dribble flashed by an unknown two-guard from Hayseed High.

When I first arrived at Washington High School more than twenty-five years ago, late bloomers and out-of-state transfers could make a huge impact during the next season because league coaches had no idea how to prepare for the unknown.

These days, if a kid is any good, anywhere, somebody's going to know about him in junior high. Or earlier. If the footballer-turned-bucketballer was blessed with any dexterity whatsoever, his speed, drive, and athletic IQ would be documented, filed, and available for any coach in any sport. Simply a part of today's culture.

As I drove south on Interstate 5 en route to Marysville and Indian River School and a waterfront listing on the Tulalip Reservation, I felt that the intriguing group of young men I was trying to throw together just might surprise some people. There was much left to do, including commitments to secure, on-court roles to determine and dictate, personalities to mesh. The possibilities, however, fascinated me.

My main potential mystery man, though, remained an unknown entity even to me. On the seat next to me sat a binder

crammed with scrawled notes, newspaper clippings and confidential evaluations offered by other area coaches of my elite-
team candidates. At the top of the stack rested a half-page
email printout I'd received from a trusted source about a five-
foot-eight point guard.

A Mexican speed merchant, Cheese Oliver wrote in a volunteer scouting report. *Reads the floor like Steve Nash. Will get
you the ball if you are open, ready or not. Surprisingly strong for
his size. Won't back down from a junkyard dog and probably eats
nails for breakfast. Tell you what, Deacon Joe can deal it. I played
against him one time, and he handed me my jock.*

Deacon Joe Gonzales, the only son of a migrant picker
and a long-gone minister, worked the private apple orchards
in Manson above Lake Chelan. He reportedly moved west of
the Cascades when his mother failed to come home one night
from the Omak Stampede. According to Cheese, Deacon Joe
dropped out of high school, earned a reputation as reliable day
laborer, and began tearing up the Tuesday night rec leagues in
Everton and Marysville.

Candidly, I didn't care if he no longer went to school. That
was beyond my control and not a pre-req for my club. I only
cared if he could go to the hoop and expertly thread the ball to
his teammates headed that way.

A peeling piece of plywood spray-painted with the address
and a crooked right arrow directed me down a dirt driveway
through a cluster of rundown shacks, soaring evergreens, and
abandoned vehicles. Two graying labs splayed beneath a can-
tilevered deck lazily lifted their heads as I coasted past. The
road terminated beside a well-kept two-story home with white
smoke twirling from a tented stove pipe perched above the

shake roof line.

As I parked and approached the front porch, I noticed the cement-based siding on the side of the house did not match the color and texture of the front.

"Who you?" shot a deep, sturdy voice from an upstairs window. A dim light in the room behind the figure afforded only a silhouette of the speaker.

"My name is Ernie Creekmore. I'm here to see Deacon Joe."

"Well, you just go on now," the man said. "We've been through all this before. Yeah, he lives here. Yeah, this is his permanent address. And DSHS got no jurisdiction on this land."

"I'm not attempting to ascertain—"

"He doesn't *have* to be enrolled in a school."

"I really don't know anything about that," I said. "I just wanted to speak with him a moment about basketball."

"Probably doesn't want to talk with you about anything. Including buckets."

The outline darted away from the window, dropping a thin, light curtain as he left. I swiped at the gravel with my shoe, jammed my hands into the hip pockets of my cords, and began a slow arching return toward the bus. A pair of surprisingly clean Dodge pickups rested under a carport, both with identical aluminum toolboxes stretching the width of the bed behind the cab. At least five cords of bright alder sat neatly stacked under a lean-to topped with new composition roofing material.

As I dipped into my jacket for keys, two individuals sauntered out of the front door and shuffled down the front porch steps. Despite the chill, the Caesar-cut taller one sported a sleeveless black T-shirt, his long, muscled biceps and forearms easily observed from across the yard, a gladiator marching toward a conflict. The shorter one hid his hands in the pouch of a black hooded sweatshirt and repeatedly flicked his brown floppy hair from his eyes and forehead with quick neck snaps.

Mutt and Jeff.

"I've heard of you," the black hood said. "I know you coached Cheese Oliver."

Ah, the peripheral benefits of a former star. "I did. And he mentioned you kicked his ass one morning at Marysville High." The bigger guy sneered a *Right on* head bob.

"Maybe. But that was just one time. 'Sides, it looked like he had a bum knee that day."

"Well, I wanted to talk with you about playing in a tournament down in Seattle," I said. "It would take a time commitment, but I thought I'd at least try to find you and see what's possible."

The big man scoffed and looked away.

"I got this, Howard," Deacon Joe whispered. "Really, man. No worries." He nodded in the direction of the house.

Grudgingly, Howard spun and glided toward the door, his long strides seemingly emphasized for my benefit. "My lady's moppin' the kitchen floor," Howard said. "You're gonna have to hang out here for now. Floor's wet."

As we settled onto to the front steps, Deacon Joe licked his fingertips a la Nash at the foul line and guided his clean, wavy hair over the top of two coffee-colored ears. Surprisingly calm and confident, the youngster appeared a dozen years older than seventeen.

He rattled off an impressive summary of the Snohomish County gym-rat scene, including a detailed critique of the better players making up local recreational league rosters. Deacon

Joe indicated that he played four nights a week, and two Saturday mornings a month, and hadn't missed a scheduled game since Thanksgiving. That day, he took off from work to unsuccessfully track down his mother in Spokane.

I zipped up my jacket and stood to stretch my legs.

"I'd like to get you out on the floor with some other guys. See how it goes one time. If it works and we feel OK about each other, then we'll see about the future. We're aiming at a tourney at Seattle Center about a month from now. If we can bring the right group of guys, we just might surprise a few folks."

"Sounds like we're set. I'll get back with you about the first session." I extended my hand. He shook it firmly and looked me in the eye.

"Say, where did 'Deacon' come from?" I asked.

He lowered his head, then looked slowly both ways, as if wanting to keep the information confidential. "I guess my father was some sort of traveling preacher. I never ever even met the man. My mother got to know him one summer workin' raisins down in Fresno, a town called Selma. We moved a lot when I was a kid, but she got tired of moving. I think she got tired of just about everything."

I nodded, an open hand resting on the side of my face. "And DJ, does anybody ever call you DJ?"

"Not unless they want to get hurt." He laughed. "That and Deke. It's Deacon Joe. Or just Deacon."

"So noted. I'll spread the word."

"To who else?" Deacon Joe said. "I mean, who else have you got on this team?"

"Not a lot in stone at this point. A few guys still considering that I'd like to see join us, much like yourself. There's a shooting guard over at Rolling Bay, Eddie McGann, a six-nine post player who's relocating soon from Arizona, and a strong forward from Loyola High, Trent Whalen."

"Trent Whalen?" He tottered back and raised his chin. "That could be a dealbreaker for me, Mr. Creekmore."

"Really? Why's that?"

"He nearly took my head off one night with an elbow up at Mariner High. If he'd connected, I would have ended up in the hospital, or worse."

"How long ago was that?" I said.

"It was right after I arrived here, maybe the first game. So, two years ago? I thought if everybody played that way west of the mountains, then I didn't want any part of it. He'd cleared a nice rebound but simply brought it down too low. I stole it, took it coast-to-coast and laid it in. A few minutes later, I reach in again and he swung those big arms like you wouldn't believe. Scared the shit out of me. Ref ran him out of the gym."

"A lot might have changed in the last year or so. I would encourage you to give him another chance."

Deacon Joe shook his head and glanced toward the sky. The clouds were clearing and the temperature dropping.

"Geez, I don't know. That same day, Whalen took a swing at his father getting into the car outside the gym."

I sighed, truly hoping that behavior was history. Deacon Joe offered a *That's what happened* shoulder motion.

"As I said, I really believe Trent has made significant improvements in that area."

"No disrespect, Coach. But it's hard to get anything done with hotheads and meatheads, and this guy was definitely both."

Big Howard appeared at the front door, a huge hand still

on the knob.

"Guy's on the phone. Wants help buckin' and stackin' a downed hemlock. You game?"

Deacon Joe nodded like a kid offered ice cream. "Gotta take this."

He turned, waved an arm in the air behind him without looking, jogged up the steps and into the house.

TWENTY-NINE

I THOUGHT WE HAD a deal," Harvey Johnston seethed. "You were going to tell me anything that may have some relevance to this case! After the hamburger-bag incident, I can't believe you kept this thing about the cake from me for this long."

I slumped into one of the twin chairs opposite his desk and interlaced my fingers behind my head. "I'm still pissed at you. You're lucky I told you anything."

"I'm doing what I can about stalling on the Hazelton inquiry. What's your excuse?"

"I simply didn't want to bother Martha at those hours," I lied. "I know how women need to get their beauty rest. I remember when reporters used to call the house late at night requesting a quote or a bunch of game stats. Disturbed Cathy."

Harvey rolled his chair away from his desk and sprang to his feet.

"Don't you dare pull the wool, Ernie!" He shook an index finger in my face. "You know that timing is everything, and you had a hell of a lot of time to call me since this occurred. For crying out loud ..."

He was on a rare roll and gripped the edge of his desk as if intending to rip off a sample.

"I've told you I've always respected your instincts with young people, but—"

"No, hear me out. If I couldn't respond to them right away,

I felt that some sort of inspiration would surface within the next day, sort of like the old 'let me sleep on it' theory. I guess I still go back to that process when the needle on my mindmeter rises above the obvious level. I usually figure I can fix it, or solve it, just as well as anybody else."

"But we're talking about murder cases here, Ernie! These are not kids contemplating the fastest way through puberty. We've got some dangerous, sick clowns out there and it's about time you separated the seashells and balloons from the sharp knives and blunt objects of the real world!"

"It's not as if a chocolate cake is exactly a blunt object."

"Don't start on me, Ernie! You know what I mean! You've got a person's handwriting on this note." He turned to his desk and rifled through papers before he located and clutched an accordion folder in both hands. "As you did in the previous piece we discussed that could be potential evidence, Ernie. Did you hear me? Evidence. This greasy little hamburger bag is no longer a stained piece of paper. Neither is your cake note!"

A light rap at the door bailed me out, at least for the moment.

"By the way," Harvey said. "We trotted Paula Soijka in here for a little chit-chat and got less than little about the last several weeks. Stonewalled us, basically. The woman had solid alibis for Hazelton and Whalen. She couldn't say enough about the old days, though. She and Samantha spent one summer sitting on the sofa, drinking beer and watching *Investigation: Discovery*."

Margie wedged her well-coiffed head through the partially open door and flashed her bright white teeth.

"What?" Harvey roared.

"The district attorney would like you to call him immediately," Margie announced. "Something about the mayor needing an update."

When Margie turned to straighten her desk, I pointed to my chest.

"Me?" I mouthed to Harvey.

He shook his head.

"Just grand," Harvey mumbled to Margie. "Any creative way you can suggest saying that I'm still empty-handed and have made no progress? God knows I've used every one in the book."

"I'm sure you'll think of something, sir. Did you want me to get the DA on the line?"

"All right. I guess you'd better." I turned to leave.

I nodded and closed Harvey's door behind me. As I looked up, Margie blocked my path leading to the hallway. She stepped closer and placed her palms on my chest. She smelled like roses. I wondered how she kept her lips so gleaming. They appeared ready to drip.

"I thought you were supposed to be making a phone call," I said, as she fingered a button on my shirt.

"You know, I might be a little jealous if I found out someone else was providing you with dessert. I couldn't help but hear all this talk about a chocolate cake." She leaned in and nuzzled my ear. "I'd like to block some time to make a little frosting."

She wrapped her soft sleeves around my neck and studied me for a moment, her breath warm against my chin.

"Margie," I whispered. "We can't do this."

She pulled me closer and pushed her soft mouth against

mine. Warm blood pumped through my body as I tasted her lips for one long moment, thoroughly enjoying the embrace. As I opened my eyes, the realization of place startled me. I clenched my fists, backed away out of her reach, and wiped her lip gloss from my mouth with the back of my hand.

"You really should make Harvey's call," I said. "He's probably waiting for the connection right now."

"Well, I am hoping we'll pick up where we left off."

"I need to speak with you about several things, but it's going to take a lot more time than we have right now." She appeared frustrated, like a batter who just witnessed a home run turn into a wind-blown out. "The cake incident is part of an investigation, a case that's been taking up a lot of my time. Then there's the team, and its practice schedule."

"I understand all that. I was just attempting to get another commitment, perhaps dinner, movie, or my special kind of dessert"—she winked and grinned—"on the calendar."

Ah, the C word. Even if just a lower-cased C. Something deep in my gut was about to come out but I was uncertain how it would be delivered.

"Margie, you know you are the first woman I've dated since Cathy. While it's been five years since she's been gone, I'm still not ready for this exclusivity thing. I'm sure I'm way outside the statute of limitations for being on the rebound, but that's the way it is. It's certainly not you, believe me—you're quite the catch. It's me. I'm not ready to do schedules."

Tears formed in her eyes and she lifted a fist under her chin. "Are you seeing somebody else? I mean, who's making you cakes?"

"I wished like hell I knew! Look, I'm not seeing anybody.

But I'm just not in a place yet to worry about having dinner only with one woman at time. The movies, the dinners have been wonderful. But I'm not ready for the exclusive one-on-one game. I'm not talking about playing a huge field, but I don't want to be labeled as going with anybody."

"It's a far different world now than before you were married, Ernie." She tiptoed behind her desk, gently lifted a tissue from an always overflowing box, and dabbed her eyes. "Most women I know expect exclusivity, especially when it comes to sex."

"Hey, I'm still clueless on a lot of stuff. You know that. To tell you the truth, for years I didn't even want to know what it would feel like being with another woman." I approached the front of her desk. "Margie, you are terrific, but I'm nowhere near assuming, or expecting, that you'd be seeing only me."

She nodded slowly and whispered, "But you can't make that decision for me."

Harvey burst through the door, his necktie pulled down below his open collar. "Is the DA's phone …? Is everything OK here?" He ran a hand over his thinning hair and rested it briefly behind his head.

"Just fine, Harvey," I said. "It's my fault. Something came up unexpectedly that I had to clear up with Margie. I was just leaving."

Harvey took a wider stance and stared at me. "Hey, before you go, did you find out where Trent Whalen was at the time Hazelton was killed?"

"I didn't think you really cared anymore because I—"
"Ernie!"
"I assume he was at school or on his way to practice."
"Didn't we already talk about what assume—"

"OK, I'm on it ... I'm on it. Let me try to get Gene Slaughter on the phone."

"Good. Do that." He paused and tugged at his chin. "How much time between the end of class and practice?"

"Depends on the day. They probably alternate court time with the girls."

Harvey closed his eyes and massaged his forehead, the tiny diamond in his wedding band resting directly above his nose. "Great. Just dandy."

THIRTY

SOME GUYS GET only a gold watch. Others are honored with a platinum press pass. When I retired after nineteen years of coaching at Washington High and twenty-six years with the school district, it presented me with a token of its appreciation far more memorable and worthwhile than the fake gold watch I did receive.

The powers that be racked their creative minds and handed me a sparkling brass key to the gym, the venerable, creaky "Crab Pot." The place felt like a sauna when it was packed to its limits on Friday nights, but quickly returned to a cold storage locker for our Saturday morning old-boy skirmishes.

More than twenty years ago, while teaching and coaching at the school, a group of faculty, staff and administrators launched a weekly full-court Saturday game that remains to this day curiously free of elbows and assholes. All participants continue to be physically well-preserved, understand the importance of ball movement, and genuinely enjoy a well-threaded bounce pass more than the possibilities of an off-balance outside jumper.

The nucleus, median age forty-five, valued and practiced the theory of finding a good shot. Out-of-town visitors who accepted the on-court philosophy were welcomed with open arms, along with family members and any "old boy" newbie who looked like he could get up and down the floor without maiming anyone.

Not only did I want my Saturday morning guys to bump and bang the teenage all-stars, but I was also eager to have the oldsters critique their games and attitudes. These men knew their buckets and they knew how to read people. Several had acted as advance scouts for me when I coached the Crabs.

Exactly five weeks before the Seattle Center Spring Hoopfest, I arranged for five likely candidates to mingle and play with our Saturday morning crew. It was past time for a practice, and an intra-squad scrimmage appeared impossible. Nowhere near a final decision on the ten all-stars who would comprise my team, the combination of old and young provided enough bodies for a full-court game and cursory evaluations.

The casual meet-greet-and-play reduced the level of first-day teenage macho and expectations because the youngsters were sprinkled among three five-man teams. And my intentions extended beyond basketball. The young guys were forced to converse with adults they'd never met, and get a taste of the old gang's continual interest in high school athletics. Plus, they'd witness how a few fathers interacted with their own sons on the floor. Of the five invitees—Deacon Joe Gonzales, Nick Chevalier, Eddie McGann, Elmo Service, and Trent Whalen— three were dad-less and I'd be willing to wager at least one more wasn't in the picture.

Elmo was the most difficult decision. My conscience was clear about the hamburger-bag cash because I had donated the money to a needy cause. I was also fairly certain that the guy behind the cash was Scott Hazelton, the man who had been clubbed to death at Lake Wilhelmina.

While the cake incident stuck in my craw, an eleventh-hour

phone call from Ivan Scuttle, Elmo's coach at Port Edwards, injected a blast of reality into my fast-closing window for personnel selections. However, after hearing the reasons why Elmo deserved a chance, I almost asked the coach what was in it for him. I'd become that jaded about kids and dollar signs, especially those with a hamburger-bag past.

"Really, Ernie," the coach said. "Where are you going to get another six-seven black kid who can run and score?"

Deacon Joe, the last player to respond to my email announcement about practice, was the first to shuffle in the door. He quietly strolled across the floor and slouched in the front row of the stands, his triple-X hooded sweatshirt draped over an alleged five-foot-eight frame. His no-eye-contact entry befitted his "I'll try it once" reply to the session. One of the regulars took him for a young janitor who showed up early to get a head start on sweeping and cleaning.

Eddie, Nick, and Trent followed. I proceeded with casual introductions and team assignments, and paid particular attention when Deacon Joe shunned Trent's handshake for a cursory fist bump. Pairing Eddie and Nick with three of our better players turned out to be an effective combination, with the older guys instinctively providing enough spacing for the youngsters to drive or post up.

Despite their history, the Deacon Joe-Trent duo quickly meshed with a trio of veteran players, thanks to the tiny guard's laser passes and ankle-cracking crossover moves. Once the little dynamo got the ball in his capable hands, he flew down the floor and casually yo-yo'd the dribble at the top of the key, awaiting Trent to anchor the low block while the others formed a triangle on the other side of the lane. The youngsters' two-man game was immediate and instinctive, a raw Stockton-and-Malone, with Deacon Joe communicating exclusively with quick nods, gentle hand gestures and eye contact.

The positive nonverbals quickly piled up. Trent acknowledged every assist, casually pointing to his teammate as they hustled back on defense. After a stellar backdoor pass, Trent swerved out of his usual return to slap Deacon Joe a low five. At the other end, when Eddie nailed his first attempt from three-point range over a lunging, outstretched hand of a former Division 2 star who was clearly our best Saturday morning player, my spine began to tingle and I knew it wasn't the MS.

The two clubs traded baskets, tying the first game of the morning. A couple of regulars had walked into the front court while the young boys had yet to break a sweat. On a side court, the group waiting to take on the winners launched rusty jumpers and angled their aged bodies against the wall, stretching legs unworked since the previous week. A portly accountant in faded, knee-length Syracuse baggies asked his teammates about Washington High's sophomore sharpshooter, then jogged over to the corner to fetch a ball that caromed away from center court. As he did, all eyes swung to the main entry a few feet away.

Elmo Service, in full Los Angeles Lakers warmups with BRYANT stitched on the back of the Forum-blue jacket, sauntered across the baseline, the metal tips of his long white shoelaces sliding along the oak floor behind his mammoth high tops. Mirrored aviator sunglasses rested atop a black Chicago White Sox baseball cap, its flat-brim strategically rotated above his right cheek. He glanced around the gym.

"Well, Mr. Service," I said. "How nice of you to join us."

"Yeah, sorry about that, Coach," Elmo said, easing a canvas bag the size of Seattle off his shoulder. "Seems some of Elmo's people spaced on the time."

"I see. Please plan on joining me after this workout for a little clarity on the rules and expectations."

He folded the glasses inside his hat, carefully stuffed them in the corner of the bag and suddenly twitched. Standing erect, he lifted his chin. "Glad I ate a big breakfast," Elmo said as he saw Trent amble toward the drinking fountain. "'Cuz it looks like this could be a long mornin'."

Trent returned, wiped his mouth with the bottom of his jersey. "Are we playing, Coach, or just talking?"

As the game ended, I introduced Elmo to his teammates for the day. The group briefly exchanged greetings before Elmo returned to his bag and pulled out matching scarlet wristbands and headband.

"Coach, it looks like you are asking Elmo to run with a bunch of retired librarians," Elmo said. "I mean, we be all right, 'cuz I'm up to the challenge. But it looks to Elmo like Elmo is going to have to carry this team on Elmo's back."

I smiled and shook my head because I thought I'd seen it all. I've coached gang members, prima donnas, and kids who wanted to quit after the first day of sprints. All-stars and academics. But never did I have a kid who referred to himself in the third person.

"Don't dis Elmo's teammates just yet. Elmo may be surprised how smoothly they get Elmo the ball."

"That's cool," Elmo nodded. "Elmo got no problem with that."

Just as I was about to visualize a double-high post

arrangement with Eddie running the baseline, Bjarne Dagmar sidestepped through the far door and slid into a row directly opposite me. Moments later, Diane Chevalier appeared through the same door and parked her tight-jeaned bottom an arm's length from the detective. She casually slanted back and propped her cowboy boots against the row in front of her. I glared at Bjarne.

"Coach, my mom told me last week she wanted to have coffee with you after the first practice," Nick said behind me. "Looks like that's today." Then, to Eddie: "Come on over and meet her. I got no idea who the guy is." The two players plopped down the bleacher steps and circled around the basket to the other side of the floor.

Eddie and Nick wrapped up their conversation with Diane and trotted onto the court. Elmo tilted his head to the side and examined Eddie.

"Let's see if the bro can score on Elmo," he said. "Gonna find out if the man's got what it takes."

The comment brought snickers and a few hoots. While Elmo cinched his calf-length shorts and adjusted his headband just so, Eddie knocked down a twenty-five-foot bomb that barely touched the net. He turned, winked at Nick, and sprinted back on defense.

"Goodness," I whispered in delight under my breath, then rose for the mandatory welcome of Diane and Bjarne. I offered my best fake smile and hello before I slid in next to Bjarne.

After a long pause, I said, "So, did you stash your handcuffs in your coat pocket, or are you just waiting for backup to apprehend both me and Trent?"

"What? No, totally off-call today." Bjarne smirked. "I'm

merely a spectator observing some impressive athletes."

"Don't leave me hanging, Detective," I whispered. "Or I'll kick your ass. Badge and all."

He cleared his throat and looked down the row. "Actually, we've received some intriguing information today."

"Really? Does this mean I'm off the hook?"

"No, not at all. He rotated on his rear, perusing the stands. "Look, this is not the time or place."

I lunged forward. Diane noticed so I lowered my voice even more. "Come on, Detective. You do not want to do this."

The gym doors swung open and Samantha Whalen sauntered in. She located Trent on the court, smiled, waved and walked toward us. Trent did not acknowledge the wave.

"Good morning, everyone," Samantha said.

"Morning," I said.

She flashed a *Really?* look at Bjarne as she turned to sit. What was that all about?

Diane stood and extended her hand, "Samantha, I'm Diane. We met one evening at Tony's."

"Yes, we did. Nice to see you again."

"I don't know if you've met Bjarne Dagmar. He works with—"

"I'm quite acquainted with Detective Dagmar, yes," Samantha said. "Actually, it seems he knows a lot about everyone."

Bjarne chuckled, his cheek flush.

"I see," Diane said.

Deacon Joe inbounded the ball. Trent pivoted at the low block, took three steps across the key and planted a rock-solid back pick on Elmo that freed Elmo's handpicked opponent for an easy bucket.

"Moving screen, man," Elmo sneered, squaring up to Trent. "Don't be pulling that cheap shit so early in the morning."

Then it happened. Trent took a step toward, his fists clenched at his sides, sweat perfectly blotting his olive-drab tank top. The taut muscles bulging in his arms and legs conjured the image of an angry young Marine Corps instructor ready to challenge a boot-camp recruit.

"You want some, Elmo?" Trent scoffed. "More than happy to go 'round with you." He then swung a fearsome haymaker perfectly in rhythm with his massive legs, butt and arms. Thankfully, it didn't find its target. The punch would have crushed Elmo's face, but his quick juke allowed the blow to land in the air to the left.

"Trent!" Samantha Whalen yelled. "What's going ...?" She stood motionless, one hand to her forehead.

I raced out on the floor, open-mouthed, having prayed this moment would never come, but Timoteo had already stepped between them and stretched out his arms like a traffic cop. "No room for this at any time, especially on Saturday morning," he said. "Now cut it out, or get out."

"Tell my mom to get out of here!" Trent glared into the bleachers. "Now!"

"Tellin' you, man," Elmo screamed. "The dude's crazy. Nothin' changed, man. His mama saw it last time, too. Zebras do not change their stripes and tigers do not change their spots."

"I think you mean leopards," Deacon Joe said.

"Whatever."

Clasping my arms around Trent, I circled him away toward the locker room. Had he resisted, he could have flung me away like a toy.

"What was up with that?" I exclaimed. "No, really, where on earth did that come from? Do you even realize the damage that could have been done?"

"Make my mom leave, Coach. Please."

Samantha jogged toward him, her flat shoes clicking on the floor. "Trent, honey! What's wrong?"

Trent wandered over to the far wall, waving her off behind him.

"Samantha, it might be best to give your son a little room," I said. "Maybe you could wait ..."

Head down, she turned and walked toward the same door she entered moments ago and slipped outside.

"I don't know, Coach. Sometimes I just lose it."

"When she's around?"

He nodded. "Yeah."

I was about to ask, "What's going on?" But then I saw a couple of the older guys slung their bags over their backs and headed for the exit.

"I love ya, Ernie," one called out. "But I don't need this. I've still got kids who expect me to feed them. I can't come home a cripple."

I waved an acknowledgment. "Sorry, guys. I completely understand. I'll see you next time."

I wondered how many of the younger guys felt the same way, yet felt compelled to stick around. I returned to Trent. Diane and Bjarne turned and stared.

"You have to remember you're part of a team. Wherever that came from, you're going to have to let it go if you want to be with us. I can guarantee that you just scared the shit out of everybody in this building. That cannot happen." Lowering my voice, I continued. "You think about that. And when you're ready, you will apologize to everybody, and to Elmo personally."

The players silently reconvened and play continued, minus Trent, slumped on the gym floor in the corner. Elmo snatched the ball off the floor and inbounded to nobody in particular under the basket.

"'Bout some help on those screens?" Elmo sniveled. "Got to talk to Elmo."

The scrappy guard running the offense for Elmo's club appeared to have had enough of the distractions. He caught Elmo's lazy pass in full stride, bolted the length of the floor and drained a foul-line jumper before Elmo reached the halfcourt line.

"This could be interesting," I muttered and took a seat in the folded-down bleachers below Nick and Eddie, still rocked by the implications of the punch. As I watched Deacon Joe become more comfortable and understanding of other players' moves, I was impressed with the observations coming from Nick and Eddie behind me:

"See how he uses his first dribble to get somewhere? Guy's a smart player."

"The guy doesn't jump very high but he gets his shot off in a hurry. See that?"

Deacon Joe found a way to involve all the players, even slowing the pace a notch to allow the older guys not only to participate in the flow but also to succeed. He instinctively knew where and when to get the ball to each player, as if he'd already compiled a mental list of individual tendencies and strengths. And his specialty appeared clear. After just fifteen minutes, the high lob became an art form. Precise, confident and timely.

"Can you believe this guy?" Nick said to Eddie. "I mean, the dude can dish. Have you seen him throw a bad pass yet? Freakin' DEFCON Joe."

"Ya know, I play a lot," Eddie said. "Maybe not in a ton of gyms because I work weekends, but I have never even heard of this guy. I gotta think a lot of other guys haven't, either."

After Deacon Joe staked his club to a comfortable lead, Elmo shed his macho swagger and became a helpful, nearly unselfish teammate. Alternating at the high and low post, he attempted only wide-open shots and delivered pinpoint passes to teammates cutting to the basket. And when his teammates' easy attempts swirled out of the hoop, he encouraged rather than rebuked, and attempted to pass the offending players the ball at the same spot on the floor for another try.

I'd heard other coaches talk about Elmo's capabilities, but I'd never seen them for myself.

At the next whistle, Trent appeared from the corner and asked if he could have the floor. Timoteo nodded.

"Excuse me," Trent began. The gym fell quiet. Players stood, hands on hips at midcourt. "Sorry 'bout what happened. There's no excuse. I've been waitin' for this for so long, that I guess I felt I had to set some kinda tone. I need to apologize to you all, 'specially to you, Elmo. Nobody deserves that." He hesitated and swept a sneaker in a semicircle on the floor in front of him. "I'm asking for a second chance. I really want to be your teammate."

No one said a word. Then, Elmo broke the silence.

"Sounds good to Elmo. Elmo knows all about teams,

coaches givin' Elmo a second chance."

"Sometimes three," Deacon Joe said. Everybody howled, the ice now broken.

Trent smiled and slapped hands with Elmo. Timoteo encouraged the teams on the floor to resume their run.

I took a deep breath, slumped back and wondered what could be. Nick and Trent as double low posts, Elmo at the foul line, Deacon Joe at the point, and Eddie wide on either wing. Nice. Maybe start with a Deacon Joe-Trent two-man game on one side, and mix in an Eddie-Nick-Elmo triangle offense to add versatility.

When the game ended, Timoteo approached. "You going to run with us, Ernie? Timoteo said. "I'm sure you want to show the all-stars that the Coach's still got some juice in those old joints."

"Actually, I was going to take Nick and his mom to the bakery for a little coffee," I said. "Why don't the guys who still want to play just shoot for teams?"

Diane waved her arm as if brushing me away. "No, no, you go ahead and play. We can have coffee anytime."

"Are you sure?" I said.

"Yes, no worries. Please, join the game."

Nick grabbed his bag, and he and Diane turned to leave. "I thought you were hoping to have coffee with Coach," Nick said.

"I was, honey," Diane said loud enough for me to hear. "But that was last week."

Bjarne followed them out.

THIRTY-ONE

EDITH SNEERED AT my mismatched sweats as I strolled through the back door of the office shortly before 6 p.m. Before I could say a word, Peggy Metzger waved me down and lifted the mouthpiece of her telephone headset opposite razor-straight black bangs.

"I'm sending a call to your desk right now," she said, pointing to my cubicle. "Then I'm out of here."

Mouthing a thank-you, I picked up the mail from my slot and headed for my chair. A moment later, the middle button blinked at the base of my black phone.

"This is Ernie Creekmore."

"Oh, Ernie? This is Paula Soijka. I have some good news and some bad news." Her words came sharp and short, as if I had requested research on a specific property.

I cringed and gripped the phone like a billy club. "OK. I guess."

"What would you like to have first?"

How about neither? "Well, my day hasn't been jammed with superlatives, so why don't we keep all the bad news together and then end on a high note?"

"Jammed with what?" she asked. "Anyway, I guess that means you want the bad news first. So, that Timmy friend of yours has not called me and I was really looking forward to meeting him."

I extended the receiver away from the desk and wiped a hand across my face.

"Didn't you say he was going to call me?" Even at a distance from my ear, she sounded curt and clear.

After a long pause, I mumbled, "I don't remember saying anything about—"

"God, we've been over this," she huffed. "It was at the bar that night …? Well, anyway, the good news is that the logo is done for the shirts and the owner of the Shell station, a guy named Kevin, has approved it. He's going to leave them on his garage door tonight so you can pick it up and check it out."

I shook my head. "I'm sorry. The what? And it's Kelvin. Kelvin Petty."

"You know those T-shirts I was making for your team? I wrapped up the design today and this Kevin guy, I mean Kelvin, said he would be the sponsor and give me the money when you approved the look."

"Did I agree to go ahead with—"

"I figured all we needed was a sponsor and people told me this guy liked basketball. We've got the Shell corporate logo on there, a basketball, a pair of sneakers. To tell you the truth, it doesn't look that bad at all."

I slumped in my chair.

"Are you still there?" Paula shouted. "All you got to do is go down there after eight. The guy said he'd tape the folder to the garage door at the back of the station."

"I wish you would have spoken with me first before approaching people like Kelvin Petty," I said. "He would not be a man I would ask about underwriting a T-shirt. He's been loyal friend to my teams and—"

"And that's exactly why I went after the guy. Look, it's a done deal. Just get down there tonight and pick the thing up. Then, cha-ching! He gives me two grand. And don't wait too long because it's supposed to rain around midnight. I don't want that artwork to get wet."

Before I could respond, she hung up.

I packed up a stack of new listings and headed to Tony's for a beer and a grinder. Scooter took my order and I headed for an empty stool at the bar.

There, I noticed Paula Soijka, partially hidden by the huge bartender and the cash register. She was shielding her face while raising a cocktail to her lips like an out-of-sync puppet. She squinted my way, then sprang up straight, spilling the drink on her yellow windbreaker. Animated conversations and loud bar chatter covered her clumsy cleanup.

"Don't worry," I hollered. "I'll pick up the stuff at the gas station as soon as I leave here."

Scooter slid me a beer and I retreated to the restaurant to avoid Paula and wait for the sandwich. By the time it was ready, I nearly needed a canoe to get to my rental car. The rain arrived in buckets, its rhythm ranging from driving to torrential. The trip to Petty's Shell Service, located on an isolated triangle of property bordering a huge county green belt that stretched to the Skagit River, took me ten minutes instead of five.

My bright lights magnified the rain, huge silver drops the size of fat quarters. A sliver of lightning lit the western sky; it was followed two seconds later by deafening rolling thunder. A rectangular envelope fastened to the side of the massive sliding door with gray duct tape, under a metal overhang.

Chugging forward, I pulled to a stop just right of the door

to avoid a river of water from a nearby downspout. I left the motor running and the headlights on, opened the door and stepped head down toward the door. As I reached to loosen the tape, a thunderous roar from behind filled my ears. Turning toward the open lot, I caught the outline of a car fishtailing my way.

I managed two quick strides toward the rental before the speeding car closed in. My head throbbed but my legs and arms were shot through with adrenaline, and they did the thinking for me. Using my car as a buffer, I pumped like a sprinter toward the far corner of the building. The phantom driver swirled his vehicle in reverse, slamming my car door closed with its chrome rear bumper as it reeled in a frenzied circle, its four tires spitting black water.

I ducked behind the building, gauging the distance to the greenbelt as the driver restored control and turned on the headlights. The car lunged in my direction, its wheels squealing for traction. I darted for the street. Leaping over the gutter stream, I caught a chuckhole in the street and fell on my right shoulder, toppling onto my back. The car flew out of the parking lot, swung wide, and zigzagged closer. Four doors, dark green or black, in a blur.

I scrambled to my hands and knees and crawled as fast as I could, my battered knees pounding over the wet gravel.

As I reached the far curb, I staggered to my feet, managed three faltering strides before diving off the hill into the greenbelt and wind-milling down the slope. Short, staccato, painful breaths returned as the car banged to a stop above me, its front tires perched over the curb. Hugging my side, I bent lower and snaked into the woods as the driver maneuvered his headlights into the trees.

Tripping and stumbling into a grove of hemlock, I slid behind the biggest one, stood as straight as possible, and tried to catch my breath. I stole a peek toward the street. Steam swirled above the car's hood, and the silhouette of a stocky man, hands on hips, loomed between the headlights. I bobbed back behind the tree, counted to five, then risked another look. The driver kicked at the ground, returned to the car, turned out the lights.

"FUUUCCCKKK!" he roared. Then he stepped toward the hill.

I froze, racking my brain to recall the entries and exits of the greenbelt. Meandering toward the river, I half-jogged with one arm extended, praying that I could reach one of the open picnic areas and a bark-covered walking trail without smacking into an unseen alder.

I took thirty paces, stopped and stood still, listening for sounds other than wind and rain. Branches crunched from the area I'd just crossed. I juked side to side like a running back avoiding a field of ghost tacklers.

A moment later I tumbled over a twisted root and slammed face first into the soft mud. On my knees, I followed the root, hand over hand, to what felt like the paper-like bark of a mammoth madrona. I sat against its trunk, my scrunched torso compounding the pain in my ribs as I wiped my face with the sleeve of a soaked sweatshirt. It draped from my shoulders like a weighted cloak.

I tried to quiet my breathing and listen for footsteps.

Scooting on my bottom around the tree, I recognized the smell of fresh wood chips, returned to my hands and knees and crawled ahead though the mud, kneeling upright periodically to clear small sticks and pebbles from my palms. After my second stop, my right hand felt the smoothness of wet grass. I rose and crept ahead until the bottoms of my mud-caked hightops brushed a patch of wood bark.

Dropping to my knees, I stretched out my arms and felt the stones that lined both sides of the trail. Arching my back, I muttered "thank you," then bent down like an aging Sherlock Holmes and shuffled down the path to the river, stopping every twenty steps to look and listen.

An hour later, I knocked on Harvey's back door and scared the daylights out of Martha.

THIRTY-TWO

HARVEY'S NEW WHITE terry-cloth bath robe, coupled with my black and blue body, had me looking like a battered boxer the morning after the bout.

"A cruise line gave me that thing ten years ago," Harvey said, taking a seat on the sofa opposite me. "I gave two talks onboard to Alaska about keeping valuables safe. We both got a free trip. Free robes. Can you imagine? I've never even put it on."

"I use mine all the time," Martha said, carrying a tray into the living room. "Do you take cream with your coffee, Ernie?" Martha said. "I have a little half and half."

"Just black, Martha. Thanks." She handed us both steaming mugs and returned to the kitchen. Harvey became all business.

"My guys picked up Paula Soijka last night," Harvey said. "She was still at the bar at Tony's and pretty well hammered. They said she was in no shape to drive anywhere, let alone maneuver a vehicle like you described in that rain. Scooter said she sat there all evening."

I blew into the coffee and took a sip. "She set me up, Harvey. Clear and simple."

"Have you given any thought as to who else might have known you were heading to Petty's Shell? It was a man's voice at the top of the bank. Right?"

"I've got no idea. And yes, clearly a guy." I placed the mug on the magazine table in front of me. "I *do* know that last night

271

was the first time I was afraid to return to my own house. This thing has gone too far. Last night was strike three."

Harvey nodded and fingered his suspenders. "I don't blame you in the least, Ernie. Frankly, I'm feeling guilty about asking you to get involved in the first place. And I'm embarrassed that we haven't done a better job of protecting you when—"

"I shouldn't need your protection, Harvey! It's freaking *basketball*, for crissake!"

Harvey frowned and looked out the window. "It's a helluva lot bigger than that now. I'm concerned about all of North Fork. There are individuals out there putting innocent people at risk." He let those words hang in the air between us, then said, "Look, Ernie. I'd never thought I'd say this but it's probably a good idea that you give up this coaching job. Back away completely. Maybe let another guy take over and—"

"And let all of this hang over *his* head? Are you kidding me, Harvey? It's not that easy. I mean, think about it."

Harvey stroked his chin and took a sip of coffee. "You're right. Any new guy would have to dodge the same BS that's hit you."

The phone rang and Martha answered the call in a back bedroom.

"Maybe not any new guy," I said.

Harvey squinted at me and placed his mug on a side table. "What do you mean?"

"Honey, it's for you." Martha tiptoed between us and handed the cordless phone to her husband. "Somebody from the office."

Harvey snapped his suspenders and barked into the phone. "Talk to me." His eyes darted from side to side. "When did you talk to him?" Another long pause. "I see." Harvey glanced at me. "Well, I was going to the Rotary Club wood cut but I'll change and come on in. Right." He ended the call and flipped the phone on the couch.

"What's up?" I said.

"My officers spoke again with the dairyman who thought he saw the vehicle that ran you off the road. It turns out that he scribbled down four letters on a gas receipt before he left on vacation and left the slip of paper under the seat in his rig."

"And?"

"It turns out he got a darn good partial. The only car with those four sequential letters in this area is registered to one Paula Soijka."

My chin hit my chest. "No way. I'll tell you what, Harvey. Whoever ran me off the road that night was the second coming of Kasey Kahne."

"Well, if she was driving, she's in a world of hurt. You may recall that she had two priors and our great state has a three-strike rule. The vehicular charge would make her third felony. And you thought you were the only one concerned about three strikes. This woman could start singing."

Restless, I twisted in my chair trying to find a comfortable position.

"Look," Harvey said. "Stay here as long as you want, take over the guest room. I'll have somebody fetch your rental car at the Shell and drop it off here. If you need a car before that, take Martha's Lincoln."

I nodded. "Thanks. I might take you up on that. I could use some air and I'm supposed to meet Linn Oliver anyway."

*   *   *

Just before noon, I picked up Linn and we headed north on I-5.

"I've wanted you to meet this kid ever since I played against him," Linn said. "You talk about a secret weapon. This guy could really make *the* difference for the all-star team."

"I wanted to talk with you about that team," I said. "I've given it a lot of thought and I'm thinking about stepping—"

"Hang on," Linn said. "Let me read you my notes while they're in front of me."

Haywood Range, poster boy for White Men Can't Jump. *The best pure shooter north of Seattle. Slower than a night in jail. Intergalactic range. Shot's an ugly mechanical-like maneuver that does not really qualify as a jumper. Launches from his tippytoes after coaxing his massive rear end as high as it can go. Looks like a set shot from a 1950s newsreel. Man does not miss.*

"If this guy is so slow, how does it fit into our fly-and-fling offense?" I said.

"We assign him a spot on the floor and he doesn't move. Deacon Joe gets it to him. Count it! Like Paul Westhead's high-octane offense at Loyola-Marymount."

"Then we're going to need another rebounder other than Trent. Can you find me the second coming of Karl Malone?"

"I've got that covered, too. But he doesn't play until next week."

"Very impressive," I said. "Especially coming from you. Now, I need to talk with you about something else."

I took a deep breath and launched into the full story.

"Think about this," Linn said when I'd finished. "You back

out now and everybody's going to think it's because of your MS."

"I don't care what everybody—"

"No, hear me out. We spread the word to everybody but the players that you're taking a leave. You'll continue to run the show. I'll start the practices and you just pop on in when you feel like it. When people ask, we'll just say that a new coach will be named soon."

"No. I will not put you in jeopardy. This is serious stuff, Linn."

"Hey, it's not as if I've never had the shit beat out of me before. Didn't you bring me back from the dead once? Besides, I'm betting by the time everybody figures it out, we'll have chosen our team and be headed for the tournament. End of story."

I shook my head. "If anything ever happened—"

"I'm also betting that you are dying to coach these kids. What a group, and wait until you see this guy."

As we turn onto the off ramp, Linn's cell phone clanged some heavy metal number I'd never heard.

"Hello. Yes, it is. Can you hold a moment? He's driving." He turned toward me and pointed the phone. "It's for you."

"Really?" I pulled over on the shoulder, slammed the Lincoln into Park and let the engine idle.

"This is Ernie."

"I called Linn because you didn't answer your phone," Harvey said.

"Yeah. I guess I left it in the rental car."

"A patrol car found Paula Soijka this morning in the parking lot of the Kiwanis Ball Fields at Riverfront Park. Looks like a drug overdose but there's still a lot of work to do. Anyway, I wanted you to know."

"Good Lord," I mumbled. "Is there no end to this? OK, we were going to scout a kid, but maybe I'll just return the Lincoln and head home." I turned to Linn and shook my head. "Harvey, is my car at your place?"

"Yep. Good to go. Swap the cars whenever you're ready."

My mind raced faster with every mile. Paula Soijka, dead. Related to the attempts on my life? Unrelated? Suicide? A confession of sorts? Or an accidental overdose? Or ... murder?

THIRTY-THREE

THE LOANER CAR provided by the insurance company not only lacked the space of my beloved and battered bus, but I also could not figure out how to open the trunk from inside the car.

I leaned across the shotgun seat, yanked open the glove box and pulled out the owner's manual. As I paged through the index, my cell phone rang.

"What?" I yelled, nearly prone across the front seats.

"Ernie, I'm so glad you located your cell," Harvey said, "but now we have to work on your greetings and salutations."

"Don't get me started. This thing is a pain in the ass, and everybody expects it to be the most important thing in my life and my constant companion."

"Only those people who would like to speak with you or leave you a message."

"Cut the crap. What's up? I'm just heading home."

"What's up is that we received a positive DNA match back from the lab from the Tim Whalen crime scene and I thought I would tell you before you heard it from someplace else. For example, a person like Greg Smithson or another reporter who actually works a beat."

"Well, that's great news! Now tell me I can stop worrying about this draining case and focus on preparing for the tournament without any more distractions."

Harvey paused so long that I worried the call had been dropped. He continued in a softer tone. "Not so fast, Coach. This will not remove Trent as a suspect. At least, not yet. We'll know more in the morning, probably about eleven. Please stop by, and then you can buy me one of those foot-long meatball sandwiches at Tony's that I'm only supposed to eat half of."

I launched myself off my elbows and sat up straight in the driver's seat. "Now wait a minute, Harvey, that's not fair. You track me down in the evening with the best message we've gotten in months and you leave me hanging? What sort of BS is that? I don't want to wait until eleven tomorrow morning, so tell me now."

"You know I'm not supposed to disclose information to anybody before it's official."

I could feel the heat in my cheeks. "Well, I'm not anybody," I roared, pleased the windows were not open. "Besides, you got me into this crazy deal in the first place. Now, hurry up and tell me what's shaking."

"All right, just keep your shirt on," Harvey said.

I could almost hear him rewinding his internal tapes.

"We were able to obtain DNA samples from two cigarette filters found above the wood trim in the interior doorways of the Hanrahan residence on West Tulip Road. We entered these and other samples from the Whalen crime scene into the FBI's CODIS program database. Until recently, this Combined DNA Index System only coughed up zeroes for us."

Harvey halted his message again. Before I could ask "Are you still there?" he returned.

"But earlier today, the CODIS manager called with what she said was a perfect match."

My shoulders dropped and I leaned back in the driver's seat. "I'm telling you, Harvey, you've made my day. No, make that my month. Now, who the hell is it?"

"I'm uncertain how much you know about this new technology, Ernie. But a DNA match at a crime scene is an investigative tool, not proof positive of guilt."

I felt like an attendee in one of his informational seminars at the community center. "And it's a very accurate investigative tool. Now, tell me, damn it!"

Harvey took another long moment, this time to clear his throat. "It's a Jesuit priest over at Loyola High, Father Benjamin Hawkenson. Older guy, came up from a parish in Tacoma two years ago."

While I knew the Jesuits were known to be America's guests and that the Northwest Province had more money than most small corporations, I grappled for a logical connection. "So, what do you know about this guy?"

"He's the school's assistant athletic director and chief fundraiser. I'll know more tomorrow."

I paused. "When are we going to talk about Paula Soijka?" I said. "And, what's the latest on Hazelton? I'm a suspect. Remember?"

"We don't know enough yet on Ms. Soijka," Harvey said. "We're just beginning to go through her stuff. And, at the moment you're the least of my worries, but your attitude is moving you up the chart."

THIRTY-FOUR

THE DEEP-TISSUE MASSAGE therapist steered clear of my ribs and lower back and concentrated on the shoulders, arms and legs.

"Watch it!" I screamed at Nada, the dark-skinned Indian woman I'd seen twice a month since moving to the area nearly three decades ago to take the teaching and coaching position at Washington High School. "This is supposed to be therapeutic."

She sighed, probably because I said the same thing every time I was on her table. "Your stress has a tendency of settling right here." She manipulated the muscles of my right hamstring with long, strong fingers that felt like steel-tipped darts. I jerked when she sunk an elbow deep into my calf, briefly snapping my head from the cradle at the end of the table. "And it's got nothing to do with your MS, I'm afraid."

"Are you sure?" I mumbled face down through the support as I settled back in, trying to fib my way around a suddenly decision-packed existence. Ten years earlier, my body seemed to handle the rigors of coaching with a lot less pain. Toss in a couple of dead bodies, attacks on my life, a perplexing criminal investigation, and couple of intriguing females, and my muscles felt tighter than a nylon crab line. And then there were the baseball-size knots in my calves that seized at night and launched me out of bed and into a clumsy stretching session.

"Of course I'm sure." Nada laughed. "You had none of this

concentration eight weeks ago and your MS numbness hasn't progressed in your hands and feet. You said so yourself. I really don't think I've seen you like this since Cathy died." I groaned and whined as she pressed her thumbs into the bottom of my heels, sending a hot-poker sensation through my stiff Achilles. "It's quite apparent that someone has not been stretching after Saturday basketball."

I turned my head away, resting a cheek on the side of the cradle.

"That someone rarely even gets to Saturday basketball anymore, let alone properly stretch after games." I splayed my arms and prepared for more misery by envisioning positive experiences. I dreamt of swimming in warm saltwater, tropical fish and irrepressible turtles all around me; of a last-second shot going through the nets to win a state championship game before a sellout crowd; of Diane Chevalier sitting across from me in a corner table at Tony's, her blue eyes sparkling above a candlelit glass of Chablis.

Nada broke the long silence and I reluctantly shuddered out of dreamland.

"I had a client once who became uncomfortably tense and tight before basketball, not afterward. He has since died, so I imagine it's permissible to speak this way."

"He'll never know," I groaned.

"He had a child who was a player and this man got so worked up before games that he scheduled our sessions a few hours before the games. I've had clients, usually business executives, who scheduled massages before important meetings but I never had another person like him."

"Don't tell me he was upset with my coaching and had to

come in here to relieve the anxiety of seeing The Fighting Crabs."

"No, his son attended a private school and since I don't know anything about sports, I couldn't tell you how the team performed," Nada said. "I wished it had taken me longer to unravel his taut muscles, because once we got him loose and feeling better, he began revealing some of his personal exploits that were far too much information for me."

She stepped away from the table, added more lotion to her hands and continued the treatment. "I mean, about halfway through our sessions, it was as if he felt nearly compelled to tell me how he and his wife no longer had anything in common, and that she had no clue that he was having sex with one of her friends."

"And I thought bartenders got all the dirt," I yelped, trying to relax my shoulders under the pressure of her spike-like fingers.

"You wouldn't believe what people say when they're in here," she continued. "But I'll tell you what. I was so embarrassed that I had to ask him on more than one occasion to stop. It didn't do any good. He usually picked right up on the inappropriate disclosures in the next session. I came very close to asking him not to come back, then I saw a story in the newspaper about him being murdered. It doesn't appear that the police have any suspects. At least, I haven't read much about it since in the paper."

I turned my head, lifted my chest off the table and exhaled. "Lord."

"How stupid of me," Nada said, finally easing her vise-like grip from my left knee. "You must have known him. He sold real estate, just like you."

THIRTY-FIVE

LOOSE, FLUID, AND feeling I could play full-court for the next three hours, and not particularly inclined to worry about who was trying to kill me, I cruised down the hallway of the county's administration building, promising myself I would increase my number of monthly sessions with Nada. And not let myself get driven out of my town, and out of the things I loved to do in it.

Margie's icy greeting brought the first tenseness of the morning to my neck, but it didn't come close to the tightness in her jaw.

"They're waiting for you in there," she said, barely parting her lips.

"Thanks. How's your day going?"

No reply. Head down, she slammed color-coded tabs on the upper corners of individual pages.

When I entered the inner office, Harvey was seated behind his desk, chatting with a young-looking priest in a crisp white collar and a nicely tailored black suit, the clergy's equivalent to Marine dress blues. Most of the priests I knew wore civvies to games and casual gatherings, and sometimes loud Hawaiian shirts over khakis.

"Oh, good," Harvey said, rising from his chair. "Ernie, I'd like you to meet Father Archibald Geiszel."

"Northwest Provincial of the Society of Jesus, the religious order that runs Loyola High School and many other fine institutions of higher learning in this country," I said, extending my hand.

The Jesuit appeared impressed, and a bit confused, by my knowledge of his position. "Nice to meet you, Coach Creekmore." His hand was lean and his grip firm.

"Pleasure."

I did my best to ignore Bjarne who eased a metal folding chair through the door and set it opposite Harvey's desk. He approached Father Geiszel and offered his hand.

"Dominus vobiscum."

The priest rose, smiled and shook his hand.

Bjarne then eyed Harvey and said, "And don't forget to frisk 'em."

The priest flinched and sat back in his chair. "A former altar boy who—"

"A former altar boy a little pissed about wayward priests."

Harvey glared at his employee. "I'm sorry, Father," Harvey said. "Let me apologize for Detective Dagmar. His courtesy and respect elude me."

Bjarne snickered while the priest brushed an invisible speck from his trousers.

Returning to his seat, Harvey said, "Why don't we just dive right in? Ernie, please." He pointed to the matching armchair adjacent to the one occupied by the priest. "Earlier this week, a member of Father Geiszel's community was taken into custody and subsequently charged with a felony offense, RCW 9A.88.110, at the King County Jail in Seattle.

"Due to the severity of this offense, a DNA sample was obtained from Father Benjamin Hawkenson via a cotton swab, and the sample was entered into the CODIS program. With this type of felony, a biological sample must be collected for purposes of DNA identification."

I blasted a fake cough and halfheartedly raised my hand.

Harvey looked up and frowned. "Ernie?"

"Sorry to interrupt, but could you explain the numbers and letters? Uh, the ones that are assigned to this particular crime?"

Harvey straightened up in his chair and glared at me. "Patronizing a prostitute is a felony in our state. Father Hawkenson has been charged with patronizing a prostitute on International Way near SeaTac Airport."

Father Geiszel squirmed in his chair and spoke, his eyes wandering and unfocused. "While some of our priests have created a myriad of legal problems for our community for years, Father Hawkenson has faced an ongoing challenge with this situation. As you probably know, he could have been arrested for this behavior in the past, but the undercover policemen in each case provided an incredible amount of leniency."

"In each case?" Bjarne said. "How many times did those big-city, Irish Catholic cops look the other way?"

"Detective Dagmar, please watch yourself here," Harvey cautioned.

"Several," Father Geiszel continued in a new whisper. "It got to a point where I was wondering what dinner I would have to leave to address the issue again."

"Yes, well, what we want to address today are the results of the DNA match," Harvey said. "Tell me, Father Geiszel, does Father Hawkenson smoke?"

"Why, yes, he does," the priest answered, seemingly surprised by the question. "It's actually become a constant problem for the other priests in his house. We ask him to confine his smoking to the back driveway, but he'll often sit on the back porch when it's raining. Never uses an ashtray. When he drinks too much, he's got this nasty habit of crushing the cigarette on the bottom of his shoe and leaving the remaining portion above the door to be smoked at some future time. He's even tried to hide the butts above the doors inside the house."

Harvey glanced at Bjarne and then at me.

"Father Geiszel, we obtained DNA samples from two cigarettes at a murder scene that match the sample taken from Father Hawkenson when he was arrested in Seattle. The site was a private residence near the river, not far from here. It is owned by a Mr. Patrick Hanrahan, who had listed the property for sale with the deceased, a real estate agent named Timothy Whalen. You may have read about the case in the newspapers."

"Absolutely, and I can't imagine the hurt and suffering it has brought the Whalen family and your wonderful community. Mr. Hanrahan is a very dear and generous friend to the Society, and to have something as awful as this occur in his beautiful home is unthinkable. Many of our priests have used the Hanrahan home for weekend meetings and retreats for the past several years."

He craned his neck and stroked a too-tight clerical collar. "As you know, Mr. Hanrahan travels extensively overseas on business. I've always looked forward to my time there and that veranda overlooking the river. So peaceful and tranquil. Confidentially, I was hoping he would gift the home to the Society, but he obviously decided to go in a different direction with this particular asset."

Harvey flipped through two pages of the file in front of him.

He turned the second page to read its backside. "I understand Father Hawkenson led the fundraising at your school," Harvey said. "Did he ever mention to you any disappointment about not securing the Hanrahan home under the Jesuit umbrella?"

"Oh, no, not at all," Father Geiszel said. "Mr. Hanrahan has been beyond generous to us."

No one spoke for several moments. Harvey continued through the folder, apparently looking for a particular section.

"Excuse me, Father," I said. "Are you aware that Mr. Whalen's son is the star player on the Loyola High School basketball team?"

"Yes, I am. And I was made very aware of that when he transferred from his previous school. We don't offer athletic scholarships, per se, but we do try to help. Mr. Whalen also asked about the possibility of a discount if he prepaid his son's tuition. Apparently, his income was sporadic, not as consistent as some of our parents' salaries. But how is that relevant to this conversation?"

"I was just wondering if that was the reason Mr. Whalen was given the listing on this property. There are many other offices closer than his and other agents with more experience in the area. Perhaps Father Hawkenson influenced that decision."

Harvey squinted at me, his hands resting flat on his desk.

"I wouldn't know, Coach Creekmore," the priest said. "You would have to ask Mr. Hanrahan." He shifted his weight in his chair and cracked a smile that bordered on sly. "I will say, though, that the Jesuit underground does run deep."

Bjarne stood and slowly massaged his forehead.

"Father Geiszel, were you aware of any arrangement, financial or otherwise, between Father Hawkenson and Tim

Whalen?"

"What do you mean by that, Detective?"

"For example, do you have any reason to believe that Father Hawkenson and Mr. Whalen were lovers?"

Father Geiszel's eyes grew wider, his words more pronounced. "As far as I know, Father Hawkenson's challenges are with the opposite sex."

Bjarne appeared to be enjoying his place, both in his line of questioning and in floating above the seated priest. "Did Father Hawkenson loan Mr. Whalen a large sum of money with the possible understanding that his son would transfer to Loyola? Perhaps Mr. Whalen failed to pay it back."

"Absolutely not! And I am rather offended that you would even infer that. It would be inappropriate, against the rules of the state's sports association, and probably illegal."

Bjarne crossed in front of the priest and stared down at him. "You have to understand, Father, that we have two unsolved murders in this town. That does not happen around here very much. So excuse me if I ask extremely leading questions about the best information now in our possession!"

"Slow down, Detective," Harvey muttered. Bjarne glared at his superior and then shook his head.

"I can tell you, gentleman, that Father Hawkenson was in the Hanrahan home on many different occasions," Father Geiszel said. "There's no disputing that. In fact, I was with him for a handful of events there, including one with Coach Slaughter." Harvey raised his eyebrows and jotted a note. "But I can categorically tell you that he was not present in the Hanrahan home on the day Mr. Whalen was killed."

"Why are you so sure about that, Father?" Harvey said.

"Because after noon Mass that Sunday, I was called to the Capitol Hill Precinct to pick up Father Hawkenson, who had been there since mid-morning. I'm sure the police records will reflect that I arrived shortly before 1 p.m. Father Hawkenson remained in my presence until supper."

"He wasn't charged?" Harvey said.

"Not that day," Father Geiszel replied. "We try to handle these things internally."

"You're certain of the timeframe?"

"Positively."

Bjarne Dagmar spun and slammed his fist on Harvey's desk. "Screw internal justice!" he barked and stalked out the door.

Harvey suggested we take a break, but the session never really resumed. After Bjarne's departure, the discussion turned to a more casual conversation about enrollment numbers and teacher extracurricular stipends and compensation. We said our goodbyes and I began to follow the priest out of Harvey's inner office.

Turning to the chief detective, I whispered, "I'd say a chat with Gene Slaughter is in order, ASAP."

Harvey nodded rapidly, then swept his hand toward the door. Margie stood, shook hands with Father Geiszel and thanked him for coming.

As I reached for the hallway door, Margie tapped me on the shoulder. I turned and faced her.

"I owe you an apology," she said, nearly whimpering. "You didn't deserve the way I treated you on your way in. It wasn't right and—"

"I understand, Margie. Really."

"Let me finish." She stopped and giggled awkwardly. "You

know, sometimes you never let me finish ... Anyway, when I think back, I did go after you a little strong. How would you say it? A full-court press?" I smiled and glanced at my shoes. "But now I am beginning to understand what you want about the re-entry thing."

"Thanks, I just—"

"What did I say about letting me finish ...? As I was *trying* to say, I put myself in your shoes and felt I wouldn't want only one man's company right off. I kind of expected that from you, and I'm sorry. I was just hoping we could see each other in restaurants, here at the office, and not run the other way."

I waited a long moment. She tilted her head to the side. "Are you finished?"

"Yes, you jerk," she laughed. "I am finished."

"Well, I very much appreciate that." I kissed her lightly on the forehead. "And I'm glad I won't have to run because I'm not very fast anymore."

THIRTY-SIX

THE NEW FACE of our franchise, the legendary Linn Oliver, corralled a group of his friends and Washington High School alumni to serve as opponents against our North Counties select team in the final full-court scrimmage before the Seattle Center Spring Hoopfest. One of the opposing players was a ringer, a former player at Washington State who just happened to be the newest cop in Harvey's department. As part of the coaching deal negotiated with Linn and Harvey, "Sparky" was to be Linn's shadow and also supervise the nightly surveillance of my home.

As I popped out of the rental to open the Washington High gym doors, I noticed Greg Smithson tapping on a silver laptop in his car, the ubiquitous blue baseball cap perched high on his forehead. Looking up from the screen, he peered through the windshield and grinned when he identified me. He turned the key in the ignition in order to lower the window.

"I guess I'd given up hope about getting you to see these guys," I said. "I appreciate you coming."

He turned off the engine. "I came down from the Everton ferry," Smithson said, closing the computer and stuffing it in a nylon backpack. "My folks have a place in the San Juans. I'm on my way back to Seattle and was eager to check out some of your mystery men."

I led him inside The Home of The Fighting Crabs and

chatted about next week's tournament while I turned on the gym lights and readied the scoreboard clock. More than two decades ago, Smithson nicknamed the building "The Crab Pot." It became a loving term for locals and a feared, claustrophobic venue for visiting coaches and players.

"It is one of my favorite places in the entire state," Smithson said, as The Cheese arrived with several talented players from my former teams. He greeted the players and blushed at complimentary comments about his coverage of high school athletics.

As Cheese organized the teams, explained the running-time quarters and call-your-own-fouls rules, I slid in next to Smithson at the scorers' table and set the overhead timer to eight minutes. The teams began to warm up at both ends of the court.

"The big kid's got good feet," he said of Nick Chevalier. "I've never seen him before."

"He transferred from Arizona," I said. "He arrived completely out of the blue."

He jotted some unintelligible notes on a spiral pad.

"Was it a stretch for you to take Elmo Service?" Smithson said, his eyes still focused on the floor. "The man is well-traveled, to say the least. He's got a huge family, a slew of cousins, uncles, his own little entourage. Some of them have been rumored to leave calling cards."

I flinched. "Such as?"

"Items of value to help influence decisions. I think that's probably why he's at his third school. I've asked Elmo about it and he said he didn't know a thing, other than his mom baking cookies for the team bus."

"Nice," I laughed. "Homey touch. Do you know if she does cakes?"

"Huh? I wouldn't have a clue."

We watched as Deacon Joe Gonzales confidently controlled the tempo, rocketing up the floor when left alone while orchestrating our limited number of set offensive plays at the right times. He didn't force any passes and pulled the ball out to reset when his teammates were incorrectly spaced.

"Your point guard looks like the real deal, Coach," Smithson mused. "Now I'm starting to get why you wanted me here. I won't say a word to anybody, but where in the hell did you find him?"

"Linn Oliver found him in a pickup game in Marysville. He couldn't stay with him at all on defense. Dropped out of school and lives on the rez with a carpenter."

"You're kidding. Great story, especially the part about being discovered by one of the state's best ever. When can I write about it?"

"Just do me a favor and hold it until after our first tournament game."

"Consider it done. But by then, you'll be big-time. You might not even talk to me without approval from your agent."

I cringed. "Don't talk to me about agents."

The alumni team stayed with the young kids for the first half, but Deacon Joe's speed and the inside play of Nick, Elmo, and Trent Whalen eventually turned the fourth quarter into garbage time and a twenty-point win for the all-stars. I thanked Smithson again, informed the players of the Thursday shootaround before Friday's first tournament game, and buttoned up the gym.

Trent emerged from the locker room, a towel tucked around his neck and into his hooded sweatshirt like a prizefighter.

"Are you the last one out?" I asked.

"Yup. Everyone else is gone. Guess I'm the slowest poke."

"Let me collect my junk, and I'll walk out with you."

Three cars remained in the parking lot. Clouds had gathered in the western sky and a light rain began to fall. I pulled the swing lever on the door shut, pushed a shoulder into the middle panel to make certain the building was now locked, and turned toward the cars.

Bjarne Dagmar strutted toward us, as did a police officer I didn't recognize, from a county-issued Plymouth. They stopped three paces from us and stood the way cops stand when they mean business: one man slightly in front and to the left of his partner.

They took a step toward Trent and the uniformed officer swung a set of silver handcuffs from the back of his belt.

"Trent Whalen, you are under arrest for the murder of Timothy Whalen ..."

Stunned, the youngster dropped his bag at his feet. "What the heck is ...?" He looked at me as if he'd just missed an open lay-in at the buzzer.

"You son of a bitch," I yelled at Bjarne. I stomped toward him. The quick move tweaked my ribs and I bent forward, clutching my side. "You've been dead set on doing this all along. It's not the right thing to do, and you damn well know it!"

"You have the right to remain silent," Bjarne continued and he clamped the cuffs on Trent, whose face was now the color of the white sweatshirt layered under his jacket. "Anything you say can and may be used against you in a court of law. You have

the right to have an attorney present before and during questioning ..."

Furious, I watched as the policeman guided Trent, tears
rolling down his face, toward the backseat of the Plymouth.
As soon as the vehicle was gone, I fired the scorebook into the
rental car and began the search for my cell phone. The drizzle
turned to a downpour as I punched in Harvey's number.

"Hey!" I screamed when he picked up. "Thanks a million
for the heads-up. What a bunch of frickin' BS and a real jerk
thing to do. I can't believe you let this happen without inform-
ing me it was in the works."

Harvey waited to respond. He always did when I came in,
or called in, hot. "I tried calling your cell several times, but you
never answer the thing. The mayor came down on the DA and
then when I was out, Bjarne convinced the DA he had enough
ammo to bring Trent in."

I moved out of the rain to the cover of the gym's entrance.
"I can't believe you weren't there to handle this. After getting me
in the middle of this, where in the hell were you?"

THIRTY-SEVEN

By THE TIME I reached the Skagit County Jail, the buzz of activity was palpable, as if some rock star had been seen scurrying down the hall to the men's room. Bjarne stood smiling with an attractive female officer in the far corner of the processing area, while Harvey carried on an animated conversation with an assistant district attorney in a glass-sided office. A moment later, Bjarne hustled down the corridor and Harvey emerged with what appeared to be a slight smile.

"Here is what we have at the moment," he said.

I moved in closer and pointed a finger to his chest. "What we've got is a young man in your custody whom I want kept under the radar, and off the local websites and the damn front page, until you play out every single other angle of this investigation."

"Hang on, Ernie. And please lower your voice. I'm way ahead of you on this."

"That would be a first," I sneered, and took a couple of steps down the hall.

"Now, are you going to listen, or are you going to just stand and stew?"

"Both."

"Suit yourself." He paused a moment and then approached me.

"When my officers went over to her residence and found

her in her so-called stained-glass studio. It appears Paula had recently gone into the retail meth business and was cooking up a nice little batch. The place looked like she'd just looted a drug store. Crumbled boxes of Sudafed, Wal-Phed, every form of pseudoephedrine you can think of, were flung everywhere. The only signs of organization were the little cubbyholes on the wall for her runners."

My mind flashed to Paula's over-the-counter drug purchases at the gas station, then to her condition at Tony's the night Samantha wooed me to the bar. Perhaps I could read teenagers in school and on the court, but my brain was blocked when it came to adult women. I shook my head and exhaled audibly, embarrassed by the miss.

Harvey turned and faced me. He looked down and ran a hand over his scalp. "Ernie, Trent had his own cubby. And there was more in it than cold meds."

"What do you mean?"

"A lot of the little boxes looked the same. But one was an open box of condoms. Trojans to be exact."

I felt my eyebrows head higher. "Well, they could've been—"

"That's not all. We found several eight-by-ten black and whites. Trent's stripped to the waist with Paula all over him."

"Lord," I muttered.

Harvey rubbed his forehead. "Right ... It appears the lady paid kids to clean out all the shelves in the county. My officers even found receipts from stores out of state."

Harvey looked over his shoulder for foot traffic, then narrowed the space between us.

"She indicated she might've had more to say. To you."

"What do you mean?" I said, arms crossed over my chest.

"Did she leave anything for you? A package? Phone message? Anything?"

"Not that I know of. I didn't see anything at the office, and you know I've been staying nights at your place."

Harvey paused and tilted his head slightly.

"She left a note in the bottom of Trent's cubby. It said, *If I'm gone, Coach will know.*"

I felt my jaw hit the floor. "What the hell does that mean?"

"I was hoping you would tell me ... Look, hit the office again, then go home and look around."

"On my way. Is it OK if I speak with Trent when I get back?"

"Fine by me, if it's OK with him. You may not have much time. Momma's supposed to be on her way with some hotshot lawyer."

"You did want me to talk with him. I'm sure you remember."

THIRTY-EIGHT

T HE MANILA ENVELOPE rested atop a six-pack of Corona in the refrigerator of my garage. On the front underlined with a blue Sharpie read:

If they come protect Trent

Inside the envelope was a single-page, handwritten note:

Coach,

Dagmar told Samantha about me and Trent. She has tried to kill me once and will try again. I love Trent and loved his father, too.

I might move or hide. I have copies of most pages.

I know you are a good man and will help Trent. I did not run you off the road. Bevacqua tried for Samantha. He is everywhere.

The rest is in here.

Paula

I thumbed through the journal, jammed with more than three years of dates, times and activities. Pages of reflections. Sticky-note reminders. A few loose pictures fell to the cold concrete, along with newspaper clippings of Trent's games and stories of his controversial transfer from Everton to Loyola. I crammed all the material back into envelope, fastened the clasp and raced back downtown.

As I emptied my pockets and tossed the envelope into the bin adjacent to the electronic screener, I waved to Harvey who was speaking to a uniformed officer in the lobby.

"Is Samantha here yet?" I said after clearing the machine and gathering my belongings.

Harvey turned and ushered me down the hallway.

"I haven't seen her. What did you find?"

"A lot."

He nodded an *It's OK* to the guard stationed in front of three small jail cells and a conference room with a metal door and a square viewing window. I peeked in the window and saw Trent, head in his hands, at the rectangular table. For the first time he appeared small.

"I'll give you a minute," Harvey said. "But don't expect much more."

I rapped on the door and went on in. Trent raised his head and rubbed his bloodshot eyes. The white gym towel remained tight around his neck. I pulled out the chair opposite him and folded my arms on the table.

"How are you doing?"

"Coach, this is bogus," Trent said, his voice rising. "I wasn't anywhere near that house. Sure, I did leave the gym that day between games, but I just went down to the Red Apple for some Gatorade and cookies and some cold stuff Paula asked me to pick up for her. I've told them that a hundred times, but they won't believe me. The same questions, for months."

I raised both hands above the table in an *I get it* signal. "I'm trying to slow this circus down as much as I can. At least one detective has been concerned all along about your anger toward your father."

Trent shifted in his seat and continued in a gentler voice. "I've told you we got into it a few times. I think I even broke his nose once, but I'd never kill the man. In his own crazy way, I guess he was trying. He stopped trying with my mom, though. They both did."

"That had to be tough," I said.

"I'm not stupid. I know they were involved with other people. That house was not a pretty place to be, so I spent as much time as I could at the gym. It was only when they tried to keep me from getting away from all the craziness that I lost it."

"I know that had to be hard for you. Speaking of the gym, do you remember if your mom came to the gym on the day your dad was killed?"

"Let's see. Now that I think about it, she did. Early afternoon. Left me a note and some money for food."

"Did she say anything?"

"Never saw her. She left it in my gym bag. Note said she was freezing. Going home."

"Did you tell the cops that?" I said.

Trent shrugged as if clueless. "Don't think they ever asked. Why?"

"Just curious."

After a moment, I scooted in closer to the table. "Trent, do you remember when you broke your dad's nose? A guy your size and strength could really do some damage. I remember that punch you threw at Elmo."

He ran a palm over his face and gripped his chin. "Maybe two weeks before he died. I regretted it as soon as I threw the punch, and even more after he was gone. We were getting out of the car in the driveway, it had begun to snow for the first time this year, and he was criticizing how I'd defended a guy. Then my mom comes out of nowhere and chimes in. Bam, I snapped. Let him have it right there." He touched the bridge of his nose. "There was blood everywhere. Down his shirt, on my jacket, drops on his good shoes. I felt like a fool."

The door flung open. Samantha bolted in, trailed leash-like by a man in a dark blue suit and Harvey Johnston. She wore black, form-fitting designer jeans and a long-sleeve denim top, gold necklace with matching earrings. She slammed a glossy white purse onto a folding chair, slid over and hugged her son.

"Honey, you OK?" She glared at Harvey and me. "This is over," she shouted. Nodding at me she said, "What the hell are you doing here?"

The room became suddenly smaller. "I'm his coach, remember. We had just finished practice when one of my players happened to be arrested in the parking lot."

"Christ," she spurted. "Well, I'm the mother and I want you out of here." She shot a thumb toward the door like an angry umpire.

Trent pushed away from the table, the metal chair nearly striking the wall. He stared motionless at the floor.

"No problem," I said. "I just wanted to keep a good kid company until someone else arrived."

She launched on to her tiptoes to get in my face. "Well, we've arrived, buster, so you can split."

I reached for the door, and then turned. "I just didn't think a mother could be such a flat-out coward. Actually, lady, you're quite a few rungs down from there."

She reached me in two quick strides. "Who the fuck do you think you are?" Samantha roared. Her lips twitched. Her body smelled like wine vinegar; her breath like gin. "I'm a cop's daughter and there were no wimps or cowards in our house, jerkoff."

"Ernie?" Harvey muttered. His eyebrows arched higher. He raised a *I'll handle this* finger toward the suit.

"You come from people who could take care of themselves," I said.

"Ernie," Harvey uttered. "I'm warning you …"

"You're damn right." Samantha jammed her hands onto her hips and locked her knees, as if awaiting my best punch.

"Actually, I believe I'm looking at the biggest wimp I've ever seen right here."

"What is this?" the blue suit declared, focusing on Harvey. "My client didn't come here to—"

The five anxious bodies in the space quickly brought the heated, clammy feel of a warming sauna. Trent removed the towel from his neck and fired it to the floor.

I maintained my phony cool, slowly enunciating every word. "I've seen the worst parenting imaginable and some over-the-top horrid behavior, but you take the cake, lady."

"Drop dead, asshole," she seethed as she bumped my chest. "Where do you get off …?"

"Samantha," shouted the blue suit, rising to his feet. "Come over here and sit!" next to me and sit down. He guided his gold silk tie down the center of his white button-down shirt.

"Shut up!" she whirled and stabbed a finger toward him, her wild eyes magnified by thick rings of black eye shadow. "I'll tell you when to talk."

Harvey stepped in front of her. "Mrs. Whalen, please ... ."

Samantha forearmed Harvey aside and glared at her lawyer. "You've bled me for ten grand already this year, not to mention the fortune for Tim's estate work."

"You are mistaken," the attorney mumbled.

"Now, I'm in charge!" She pointed across the able.

"Yeah, right," I mumbled.

"Just hold it! And I mean everybody!" Harvey roared.

Leaning against the door, I casually slipped my hands into my front pockets and crossed my legs as if waiting for a bus on Division. "I mean, any mother who'd let her son be charged for a crime she committed," I said.

"I would do nothing of the sort!"

"It's worse than that, though," I laughed. "A premeditated frame job. You set up your own son."

"Ernie, that is enough!" Harvey yelled and stepped between us like a referee separating two fighters.

"Don't worry," I said. "I'm out the door."

"I didn't set up anybody!" Samantha shrieked.

"Samantha, I'd advise you not to say another word," said the blue suit, attempting to remain calm. He placed his leather attaché case on the end of the table.

"Really, how can you possibly sleep at night?" I continued.

Harvey turned and glared at me, then slammed an open hand into my chest. "Look at me," he fumed. "I mean LOOK at me! That's it." His other arm remained outstretched to hold off Samantha. "Let my detectives do their job!"

"I sleep very well at night, thank you," wailed Samantha in a sing-song fashion, her head wigwagging from side to side. Then in a raucous scream that bounced off the walls, "Because

Trent's son-of-a-bitch father—Trent's cheating, scamming dad—is six feet under! Man, did I make a mistake getting involved with that loser!"

"I guess that isn't it, Harvey," I smirked. "Maybe Samantha's ready to tell us about her mistake in leaving the arms of her lover too early the day Tim was murdered?"

Trent grimaced and rubbed his eyes. "Mom, is this another—"

"Samantha, absolutely do not respond!" the lawyer bellowed. He cupped his hands and slid them over his slicked-back hair. "Mr. Johnston, I must insist you remove Mr. Creekmore immediately! He has no place here."

"At least I know my place," I said. "No worries. I'm leaving."

Harvey shoved me into the door and held his forearm across my waist. Before he could speak, I kept rolling.

"And friends. You had to be pissed because he was also bunking down with your best friends."

"You bet I was pissed, especially that Sunday when I found an Alaska Airlines package to Mexico for him and some bitch from the North Fork Garden Club. You bet your ass I wasn't going to let him get away with it! The bastard drained our bank accounts on basketball and women. Hoops and hookers. No camp was too expensive; no bargain-basement babes, either."

"But you were no dummy, were you," I chided. "You found the key to the basketball money, didn't you? Surround yourself with someone who'd broker out your own son and send you the cash."

"You're damn right! My stupid husband wouldn't do it. No, he spent our savings instead." She leaned closer and pointed a finger in my face. "And there would have been a hell of a lot more if it weren't for you!"

The lawyer reached across the table and grabbed her arm. Scowling, she yanked it away.

"Chief Detective Johnston, I fail to see how any of this really and truly involves your office," the lawyer announced. "If you are not going to arrest my client, I demand that—"

"Mom?" Trent whispered, his face creased in wonderment and disbelief. "Did you really—"

"And Samantha," I said, "don't leave out the smooth move of showing up at the gym, taking Trent's jacket, and then wearing it into the open house."

"Samantha! We must leave this room immediately. And I mean now!"

She grabbed her white purse. Instead of stepping toward the door, she reached in and waved a pocket .22 caliber handgun around the room. She backed into the corner above her seated son.

"Mrs. Whalen," Harvey said, his hands raised. "Please put the gun down. This is not going to get you anywhere."

"Mom! What are you doing?"

"Oh, my God," the lawyer mumbled.

"Sit tight, Trent. This is going to get me out of here." She glared at Harvey. "And he's going to be my chaperone."

"There's no way you can—"

I cut Harvey off. "Oh, yes, you were at the open house." I nodded toward Samantha. "But you could've cared less about the place. You were only looking for the host."

"Why the jacket?" I continued. "Ah, a sort of clever disguise. Go in draped in a bulky letterman's jacket and sunglasses and come out dressed as a visiting realtor. Really, what could be better? Your son's jacket with traces of your husband's blood on it. Why not—"

"Because I was shivering. That's why, you asshole. I was cold. I had to go out in the cold and do the job that fuckin' Bevacqua was hired for but didn't have the balls to do!"

Suddenly, Trent exploded skyward, his elbows extended as if blocking out a mammoth opponent for a game-saving rebound. The power and surprise of his move jarred the gun from his mother's hand and sent it flying across the table. I lunged for the pistol as Harvey scrambled behind Trent and pinned Samantha to the wall.

"What a terrific mom and wife," I mumbled from my knees as I lifted her gun from the floor. Harvey clinched the woman's arms behind her.

"Sir," Harvey said to the attorney, "do me a favor and open that door. Stand there so I can see you and you can see me and your client. Call out to any officer in the hall for assistance."

The blue suit leaped toward the door and swung it open. "Help! We need help in here!"

Trent slumped in the lawyer's former seat, glowered at his mother, and buried his head in his hands. "I can't believe this," he murmured.

I rose and stood next to him as Bjarne bolted into the room.

"You said you'd be here to protect me, you bastard!" Samantha screamed. "You said you had it all covered. Well, now we're covered in shit."

"Nobody move!" Harvey yelled. "Detective Dagmar, hand me your badge and firearm. Now!"

"Don't give up your gun, you fool!" Samantha barked. "Get us out of here!"

Another cop poked his head into the room. Bjarne eyed the beef at the door and shook his head and handed Harvey his gear.

"Stand behind Trent and don't move an inch."

"You wimp," Samantha sneered.

"Officer, please take Mrs. Whalen into custody," Harvey said. The cop whipped a pair of handcuffs from his hip. "Wait for me right there in the hall."

Samantha twisted and squirmed, testing the range of her restriction. "I was a great mom until I made one stupid mistake," she said, nearly spitting her words over her shoulder at Harvey. "I left home without my fucking trench coat." She lowered her head and her voice. "Those damn nosy riverfront people, always checking out anybody who approaches the stately Hanrahan estate. I never wanted Trent to be any part of this. I just grabbed his damn coat when I went looking for him at the gym, figured he was warm enough wherever he was. He always wore that thick hoodie under the jacket anyway."

"This way, ma'am," the lead cop said as he aimed her toward the hall.

Harvey lifted his hand. "Just a second, officer," Harvey said and nodded toward Samantha. "The jacket you wore into the house—"

"Had a big block L on the front!" Samantha barked. "I didn't want to take a chance that the neighbors would remember it. Yeah, I should have thought of that sooner, but I sure as hell didn't want to wear it both ways. I yanked a women's blue parka off the rack by the back door and kept moving."

The lawyer extended both arms across the table. "Samantha! Think about what you are doing!"

She snorted and shook her head.

Harvey rocked back and forth like the only kid who knew the answer in a spelling bee. "And the murder weapon? What did you do with the murder weapon?"

"What?" the attorney shouted. "Samantha, I strongly advise you not to say another word! We need to have a confidential conversation. Now!"

She continued as if she hadn't heard a thing. "I strolled down the lawn to the river, skipped a few rocks from the top of the levee, skipped in my dad's old twenty-two—"

"Samantha!"

"… like it was just another stone, then skipped a few more rocks just in case the local looky-loos were eyeing me."

"But you didn't leave the scene right then?" Harvey said.

"Lord in heaven, Samantha," the lawyer moaned. "What are you doing?"

"No, I walked back in the front door, removed the parka and buried it under an old top coat on the coat rack. Then I drove home."

No one said a word. Harvey raised an eyebrow toward the attorney, who could only shake his head and rub his closed eyes.

Trent eased back into his seat, arms at his sides, fingers nearly touching the vinyl squares below him. "Jesus, Mom," he whispered.

Harvey followed Samantha and the cops to the door and exhaled audibly as the group lingered.

"I've gotta get out of here," Trent said.

Harvey laid a hand on his shoulder. "Stay put for a second, son," he said, then raised his hand as if hailing a cab. "Jerry, come on down here a second, would you?" I handed the pistol to Harvey, who shot back with, "Thanks for doing nothing that I asked."

Another policeman entered the room. "Officer Taft," Harvey said, "please stay here with Detective Dagmar. I'll be back for Trent in a moment." He turned to Samantha. "Under the circumstances, Mrs. Whalen, I'm sure you will want to take a few minutes to confer with your attorney. After we get you processed, I will find you a vacant room and provide some writing materials."

"Are you going to arrest my client?"

Harvey interrupted the attorney's formal spiel. "I'm sorry. Are you deaf? I believe you just witnessed what she said. For the record, yes, we are. And that's going to happen right now." He signaled to the cops to take Samantha away.

I followed the trio as they headed down the hallway with Harvey a few steps behind. Before they reached the front counter I said, "Samantha." She turned and faced me. "When's the last time you saw Paula Soijka?"

"That bitch seduced my Trent," she snarled. "Just ask Dagmar. Seems he knew us both rather intimately."

"Coach Creekmore!" Harvey said. "Could you leave the questions to—"

"Made that bitch pay!" Samantha yelled. "Followed her and juiced her. Big-time!"

When they'd gone, Harvey turned toward me, his mouth wide open.

"That was some show," he said. "What else can happen today?"

I smirked and looked down. "Rather sad, if you ask me."

Harvey reached into his coat pocket and pulled out his cell phone. He stepped toward the door, backed it open and spoke loud enough for all to hear.

"Yes, this is Chief Investigator Johnston. Find Bobby Bevacqua and bring him down here. Now."

Harvey paused a moment and then stared at me. "I'm going to wait to add up all of my stop signs that you blew through in there. Yes, I wanted you to speak with the young man all along, but I was not expecting you to speak to his mother. Especially in that manner."

I shrugged and picked at a callous on my palm. "I was guessing about Paula."

"I had a feeling you might be."

We walked and talked, circling to a stop in a vacant waiting room opposite the semi-circular front counter. I handed him the journal and said it would show that Samantha helped fund Paula's meth business in exchange for Paula covering for Samantha the day Tim was murdered. When Paula faced a possible third felony, Samantha got nervous that Paula would come clean and blow Samantha's alibi for Tim's murder in exchange for no jail time. The partnership absolutely imploded when Bjarne informed Samantha about Paula's affair with Trent.

"We're going to have to get Trent some professional help," I said. "Sooner rather than later. How much can a kid go through?"

"There's a terrific young counselor upstairs," Harvey replied. "I'll get on it right away."

He pulled out a chair, placed the journal on the table and began paging through it.

"Paula might have loved Tim, but she loved meth more,"

316 | HOVERING ABOVE A HOMICIDE

Harvey said. "That crap will do that do you." He stopped his finger under an entry near the back cover. "Paula writes here she got scared about Samantha when we brought Paula back in for questioning about running you off the road. Says here, *I might have to talk to stay out of jail.*"

I hovered above Harvey's shoulder. "What's the last thing she wrote?"

Harvey flipped to the back page. *Breakfast, walking in Riverfront Park.*

"My take is that Samantha had her puppy dog Bevacqua tail Paula," Harvey said. "When Paula got to the river, he called Samantha who did the deal herself. Bevacqua had already screwed up too many times."

I walked to the end of the table and flopped into a chair. "What I don't get is, what the hell was in this for Dagmar?"

"Macho power thing," Harvey said without looking up. "It's happened before. I guess he also thought he was some kind of super swordsman. Probably thought he could move back into first place with Samantha by keeping her out of jail."

Harvey whipped through several pages and grabbed a handful. "Man, there's a ton of stuff in this section alone. It's going to take a while to get through it all."

I settled back and slouched lower. After a long pause I said, "Could you believe Samantha was bold enough to bring a gun in here?" I said.

"Bold enough or dumb enough? It's a very good indicator, though, that she hasn't been thinking clearly."

"Don't let the reporters hear that quote." I said. "It'll give the lawyer some ammo for an insanity plea."

"What was insane was the security in this building. Remind

me to speak with the top floors about our screening process. What a zoo that turned into."

"I'm betting she got some help from Dagmar. He probably brought her and the suit through your employees' entrance."

Harvey groaned, closed the book and tapped his fingers on the cover. I tried to digest the past thirty minutes, then said: "I have a feeling you should get Gene Slaughter in here for a little heart-to-heart."

Harvey looked up. "The Loyola coach? What makes you think so?"

"It's something you always say about following the money."

"What?" Harvey said. "You mean sweat him and Bevacqua in separate rooms and compare stories?"

"Might be interesting."

THIRTY-NINE

Exactly fifty-five minutes after Samantha Whalen's ego propelled her into an arrest for two murders, county deputies ushered Gene Slaughter into the waiting room. He was dressed as if headed out on the town. Cordovan brogues shined below his cuffed gray trousers; his blue pinstriped button-down shirt and navy blue blazer were resplendent and unwrinkled. He froze in his tracks when he discovered I was the person partially hidden by the door.

"What's *he* doing here?" he said to Harvey, still in the hallway.

"Everybody seems to be asking me that today."

"Coach Creekmore will be sitting in with us for a while," Harvey said, showing Slaughter to a chair.

"What's his official capacity? Is he some sort of undercover investigator?"

Slaughter hesitated where to sit, then walked around the table to a brown metal chair. Harvey dropped into a similar seat opposite Slaughter and pulled out an adjacent chair. "No, not at all," Harvey said. "He was helping me answer some basketball-related questions."

"Well, maybe I can help, too," Slaughter said.

"Let's hope so," Harvey said.

"But before we get started, am I being charged with something I don't know about?"

"Should you be?" Harvey said.

"Of course not." Slaughter laughed nervously. "But you have to admit, this is pretty strange."

Harvey paused, then spoke. "Where were you the afternoon Scott Hazelton was murdered?"

"Waaaiitt a minute," Slaughter howled. "Am I a suspect in this mess? If so, it sounds as if I might need an attorney."

"Well, that's up to you, sir. But if you committed no crime, you have nothing to worry about."

"I'm uncertain what time and day his death even took place!" Slaughter barked. "I do know my afternoons are loaded. After lunch, I have fifth- and sixth-period classes, both Honors Economics, and then practice. Someone at school would be able to confirm my presence each and every day."

A uniformed officer knocked and slid his head and shoulders into the room.

"What have you got?" Harvey said.

"Sir, we've been unable to locate Mr. Bevacqua. Efforts are ongoing."

Harvey nodded and scribbled a note. After the officer closed the door, Harvey said, "Has Trent Whalen attended every practice?"

"He has. And I know for a fact he tutors freshmen in the classroom adjacent to mine in the afternoons."

"Most of the afternoon or all of the afternoon?"

"He tutors from eleven to twelve-fifteen. And then again from one to two-fifteen. He's on the court with me at three."

I could almost see Harvey's brain churning. The timeframes did not allow Trent to travel to Lake Wilhelmina and back. "You're sure? Detective Dagmar covered this ground early in the investigation."

"I'm positive."

Harvey took another note. "Did you offer a cash incentive to Trent Whalen to transfer from Everton to Loyola?"

"If I did, would it be a crime?" Slaughter smirked.

"Not in this county," Harvey said.

Slaughter straightened an already perfect collar. "Well, I did not offer Trent a cash incentive, or any other incentive for that matter. To my knowledge, the school didn't either. So, there you have it."

"Did you ever ask the school president, or Father Hawkenson, if they had knowledge of incentives?"

"No, I never asked them."

"Did you entice Trent in any way?"

"Full transparency here. I had dinner one night at the Hanrahan house and Tim Whalen was invited. He brought Trent."

Harvey pivoted in his seat and raised his eyebrows in my direction. "So, the timing of that dinner was inappropriate?"

Slaughter spread his palms out on the table. "Inappropriate? Probably not. But let's just say if I were a coach at another school, I'd find it extremely curious." He leaned in closer and interlaced his fingers like an altar boy. "Not everybody cheats, sir, but absolutely everyone jaywalks."

Harvey cleared his throat and looked at me. "So, I'm sure the Everton coach was not pleased when he got word Trent was leaving his school."

"No, I'd say Bobby Bevacqua was livid," Slaughter said. "The man chewed me a new one on the phone and said he was going to turn me in to the state association for recruiting violations. He said he knew members on the board were tired of the Catholics poaching kids from the publics. It turned into big-league blackmail."

"Really?" Harvey said. "What did he have on you?"

"Some hotshot booster photographed most of the evening with his cell phone. I didn't even know this man or see the cell. This guy thought he would be a hero among his buddies by showing off the big, strong body that was going to turn us around. Well, one of his buddies tells Bobby about it. The booster got video of me with my coat on, then later in the study with my coat off. He made it look as if I had met with Trent on more than one occasion."

Harvey lifted a piece of paper from his shirt pocket with two fingers and scribbled a note on the top fold. "So what was the resolution to making all of this go away?"

Slaughter sucked in a deep breath from the corners of his mouth and forced the exhale through his nose. "Look, I couldn't afford to get fired, or even face the negativity of an investigation. This kind of publicity puts even a clean-Gene coach on the hot seat. We were barely making the payments on the farm as it was. Bobby made me recruit and send him at least three Canadians for a team he was putting together in Vancouver. It was more of a gentlemen's agreement that would pay three thousand dollars per player. Apparently, some deep-pocket real-estate developer up there wanted more exposure for Junior Olympic-aged players."

"So you agreed?" Harvey said.

Slaughter slumped lower.

"Mr. Johnston, I needed the money. Quite frankly, I still do. What made the arrangement appealing for me was that I had a pipeline into British Columbia. I played summer league with some guys from Simon Fraser University. They have an impressive network of young candidates. That's why I asked Coach Creekmore about Canadians. Getting a good kid north of the border to play on a team at the Seattle Center tournament? That would quickly establish a big-time reputation that could be the building block for a team and eventually a tournament in Vancouver."

I pushed back in my chair and put my hands behind my head. "Help me understand this," I said. Slaughter frowned. "Not only do you have agents looking to land their players on select teams to increase their exposure, but there are private companies wanting to back teams and tournaments?"

"You bet." Slaughter nodded. "Major corporations have seen the buzz that sneaker companies have created in backing kids' teams, so they are becoming more of a presence in select leagues." The man spoke like a university professor and presented like a boardroom exec. I could see how players and parents might leap at his living room pitch to join one of his teams. "Those are the same people who like to put their names on professional stadiums and arenas."

He focused his gaze on Harvey.

"I'm sorry, Mr. Johnston. But if none of this is illegal, what are we doing here?"

Harvey extended his arms over his head and sighed. "I'm trying to determine what transpired behind the scenes during Trent Whalen's basketball years. You are under no obligation to be here. We were just hoping for your cooperation."

Slaughter sighed. "OK. Go ahead."

"Thank you," Harvey said. "So, how was all of this arranged?"

"At first," Slaughter said, "it was all run through Scott Hazelton. We met at Bevacqua's uncle's place at Lake Wilhelmina. We made in-depth background charts of both U.S. and Canadian kids. Then Bobby got the idea he could do this all by himself and started representing his own players and going after corporate money. He even hired a runner, a slick talker he found in a north-end bar. Bobby told me, 'Why pay the middle man?'"

"When did Bobby split with Hazelton?" Harvey asked.

"Bobby started to get a little edgy when Hazelton began looking at lake properties for sale. Hazelton said he loved the area and often stopped at homes with informational fliers out front."

Slaughter flinched and continued. "I noticed a significant change about the time Trent transferred to our place. Bobby said he thought somebody had paid Hazelton to make that happen, but I wasn't so sure that was the case. Then Hazelton promised Bobby the select job that Coach Creekmore eventually received."

I shook my head, wondering how the dots connected. "Why in the world did Hazelton think he had that much juice with the coaches' association to influence such a decision?" I said.

"Hazelton did his research and said that Bobby was the only viable candidate in the area," Slaughter said. "Some coaches had conflicts during spring break. No offense, but you were retired and nobody thought you'd be coming back."

"True," I admitted. "Things change."

Slaughter waited a moment and folded his arms across his chest. Somehow, his coat refused to show even the early stages of a wrinkle. "If you ask me, I think Bobby paid Hazelton to get the select job," Slaughter said. "When Ernie was named, Bobby got upset and started going after players that he knew Hazelton had targeted. Elmo Service, a rebounder from Edison, a shooting guard named McGann. I'm sure there were others. The players had no idea."

Slaughter went on to say that a majority of parents paid hundreds, if not thousands of their own funds so that their kids could join select teams. The few stars that make or break a coach or select tournament were lavished with incentives. Agents and brokers often targeted the players from broken homes or single parents with cash-flow problems. They viewed their children as a solve-all cash cow.

The info stung, proof positive the world of Manny Cossetti and Scott Hazelton was alive and well. But I still couldn't wrap my head around it. Players weren't clueless, nor were their high school coaches. My arms shot out as if giving a sermon. "What do you mean, the players had no idea? If the guy was planning to represent them, wouldn't they know?"

"Not necessarily," Slaughter deadpanned. "Being classy from the get-go is old school, Ernie. See, Bobby thought he was a slam-dunk for your select coaching job. His plan was to get the players on his own team, then tell them he was the only person responsible for getting them there when Hazelton already had done the heavy lifting. Once that was accomplished, he would do even more for them in the future. When he didn't get the job, he got desperate. He began seeking other methods of obtaining clients."

Harvey stood and paced behind the table. "I am assuming you hit your quota of three Canadians and got compensated for your efforts?"

"I set up the introductory dinner meetings with Bobby and the players, but I haven't been paid. I also discovered that Bobby went behind my back to a group of Canadian sponsors who committed fifty grand if he would organize a tournament in Vancouver and bring in his own team. I can't find Bobby and he doesn't answer his phone. I even stopped by his apartment. The lights were off and his car was gone. But it's spring break in his district, and everybody's gone."

"What sort of vehicle is Bevacqua currently driving?" Harvey asked.

"Chevy Tahoe. Black."

FORTY

THE NORTH COUNTIES selects rambled through the first three rounds of the Seattle Center Spring Hoopfest, burying three well-coached teams before dropping the final in overtime against one of the finest collections of talent I'd ever seen. Trent Whalen was a force at both ends of the floor and was named to the tournament's all-star team.

The media loved us, starting with a Greg Smithson front-page game story coupled with a sidebar feature on Deacon Joe Gonzales in *The Seattle Tribune* after our first-round triumph over Yakima Valley. Deacon Joe dished out seventeen assists that night, highlighted by a handful of no-look bounce passes to Nick Chevalier that the big guy converted into easy lay-ins. Deacon Joe also shined in the post-game press conference, inserting "ma'am" and "sir" into all answers, including one from a longtime friend of mine, a community college coach who asked about assisting Deacon Joe in the completion of his high school diploma.

Haywood Range put on a shooting clinic in the quarterfinals, nailing his first four three-point attempts before finishing the game with thirty-one points in our victory over Longview-Kelso, the game that proved we were not to be taken lightly. Haywood was a last-minute starter for Deacon Joe, who tweaked his ankle in pregame warm-ups. With Deacon Joe down, Eddie McGann brought the ball flawlessly up the floor under big-time on-ball pressure, instilling even more confidence in our guys and fear in the eyes of our opponents.

We had more than one thoroughbred guard to go with our imposing front line and we punished every defense with speed and shooting. I could almost hear the internal gears turning as coaches in the stands debated how to best defend us. It was exactly the scene I'd prayed to witness and it was unfolding on the court in front of me and in the seats behind me.

Steady Eddie found an extra gear in the semis against Aberdeen-Hoquiam, gathering twenty-five points, eleven assists and thirteen rebounds in a game that was over midway through the third quarter. Perhaps the more impressive performance was turned in by Billy Milligan, a rebounder Linn Oliver recruited who came off the bench to hold Jonathan Quigg, Aberdeen's six-foot-eight star, to four points and three rebounds. Milligan was so effective in the first half that I felt I couldn't afford to take him off the floor, providing both Nick and Trent valuable rest time in the four-game, four-day affair.

The championship game against Seattle Metro was one huge highlight film, a nail-biting classic that was as hard-fought as any game I'd coached, played in, or seen. Deacon Joe spearheaded a full-throttle offense, roaring down the floor to find his designated shooters in their favorite spots around the perimeter. Trent brought the crowd to its feet with a rim-rattling, rebound dunk of an Eddie McGann jumper in the final seconds of regulation, sending the game into overtime. Weary and worn, the teams exchanged leads until the final seconds when Seattle Metro called timeout and crafted a play for its star forward, Fennis Chenier.

Chenier, who announced that he would accept a full ride

to Villanova earlier in the day, took an inbounds pass near half court with four ticks left on the clock. At six-foot-five with a fullback build, Chenier pounded three left-handed dribbles to his left, then instantly rotated toward the bucket, elevated and lofted a textbook jumper over the outstretched hand of Eddie McGann.

The ball floated through the net as time ran out. Seattle Metro 72, North Counties 70.

The silence in our spacious locker room made the room feel even more cavernous. Range sat with a white towel over his head in front of his cubby, the remaining players with their faces in their hands or staring down at the green and gold carpet. Even though some people might think that players really don't care all that much about all-star games, these guys did. I took it to mean that they cared about each other and their mission of pulling an upset over a big-time team.

"I never asked you to be the best of friends off the court," I said. "My goal was that you give each other an even shot at being a terrific teammate. You far exceeded that goal and it is what set you apart in this tournament. It showed. Anybody with a remote notion of what makes team chemistry noticed what you had in the first quarter of the first game."

Nick Chevalier wiped his eyes. After a moment he said: "I might have helped if I hadn't come so late to the party. Shoulda got my mom to move here last year."

A few players chuckled. Eddie McGann snapped a towel at Nick's shoulder. "You showed up big-time, big guy."

"That team you played today had more talent," I continued. "But the best team did not win today. The best individuals won and that's going to happen sometimes in an all-star tournament. But what set you above that team was far more important. It may not feel like it now, but it will down the road. Over an entire season, it is irreplaceable."

Trent Whalen, his bottom braced against a locker, hands on his knees, raised his head. I caught his eyes and didn't let them go.

"You all showed leadership, despite the hardship," I said. "Despite the drama you had no control over. After that first practice, you didn't pick and choose when you wanted to be responsible. You all displayed a desire to get better, as individuals and as a team. Even the man who renders excellent service."

The players laughed and hooted at Elmo. Deacon Joe shoved him from the side.

When Elmo looked up, I said, "See what I'm sayin'?"

The locker room roared. The players gradually started to rise and begin their goodbyes. Before I opened the locker room to the working press, I thanked the players as a group and individually for what they had accomplished and for making my re-entry so memorable. I then asked those who might be interested in future tournaments and a possible travel squad to telephone or e-mail me within the next few weeks.

"That is, without a doubt, the best finish I've ever seen," Harvey said, circling in after the last microphone was pulled away from my chin. "Those kids played their hearts out. Made you look pretty good, too."

"Thanks, Harvey. I knew we'd surprise some people, but I never thought we'd stay with a team like that for as long as we did. There were three future pros on that metro club."

A short, squatty figure backed into Harvey, knocking him off balance. "Actually, I counted four," Manny Cossetti blurted, peering down at his clipboard. "Oops, sorry about that, Mack."

"It's Harvey."

"Right. Anyway, I could help almost every player on that squad to get a ride somewhere. Maybe I'll just go to a mid-major and offer 'em a team discount. Ya falla?"

I smiled. "Those guys were quicker than quick, but our guys played smart and raised some eyebrows."

"Speaking of smart people," Harvey said, pointing away, indicating a private moment. Manny held up a hand and scurried away. "Your friend, Bobby Bevacqua, failed in the smart category. We've received reports that he motored an eighteen-foot Sea Ray into Sidney Harbor on Vancouver Island two nights ago. He left the vessel at the marina without notifying Canadian Border Services. When Bevacqua returned in the morning, he found out he faced a fine, and the border officials picked up our APB on his passport. From the gear they found on that boat, it didn't look like he planned on returning soon. Anyway, extradition discussions are already in the works. The process most likely will take a few weeks."

"Not a shining star of the coaching community," I said.

Harvey pulled a notebook from his sport-coat pocket.

"We questioned Gene Slaughter aggressively in an attempt to get more information about Trent Whalen and to produce the name of Bevacqua's runner," Harvey said. "Turns out this Howie Blackwell is a two-bit thug from Snohomish who takes college bets out of the backroom of a tavern on Highway 9. When we arrested Blackwell for your attempted murder at the gas station, he copped to tossing the rock through Margie's window and some late-night phone call that I don't think I heard about."

"Didn't I tell you about that?"

"Actually, I believe you did. For once."

I chuckled and nodded. "What did you find out about the bucks in the hamburger bag?"

"Blackwell said that was all Bevacqua," Harvey said. "Plus, Blackwell has a rock-solid alibi for the timeframe Hazelton was murdered."

"Are you sure?" I said. "I'd hate to call any coach a killer."

"Sorry, Ernie. But two different people confirmed the guy was nursing several beers at The Cedar Stump in Arlington the afternoon Hazelton went down. One of my officers who has been known to stop at The Stump for a cold one on the way home from work was one of those people."

My thoughts raced back to the lake and the visit with Warren Gustaffson. I shook my head when I remembered the mention of the black Chevy nearly crushed by a tree in Henry Bevacqua's driveway.

Harvey motioned to a section alcove leading to the loge seats. We ducked behind a corner and checked for stray fans before speaking.

"We now believe that Bobby Bevacqua killed Scott Hazelton and tried to frame you for it. Bobby and Hazelton wanted you out of the way and went to the lake to kill you. Bobby got greedy, killed Hazelton, and tried to stick it on you. It was the ultimate step he could take for Samantha. He'd be her hero and her puppet in her son's future."

"He'd be Trent's agent plus Trent's all-star coach."

"Correct."

"That's quite a bit of coordination," I said.

"Think about it. It was a very short distance for Bevacqua

to cover and he knew you would be coming from town. You were probably coming down South Shore Drive at the same time when Bobby was looping the other way around North Shore. He jumped in his black Tahoe and drove away. Samantha obviously wanted you gone so she snuggled Dagmar to put the screws to you."

"She also snuggled Dagmar away from thinking she was a suspect in her husband's murder," I said. "Unfortunately, he zeroed in on Trent."

I shrugged and leaned against the wall.

"And that's not all," Harvey continued. "We have made a decision to charge him with attempted murder. That would be *your* attempted murder."

I moved closer. "You think he was the Shovel Man?"

"We do. Howie Blackwell told Detective Dagmar that Bevacqua asked to borrow his white hightops the day you were assaulted. Bevacqua fed him some line about he had a dirty job to do and didn't have time to go home first."

"It sounds as if Bevacqua wanted to frame him, too."

"We do not know that for certain, Ernie," Harvey said. "But we do know he wanted your coaching position in the worst kind of way."

I smiled and looked away.

"What?" Ernie said.

"It's funny. Howie Blackwell told me that I had a job some coaches would kill for."

Harvey cleared his throat. "You probably know that Bjarne Dagmar has been charged as an accessory in both the Whalen and Soijka murders. We didn't have enough to nail him in the Hazelton case."

"Not great publicity for your department."

"Tell me about it. Plus you were right about her gun. One of my officers who runs the electromagnetic scanner downtown said Dagmar allowed Samantha Whalen, at her request, without questioning it, to enter the building with her attorney through our restricted entrance behind the building. Longtime romantic links between the two did surface, through her e-mails. That had to hinder his investigation, leading him to center his efforts on Trent rather than on Samantha."

Minutes later, I gathered my gear, allowed the remaining players some time to themselves, and headed for the exit. Small groups of parents and fans were clustered outside the locker room door and I waved and nodded to their shouts of thanks and best wishes.

Off in a corner, Diane Chevalier chatted with an elderly black woman, whose stylish blue and beige two-tone pointed shoes matched her pants and blazer. Her white hair was pulled back behind her head in a bun.

Diane approached me with her hand outstretched.

"I need to apologize for getting off on the wrong foot with you," she said. "I was foolish and immature and I am sorry."

I shook her hand. "No apology necessary."

"No, I mean it. I also want to thank you for what you have done to bring these kids together and for going to the mat for Trent. As you know, Trent got approval to live with us while Timoteo works on his case. I don't know a hell of a lot of guys who would have helped with any of that."

I stepped back and considered the statement. "Maybe that's because you don't know me."

She smiled and wiggled her head slightly. "And that's

something I'd like to change."

The little black woman scurried up behind Diane. "I also want to thank you for what you have done for my grandson, Elmo," she said. "He's got a new head on his shoulders. His mama would have been proud."

"My pleasure, ma'am. You saw that Elmo is a key member of that group in there."

"I did, and I saw it landin' a few weeks ago on his attitude. It seems he's standin' up a little straighter. So you can see why it was a pleasure for me to make you Granny's famous chocolate cake. By the way, did you like it?"

"I sure did, ma'am, and shared it with some of my best friends."

"And a lot of those friends know where to find the key to your house. You might want to switch that location someday."

ACKNOWLEDGMENTS

T HIS BOOK COULD not have been possible without the following individuals who provided creative insights and useful information for this effort. I called upon them often and their patience, interest and kindness have been extraordinary: Jim Thomsen, George and Jean Johnston, Kelsye Nelson, Archana Murthy, Christina Tinling, David Madsen, Rob Morrell, Craig Smith, Linda Owens, Leigh Robinson, Bill Cameron, Bruce Brown, Tom Lowery, Kevin Hawkins, David Schlosser, Brian Jansma, Paul Bossenmaier, Joanne Elizabeth Kelly and to high-school basketball coaches everywhere who have their hearts in the right place.

ABOUT THE AUTHOR

H OVERING ABOVE A HO-
MICIDE is the second book in
Tom Kelly's Ernie Creekmore
series featuring the adventures
of legendary high school basketball coach turned real estate
agent and amateur sleuth. The
book finds Ernie trying to solve
the murder of a "helicopter"
parent whose body is discovered
in a vacant home for sale.

The first book, *Cold Crossover*, introduces us to Ernie who
gets word that his former start player—Linnbert "Cheese" Oliver—has gone missing from a late-night ferry boat.

Before launching into fiction, Tom served *The Seattle Times*
readers for 20 years, first as a sportswriter and later as real estate
reporter, columnist and editor. His weekly features now appear
in a variety of newspapers including the *Miami Herald, Hous-
ton Chronicle, Louisville Courier-Journal, Tacoma News Tribune*
and *Spokane Spokesman-Review* plus hundreds of websites.

His ground-breaking book *How a Second Home Can Be
Your Best Investment* (McGraw-Hill, written with economist
John Tuccillo) showed consumers and professionals how one

additional piece of real estate could serve as an investment, recreation and retirement property over time. His other books include *Real Estate Boomers and Beyond: Exploring the Costs, Choices and Changes of Your Next Move* (Dearborn-Kaplan); *The New Reverse Mortgage Formula* (John Wiley & Sons); Cashing In on a Second Home in Mexico (Crabman Publishing, with Mitch Creekmore); *Cashing In on a Second Home in Central America* (Crabman Publishing, with Mitch Creekmore and Jeff Hornberger), and *Bargains Beyond the Border* (Crabman Publishing).

Tom's award-winning radio show "Real Estate Today" has aired for 20 years on KIRO, the CBS affiliate in Seattle. The program also has been syndicated in 40 domestic markets and to 450 stations in 160 foreign countries via Armed Forces Radio.

Tom and his wife, Jodi, Dean of the Humanities College at Seattle University, have four children and live on Bainbridge Island, WA, where they back the runnin', gunnin' Bainbridge High Spartans when not wrestling with grandson Myles.